The SILVER GHOST

Also by Chuck Kinder
Snakehunter

Chuck Kinder

The SILVER GHOST

HARCOURT BRACE JOVANOVICH
New York and London

Requests for permission to make copies of any part of the work should be mailed to:
Permissions, Harcourt Brace Jovanovich, Inc.
757 Third Avenue, New York, N.Y. 10017

A portion of this book previously appeared in *TriQuarterly*.

Printed in the United States of America

LIBRARY OF CONGRESS CATALOGING IN PUBLICATION DATA

Kinder, Chuck.
  The silver ghost.
  I. Title.
PZ4.K513Si [PS3561.I426]   813'.5'4   78-22259
ISBN 0-15-124067-1

First edition

B C D E

for Cecily aka Trigger
the gunmoll of my heart

contents ➤

I'm a legend in my own mind . . .

Martin Mull,
in a comedy routine
on American Bandstand

prologue ➤
the silver ghost

Now, Judy's wealthy family owned several cars, a Cadillac, two Lincolns, Fords that seemed to just appear and disappear randomly. And then there was the *Silver Ghost*, a car famous far and wide. Judy's older brother Frankie, famous far and wide himself as perhaps the area's wildest ass, drove a '55 Porsche that could burn anything in the county. It was painted the German racing color, metallic silver, and on its doors were the foot-high numerals *1-3-0*. Frankie had returned from one of his mysterious trips driving it, claiming he had bought it in California and had driven it back across country, claiming it had been smashed up in a spectacular accident and that he had had it rebuilt. Look at the speedometer, Frankie would say. It was frozen at 110. That's how fast he was going when he smashed up, Frankie claimed. Yes, James Dean was doing a cool 110 when he blasted off to that great starfield in the sky, Frankie would say solemnly.

Because Jimbo Stark was not like those country club punks Judy had usually dated Frankie liked him. And now and then Frankie would actually loan the Silver Ghost to Jimbo for a heavy date with Judy. Frankie would actually let Jimbo slide behind the wheel of the Silver Ghost, turn its magic motor on, and cruise it haunting into the starry, technicolor, teenage night.

Now, you have to remember it, perfectly, like this. You have to imagine it, perfectly, just like this. So listen. Listen closely. Distant sweet summer evenings. You have to remember, or imagine, perfectly, distant sweet summer evenings. Perhaps with a whisper of coming rain in the air, maybe thunder far off in the hills across the river. You have to imagine perfectly what it was like to haunt through those distant bluegreen summer evenings of Jimbo Stark's tropical teenmemory in the Silver Ghost. Radio on. Windows down. The last sweet dark air that ever mattered washing into the glowing, rushing interior of that silver shell as if to drown out any possible future you will ever know.

Judy, pressed as near to you as possible, is wearing perhaps the bright yellow, sleeveless summer dress that breaks your heart. Now and then she reaches forward to dial in a new hit lovesong on the radio and you can see the delicate muscle of her tanned arm flex in your memory forever. Her shoes are off and she has her brown bare legs tucked up under her and in the soft golden dashboard light her knees glow. In her fragrance you can smell her afternoon of swimming and sunbathing and the bubble bath she lingered in later. You can smell that she has washed her hair and perfumed between her breasts for you.

Sometimes she leans over to kiss the edge of your mouth and you can smell her sweet beechnut breath. When she does this she slips the fingers of her right hand between the buttons of your shirt and gently strokes your chest. Her fingertips are both cool and moist at once. She unbuttons your shirt, then lets her hand roam slowly over your chest, her thumb stroking briefly your left nipple, to your left armpit where she plays gently with its damp hair. She rolls it absently in her fingers, sometimes tugging lightly. You turn to look at her. Her eyes are wide and blue black. Between her slightly parted wet lips the white edges of her teeth shine.

With one hand you fire up a cigarette, either a Camel or a Lucky, then, wrinkling your forehead and arching your eyebrows, you cruise the Silver Ghost toward the technicolor teen-movie dreams of downtown. Like schools of bright tropical fish, the lush neon lights along the street gather, flow, then fade dreamlike in the windshield's blue wake. Perhaps James Dean did not really blast off to that great starfield in the sky in this *exact* Porsche. Perhaps not. But it does not really matter, and you are confident in your heart that if ever there was any car conceived which has half a chance to somehow actually flash beyond that vanishing point shimmering at the end of all highways it is this Porsche, the Silver Ghost. Finally, with your confident James Dean moviemask assumed, you cruise the Silver Ghost across town to haunt the Beacon Drive-In, where you begin to circle sharklike through the mysterious, Caribbean bluegreen lights of its parking lot: circling, circling, circling this slow-motion memory carefully, your Silver Ghost speedometer frozen forever at 110 as you become carefully, perfectly yourself. Finally Judy asks you to pull in somewhere so she can order some french fries and a double cherry Coke.

part one ➤

jobs, 1959

1 ➤
outlaw of love

Jimbo Stark lay on his bed in the dark, smoking. It was Judy's turn to make their weekly Monday night long-distance call. An ashtray rested on Jimbo's chest and he frequently tapped his cigarette, keeping its tip glowing. Now and then he waved the cigarette in the air, drawing with its ember random, brief afterimage shapes in the darkness, shapes like those ghosts of flame he could remember as a squirt weaving into the evening air with sparklers. I wish I was a squirt again, Jimbo thought. A squirt running through freshly mown grass on summer evenings, playing kick-the-can, hide-and-seek, not a goddamn care in the world. A squirt who still had hope. Sometimes Jimbo felt he did not have hope in anything any longer and he was lonelier than ever before. He had been banished to live at his grandmother's home in this southern West Virginia boon-dock coal-mining town and he was lonely in this his senior year as the small local highschool's only poet. It was Judy's turn to call, goddamn it!

   Jimbo clicked on his bedside lamp. He sat on the edge of his bed and fired up another cigarette. He ran his fingers back through his thick, dark hair and for a few moments just sat there holding his head in his hands. Finally he got up and walked slowly over to the window and for a time looked out at the bare branches of the frontyard maples moving in the gusty rain. The lights from the coal tipples on the hill across the

narrow valley looked hazy through the wet glass, a halo
sparkling about each one. A freight train rumbled along the
tracks through the valley, hooting its whistle as it approached
the small coal town's first road crossing. Jimbo pressed his
hands flat against the slick, cold glass to feel the train's vibra-
tions. He shut his eyes and pressed his forehead against the
glass also. Jimbo Stark was in despair.

Indeed, Jimbo Stark felt more despair than even usual. He
had felt more despair than even usual from the moment he
heard Judy had been elected by her St. Joe classmates, for the
second straight year, as the Valentine Ball's Queen of Hearts.
Being Queen of Hearts meant Judy was to wear a lovely crown
of tiny silver valentines and would with her lucky escort lead
off the Ball's first slowdance. Last year Jimbo had been the
lucky escort who led off the Ball's first slowdance with Judy.
The band last year, a local group called the Throbs, had
played a medley of oldie-but-goodie lovesongs, Earth Angel,
You Are My Special Angel, Teen Angel, and Jimbo and Judy
had slowdanced all alone around a slowly melting ice cupid in
the center of the lavishly decorated gym. Mirrored bluegreen
lights had flowed like small Caribbean moons over the huge
silver hearts hung on the gym's cinder-block walls, had flowed
watery over Jimbo and Judy, making them for those magic
moments of their slowdance as mysterious as a moviecouple.
Judy had never looked more lovely, her blond hair luminous.
Jimbo had pressed his face into her glowing hair, his breath
thick with more blondness than he had ever known. At the
song's end Judy had for a long moment just stood there in the
center of the gym looking up into Jimbo's eyes. Her own eyes
were tropical in the bluegreen light. In her tropical eyes were
islands with torchlit long canoes passing between them. The
ice cupid melted under the small Caribbean moons of light
slowly bluegreen. A long moment, a freezeframe, somewhere
forever. Then, with a sudden gay laugh, Judy rose on tiptoe to
kiss Jimbo's mouth. Being wonderful witnesses, all the other
couples, who had stood about patiently watching Jimbo and
Judy's slowdance, applauded. That was last year. This year,

two hundred winter miles away, Jimbo felt despair.

This is so chickenshit, Jimbo thought and stepped back from the window. What was he doing to himself? Poor little chickenshit feeling so sorry for himself. Moaning like the stars were falling. Perspective. He needed perspective. And bravado. Perspective and bravado. Like, man, would James Dean, old Captain Rebel Without a Cause, moon around like a punk over some silly highschool honey? Would old Captain On the Road Jack Kerouac mope around like a dope? Hell no, man! Jimbo said aloud, snapping his fingers and trying to laugh. Not old Captain Jimbo Stark either, by God! Teenage soldier of fortune! Captain Badass Beatnik Poet! Not this cat, man! Jimbo hooted again aloud. Snapping his fingers and bobbing his head like a boxer, Jimbo bopped over to his chest of drawers and got out the pint of vodka he had stashed under his socks. He took a big hit and smacked his lips as tears flooded his eyes.

Well, one good thing about living in the boonies with his dear old granny anyway, Jimbo thought, was that she didn't search his room like his dear old mom had done at home before his old man, old Captain World War Two, had tossed him out in the cold on his ass. Like the time his dear old mom had found his love poems. Un-Christian poems, she had declared and burned them. Love poems, of Judy's blondness, of blankets and Judy's warm breasts and drive-in movies on softly raining summer nights, burned. Christ! Crap! Well, that's what cancer will do to you, Jimbo thought. Make you get all goofy about religion. Going to every two-bit tent revival that hits town. Visiting shut-ins like a hobby. Jesus, Jimbo thought and smacked his forehead with his palm. My poor old lady. My poor mother.

Suddenly sad again, Jimbo sat down at his desk. For a time he held his head in his hands; then, finally, he got out the poem he had begun days before but had not been able to finish. A poem about a certain gazebo and loss. Who would have thought how lovely / those old stones / how gently / how lovingly shaped those slender rails. Crap, Jimbo thought. He took another long hit of vodka, then put the bottle back under the socks in the drawer. He flopped on the bed and fired up another cigarette. Finally, after several more cigarettes, Jimbo rolled onto his stomach and felt around under the bed for the sock. Well, here goes your basic terminal case of the hairy palms and pimples, Jimbo thought, rolling onto his back and unzipping his jeans. The sock was one of a stupid pair his grandmother had given him for Christmas, punk-kid socks, green with yellow rocket ships shooting up their sides. The sock was stiff as a corpse and Jimbo crunched it gently in his hands until it softened. Jimbo shut his eyes. Jimbo opened his eyes. The hell with Judy, he thought and with a sigh tossed the sock back under the bed.

It seemed so long ago now, that distant, mythic Friday night when Jimbo had first met Judy at a party and his life had done a flip-flop. It had been a St. Joe party and Jimbo had led his crew of Central High rowdy badass buddies there to crash it and maybe kick some chickenshit Catholic punkboy butt. But as soon as they had stomped in the door Jimbo spotted Judy. She was bopping with one of the Catholic punkboys. As soon as the record was over Jimbo had arched his eyebrows and wrinkled his forehead and let his lower face collapse into smiles, which was his perfectly Cool James Dean moviemask, mastered after earnest effort, and he had slouched Coolly over to Judy and asked her to dance. To everyone's surprise she accepted. Jimbo could sense she was nervous. Letting his lower face collapse into smiles and using his very best bashful voice, he told her he was not exactly some hot-trotting Fred Astaire on the old dance floor and he sure hoped he wouldn't crunch one of her delicate glass slippers. Then he twirled her gracefully under his arm and went quickly into one of his Cool, fancy shuffles. Judy giggled and Jimbo wrinkled his forehead. He told her he liked her haunting perfume. He pulled her close for a few steps and told her it was the same scent she wore that distant incarnation ago when the stagecoach she was on stopped to pick him up in the middle of nowhere. What in the world are you talking about? Judy asked, a cute little perplexed frown on her face. The incarnation when you were a saloon girl and had just been run out of a dusty two-horse town by the local Christians, Jimbo explained each time he twirled her near. And I was on foot in the badlands because I had had to shoot my lame horse. And your stagecoach stopped for me. And like you I too had a past. For years I had been running with a wild bunch all through the Old West. My hobby was shooting up saloons. My fast gun had become famous far and wide. I was known only as Ringo. I'd often come across my picture on posters tacked to cotton-woods down by the stream. I wasn't all bad, though. I'd never drilled a cowpoke who hadn't thrown down on me first. I'd never ridden a horse into the ground. I was always polite to saloon girls. It was love at first sight between us. You had big orange feathers in your fancy saloon girl hat and your wrists looked just as delicate as glass and you were wearing this same haunting perfume. You are a nut! Judy said and laughed and Jimbo twirled her again and again, her blond ponytail bouncing, bouncing. Then, while his rowdy badass buddies glowered drunkenly from a corner, Judy and Jimbo danced the night away. The room was awash with babble about them. Judy told Jimbo she had heard a lot about him. He explained to her that he was misunderstood. She told him he had a pretty wild reputation. He confessed to her that he secretly wrote poetry. She told him that he didn't seem as wild as everyone said. Jimbo asked Judy to run off with him to Asia where in a hidden valley he had a shimmering magic palace of silver. Judy giggled. When one of Jimbo's rowdy badass buddies tried to pick a fight with one of the Catholic punkboys Jimbo broke it up and saved the party from shambles. Two weeks later Jimbo and Judy were going steady.

It is the late 1950s and America is a lush, electric, song-filled garden for teenage truelove, and Jimbo and Judy fully expect that their own truelove will grow and grow until the end of time, until the twelfth of never. And all of their best friends, all the other couples in their crowd—Pace and Penny, who by that time have gone all the way eleven times, Bob and Sally, who have gone only to second base, Boots and Peggy Sue, who fingerfuck relentlessly—they all believe also that Jimbo and Judy's truelove will grow and grow until the end of time, until the twelfth of never. After all, they make such a cute couple, Jimbo tall, thin, dark, and Judy petite, blond. And they dance together so perfectly. Teenagers in truelove, they are romantic perfectly. They make plans for the future. They design and redesign the shimmering dreamhome of their future. They spend hours deciding upon the names for their twelve children, their six boys and six girls. They speculate about their twelve children's glorious futures. We'll need at least one major leaguer in this old family, Jimbo says. And how's about a scientist or two? And a covergirl who will go on to break into the movies and become a big star, Judy suggests. And a doctor and a lawyer, they readily agree. And maybe a college professor. And maybe one of the girls will marry a senator, or, better yet, maybe one of the boys will actually be a senator who just might go on all the way to the White House. It could happen. Anything could happen in America.

Because they go to different highschools, Judy to Catholic St. Joe's, Jimbo to Central High, Jimbo each lunch hour and every day after school without fail hops slow freights in the trainyard for rides across town to St. Joe and Judy's waiting arms. When she sees Jimbo walking up the hill from the tracks Judy runs to hug him. With a cute gesture of slight reproach she takes the cigarette from behind Jimbo's ear, then kisses him tenderly and for a long time they look lovingly into the depths of one another's eyes.

Some afternoons after school Jimbo and Judy walk around downtown hand in hand window-shopping. Through the shining membrane of glass they look at china, at silver, at their own reflections. They select patterns. They study the trays of rings. There, that's it, Judy says one afternoon. That's our ring. They have been standing in front of Goldstein's Jewelry display window for what seems to Jimbo hours. Judy's blue eyes have been grazing the glittering points of light within. Jimbo has been rather absently observing the watery reflection in the glass of the traffic flowing behind them and thinking vaguely of fish. The ring is a diamond with a heart of small perfect pearls shaped about it. That's the only ring in the whole wide world for us, Judy says, her voice husky. The only ring in the whole wide world costs four hundred bucks. Four hundred buckeroos, Jimbo thinks to himself, studying his reflection in the glass. Four hundred fish. He arches his eyebrows. He wrinkles his forehead.

On Saturday afternoons Jimbo and Judy often go to bop and slowdance on Bebop Billy's Channel 8 Happy Hop, where more than any of the other couples in their crowd they are stars. Indeed, the small red light on the gliding camera glows like grace upon them much more often than upon any other couple. When the camera settles like this upon them they look deeply into one another's eyes and shyly smile and Jimbo knows that once again their love is its own program on teevee, its signals pulsing out like light into space, becoming real in some new set forever.

It is the late 1950s and truelove can still do this, can be like a teevee serial, renewed forever. America is not yet a rerun. America is a lush, electric, song-filled garden for teenagers in truelove. Long-playing records are a dozen years old by then and stereo albums have just become available. A Columbia University professor has declared that a biological urge as relentless as electricity inspires the following of Elvis Presley, a teen idol with blue suede niggerfeet. Stars are discovered and identified on random South Philly streets. Such as Fabian, who, although only recently discovered by teevee, has been voted by the American Bandstand audience as the Most Promising Teen Male Singing Star. Pat Boone, a teen idol with feet of white buck, has announced that he will kiss the girl star in his next movie. The sales of padded bras have soared. It will be a wholesome love scene, Pat Boone makes clear. And it may be a good thing for teenagers to see a wholesome kiss, he adds, to offset the less wholesome kissing that goes on in some movies. Because of American Bandstand all of the new dances are discovered in South Philly, as though they have been waiting there forever for teevee to make them real. In addition to his daily American Bandstand Dick Clark initiates a Saturday night rock-and-roll show where each week he identifies new stars and proclaims the Top Ten of the land. Buddy Holly, Richie Valens, and the Big Bopper fall flaming into a midwestern cornfield, but they do not vanish. Frank Sinatra, an aging star with blue eyes, declares that rock and roll is lewd—in plain fact dirty. Dick Clark makes certain that American Bandstand is not lewd, not in plain fact dirty. Smoking is not allowed. Girls in tight sweaters are banished. Bob and Justine are the starring blond couple on American Bandstand. Their blond love shines from the teevee like neon. They lead off a lot of fast dances. Kenny and Arlene, both Italian, are the starring dark couple. Often they are the Spot Light Slow Dancers of the day. Arlene wears a dark jumper and a prim white blouse, the uniform of a local Catholic girls' school, which somehow makes her black eyes seem only that much more mysterious. There are rumors about how far Kenny and Arlene go. They get fan mail.

On Bebop Billy's Channel 8 Happy Hop Jimbo and Judy also get fan mail. Often Bebop Billy gives them their fan mail right on camera. Sometimes he even reads it to them out loud. How did you two lovebirds meet? Bebop Billy reads from a viewer's letter. She was on a stagecoach which stopped for me in the middle of nowhere, Jimbo says, arching his eyebrows and wrinkling his forehead. I was a gunfighter and she was a saloon girl with a past. It was love at first sight. Judy giggles and covers her face with her hands. The other couples in the teevee studio laugh and applaud with approval. Bebop Billy laughs and slaps Jimbo on the shoulder. Jimbo's lower face collapses into smiles.

How long have you two sweethearts been going steady? Bebop Billy reads from the same letter. Since the summer of '86, Jimbo says. We started going steady just two weeks after we fell in love at first sight on that stagecoach. Bebop Billy laughs, then reads from another letter: Judy, has anyone ever told you that you look just like Sandra Dee? Oh no, never, Judy says, again covering her face with her hands. Jimbo smiles, thinking of Judy's secret scrapbook, starring Sandra Dee, with its glossy collection of Sandra Dee movie magazine covers. And what about you, Bebop Billy asks Jimbo, our viewer here writes that you are a deadringer for Tony Perkins: has anyone ever told you that? Well, now, Jimbo says, wrinkling his forehead, at one time or another I've had honeys tell me I was a deadringer for about every handsome hunk of star who ever hit Hollywood, by golly. But usually they tell me I look like the late, great James Dean. Jimbo flexes his muscles for the camera. Judy giggles. All the other couples, being swell witnesses, laugh. Bebop Billy laughs. Indeed, Bebop Billy beams, beams. Always beaming, Jimbo thinks, and in spite of it old Bebop Billy looks, up close, whipped out as hell. Almost sad somehow. His sportcoat although pink and in style is slightly rumpled. His handsome host face is red and puffy and he is sweating profusely. Being in television must take a lot of juice out of you, Jimbo thinks.

Well, here's one last fan letter, Bebop Billy says, and this video viewer wants to know if you two teenagers in love plan to be married someday. Yes, and we plan to have twelve beautiful children too, Judy says, sucking her breath in as she talks the way she does sometimes, more heartbreakingly cute than Sandra Dee would ever in any movie of her life dare to be. Jimbo's unruly dork begins to stiffen. Down, boy, he thinks.

Well, Bebop Billy says, I understand that today is a very, very special day for you, little lady. Right? The big, big day. Your birthday, right? And what's more it's not just any old birthday. Gang, our little Judy here is today Sweet Sixteen! Right, honey? Sweet Sixteen! Judy giggles. Jimbo's lower face collapses into smiles. And, Bebop Billy says, beaming, beaming, a little birdie told me you've got a sweet surprise coming. Right, Jimbo? A little birdie told me that Jimbo here has something very, very special for you. And what's more he wants to give it to you right here on camera so that you two lovebirds can share this happy moment with everyone out there in teeveeland. Right, Jimbo?

Right, Jimbo says, fingering the only ring in the whole wide world in his sportcoat's side pocket. Right. Jimbo arches his eyebrows. Jimbo's lower face forever in some new teevee set collapses relentlessly into smiles.

Jimbo threw off his bedcovers and lay there naked in the cold. How could she do it? he thought bitterly. How could she pull such a stunt like that? After all they had meant to each other. After all he had done for her. After all he had given up, had lost for her. He had started on his life of crime for her. A life of pulling jobs. He had even stolen the Second World War to buy her that ring she loved, which was not his biggest job, but it was the job he felt the most guilty about. He had stolen the Second World War from his old man and sold it off to the neighborhood squirts toy soldier by toy soldier and this had cost him dearly. And then she asks Hutch Bodine. Hutch Bodine! Judy had asked Hutch goddamn Bodine to be her lucky escort and to lead off the Ball's first slowdance. Jesus Christ! Jimbo thought. Of all the guys in town. And they had gone parking, she admitted. But mostly they had just talked, she said. Sure thing. Well, yes, they had kissed a few times. Just a few times. Hutch goddamn Bodine's slimy goddamn tongue! Christ! Christ!

Jimbo sat on the edge of his bed and held his head in his hands. Well, yes, we did kiss a few times. Did you frenchkiss? Oh, I don't know. What do you mean you don't know? Either you did or you didn't! Well, I don't remember. Maybe we did. Maybe Hutch goddamn Bodine's goddamn tongue. Jimbo started to shiver. Hutch Bodine's tongue loomed huge and dripping. Jimbo kicked away the throw rug beside his bed and with a racking shudder lay down on the freezing linoleum floor. He shook. His teeth chattered. Judy's fingers moved through Hutch Bodine's hair. As Hutch Bodine slowly unbuttoned her blouse Judy pulled his face to hers, their open mouths clinging, their tongues touching, tasting. When Hutch Bodine put his hand on her knee Judy for a moment stiffened; then, with a slight shiver, she sighed and parted her legs. Jimbo did sit-ups until his stomach muscles cramped. Jimbo did sit-ups until he lost his goddamn hard-on. He lay there on the ice-cold floor sweating, shivering, choking back vomit, his stomach muscles contracting convulsively. He was disgusted with himself. How was it possible? How could he think about Judy making out with Hutch Bodine and get a goddamn hard-on? Jimbo rolled his head back and forth on the floor. He tried to cloud the horrible thought from his mind. He lay there on the ice-cold floor and tried with all of his heart to conjure summer. Summer memories. Summer gazebo memories . . .

Judy's wonderful home. A mansion over on the bluffs above the river, white pillars along its front, broad tree-filled yards all around, french doors opening onto old brick, flower-bordered patios, an ancient gingerbread gazebo perched out back on the bank above the river like some strange assemblage of bones. They would spend whole evenings out in that old gazebo's swing necking, or planning for the future as if it were real, or sometimes just playing make-believe, like pretending those tiny lights blinking from boring Ohio across the river were really secret signals just for them from some mysterious dreamshore of Hollywood. Or sometimes a tug would be pushing coal barges down below on the dark water, silent and ghostly in the distance. And in his special spooky Boris Karloff voice Jimbo would tell Judy that the tug's lights were really the glowing eyes of some awakened ancient river beast who was rising slowly up from the cold murky depths to stalk dripping and dank through their love movie hoping to carry off the beauty Judy to the tip-top of the Empire State Building and die there for love. And Judy would shiver and giggle and cuddle like crazy. Summer memories. The sweetness of it all, swinging and necking and planning and feeling as romantic as a hit lovesong.

> > >

At last it was dawn. Jimbo got up stiffly from the floor. In the near darkness, still shivering, half sick, Jimbo dressed quietly in the clothes he had carefully laid out the night before: his favorite pegged jeans, the blue shirt Judy had given him for Christmas, his red windbreaker. Jimbo's hands shook as he fired up a cigarette. Jesus Christ, he thought. I've got to get cool. Taking deep drags on the cigarette, Jimbo walked quietly on the balls of his feet over to the window and pulled back the shade. Oh holy shit, Jimbo hissed as he gazed through the ice curtain on the glass at what looked like six feet of new snow. Telephone lines sagged with snow and the dark branches of the frontyard maples were piled high. Below in the valley the trainyard looked like a white meadow and the lines of parked coalcars looked as if they were packed with snowballs. The tipples across the narrow valley looked very black against the white hillside. Like spiders, Jimbo thought. Hunched there like hungry black spiders. Or gazebos. Strange black-boned gazebos. Now that's one for the poem, he thought. Fuck the poem. Six goddamn feet of new snow. In the washed-out white air the smoke from the huge slag heaps below the tipples could not even be distinguished. There's more to come all right, Jimbo thought, looking at the closed-in, snowy sky. The night before, when he had walked down the tracks into town to buy, with his last five bucks, the biggest box of valentine candy he could find, the sky had been clear. Not a cloud. Only coal smoke. And coal smoke did not snow. So now what? Jimbo sat wearily down at his desk. So now what? Jimbo fired up another cigarette before realizing his first was still smoking in the ashtray. He arched his eyebrows. He wrinkled his forehead. Well, just screw it, Jimbo thought. Snow is snow is snow. Nothing can hinder old Captain On the Road! Rain, sleet, snow. Nothing! Captain On the Road will not fail the mail! Jimbo jumped up and bounced around the room on the balls of his feet, shadowboxing. He put Patterson away with a quick left-right, then bounced over to his chest of drawers and took out two extra pairs of thick socks and a heavy V-neck sweater. From the back of his closet he got out his old motorcycle boots. Jimbo zipped up his red windbreaker. He dropped to his hands and knees, did twenty quick push-ups, then reached under the bed for the paper sack. He walked over to the window, then took the large heart-shaped box of valentine candy out of the sack and tilted it about in the dim morning light. The box glowed blood red and the light glinted the little silver decoration cupids into dance. When he heard his grandmother coughing from her room down the hall Jimbo quickly stuffed the red heart of candy into the paper sack and carrying his motorcycle boots, he tiptoed from his bedroom.

The blizzard that had swept into the area was the worst in years and there had been little long-distance traffic, only short lifts, and it had taken Jimbo thirteen different rides, much stamping from foot to foot in the knee-deep snow by the road, and nearly sixteen hours to hitchhike the two hundred miles. Jimbo's last ride had picked him up at a desolate country crossroads where only twenty miles out of town he had been stuck freezing for nearly three hours. Stuck freezing and thinking of winter survival. Thinking about some old prospector shuffling on snowshoes across the frozen wastes of some Alaskan miles-thick glacier: shuffling and dreaming his ancient goldfield dreams of glory holes. His half-wild wolf-dog lopes along beside him. Bone tired and half frozen, the old prospector stops to build a fire and rest. His last match sputters out. It is all only a winter dream anyway, the old prospector sighs to himself and shuts his eyes. The half-wild dog sniffs about the old prospector's still form for a time, then lopes off into the wilderness. The old prospector sleeps deeply, perishing. *Perishing.* Captain Rebel Without a Cause On the Road *perishing.* Buried by this relentless winter like a lost polar explorer. They found him that spring in a melting snowbank by the road. They found him with his eyes frozen wide open, facing north, only yards from the true Pole. Services pending his thaw. Please, no flowers, no fuss. Never, man! Never! Not Old Captain Rebel Without a Cause On the Road, man!

When he saw the approaching headlights Jimbo stalked to the center of the road. This is it, man! Jimbo yelled. Old Captain Rebel Without a Cause On the Road is through with this punk Captain Snowman shit! This cat either stops for me or runs my ass down! Imagining himself as the driver might see him, a strange apparition looming suddenly in the headlights from the swirling snow, Jimbo stood in the center of the road waving at the rapidly approaching car. This cat is really moving in this snow shit, Jimbo thought, then suddenly realized the car was sliding sideways toward him. Jimbo jumped from its path and half slid, half stumbled backward into a snowdrift. The car slid past him almost out of sight before straightening and coming to a stop. Jimbo jumped up and began frantically raking snow from around his windbreaker's collar. You dumb cocksucker! Jimbo yelled, shaking his fist at the car and jumping up and down as snow slid under his coat collar and over his bare skin. You dumb asshole cocksucker! Jimbo yelled. The car idled in the center of the road, its exhaust belching clouds of fumes. Wonder why the dumb cocksucker is just sitting there? Jimbo wondered and then it occurred to him the driver just might be a little pissed himself. Or maybe he had heard Jimbo call him a dumb cocksucker and was unhappy about that. The car was an old four-door black Plymouth with pieces of cardboard stuck in place of its back doors' windows. Well, make your move, cocksucker, Jimbo thought, arching his eyebrows and wrinkling his forehead. The driver honked. Oh holy hot shit! Jimbo yelled and ran toward the Plymouth. Old Captain Rebel Without a Cause On the Road has it made in the shade, daddy! Jimbo yelled just as he slipped and fell again. This time the box of valentine candy, its paper sack long melted away, flew from Jimbo's hands. By the red glow of the taillights Jimbo saw it hit the rosy snow and bounce under the Plymouth. Oh Christ, no, Jimbo hissed, getting stiffly up off his knees. Not this! Not this too! For most of the past dozen hours of his life Jimbo had stood by the road clutching that huge heart-shaped box of candy feeling like the world's biggest goddamn sap. Captain

Crazy Person was more like it. Which was probably the reason so many cars had churned on past his frozen ass without pity. A kid in a thin red windbreaker hitchhiking in a blizzard. A kid hitchhiking in a blizzard, clutching a goddamn box of valentine candy. A crazy person. He had to be an escaped crazy person.

When he stumbled up to the waiting Plymouth Jimbo was grinning so hard it hurt. It's under the car, Jimbo called to the driver, pointing under the car and shrugging his shoulders over and over. The driver, his gaunt whiskery face yellow in the dashboard light, scrutinized Jimbo with narrowed eyes. What's that? he called, making no move to roll down the window. It's under the car, Jimbo called, flapping his arms like helpless, foolish wings. It rolled under the car when I fell down. What did, boy? the driver called, his eyes now slits of suspicion. My box. The box I was carrying, Jimbo called. The driver blinked his wet eyes several times at Jimbo as though trying to focus them, then looked ahead up the snowy road illuminated in the headlights. He took a drink of some cloudy-looking liquid from a mason jar he had been holding between his thighs. Well, boy, he said at last, after reaching over and rolling down the window, you want me to pull her up? No. No thanks, Jimbo said. It might be under a wheel or something. It might be squashed. I'll have to crawl under and get it I guess, Jimbo said, and arching his eyebrows and wrinkling his forehead, he dropped to his knees in the snow beside the car.

The old Plymouth was unheated and cold wind whipped in about the cardboard stuck in the back windows, hitting Jimbo's neck. He had not been dry for hours and he could not stop shivering. He studied his raw, bloody knuckles in the dashboard light. He had had to smash the dirty, frozen snow under the car with his fists before he could crawl beneath it to grope around for the candy box. It rested on Jimbo's lap and now and then he tentatively touched one of the oil smears on the once glossy red surface. He had tried to wipe the smears away with his coat sleeve but had only smudged and spread them. Some beat-to-hell box of valentine candy, Jimbo thought with a tight, bitter smile. Captain Crazy Person and his sappy love movie. Jimbo blew on his knuckles, then tried lightly sucking them. Nothing helped.

The old driver had not had much to say since the first exchange of general information when he told Jimbo he was a disabled miner with a black lung cough who had been widowed twice. Mostly the old driver just sipped from the mason jar and whipped the Plymouth along, the snow sweeping into the headlights from the darkness, filling the windshield thickly around the small semicircles of the slow wipers' tracks. The Plymouth slid often enough to keep Jimbo from relaxing. After a time the quietness rubbed Jimbo's already raw nerves and he began trying to make small talk but without much success until he told the old driver how surprised he was at the lift. Especially after the way he'd been standing in the middle of the road waving like a crazy person.

I always stop, the old driver said. I always stop just in case, he added and sipped from his mason jar and then was silent.

In case of what? Jimbo finally asked.

You might of been a spirit.

What? Jimbo asked. A what?

A spirit. A spook. You know, a ghost, the old driver said and took a sip from his mason jar. Then, after a few quiet moments he cleared his throat and commenced to tell Jimbo about that strange night years ago he would never forget for as long as he lived.

He and some buddies had been honky-tonking but he wasn't all drunked up. That's why he was driving while his buddies snoozed. He was barreling over some shortcut backcountry roads he knew. All of a sudden a man was right out there in the middle of the road caught up in the headlights. Clear as day. The man's shirt was almost torn off and his head was bleeding and his eyes were wide and right down crazy looking. Then suddenly the man just disappeared on across the road. He had braked the car as quickly as he could and woke up his half-drunk buddies and they had got out and

looked up and down that road on both sides for a solid hour.
But there was nothing to be found. No bloodied-up man. No
wreck. Nothing. His buddies told him he was crazy or drunk
one or maybe both. They stopped at a truck stop diner a few
miles on up the road for coffee. His buddies were kidding him
he better drink a couple gallons of coffee black. But he had
gotten the last laugh, so to speak, for when they got to telling
the story on him to the other folks in the diner the counterman
suddenly went all pale. Then the counterman had told them a
terrible wreck had happened on that very same straight
stretch of road just a month earlier. A fellow who must of
been speeding like a demon and drunk as a skunk to boot had
somehow run his big Buick up the embankment on the right
and flipped it. But they couldn't find the fellow. He was
nowhere around. And they didn't find him until a trooper
happened to look on the other side of the road way down over
the hill. That's where they found his body, way too far from
the wreck for it to have been thrown there. Well, everyone
sitting in the diner that night got pale at the same time. There
wasn't a soul in the diner who didn't realize just as sure as
sunshine a ghost had been spotted that night.

That's some ghost story all right, Jimbo said.

Well, the old driver said, I took that fellow's ghost as a sign
from God. I had never before taken religion too serious, you
know. And I still ain't what a body would call a churchgoing
man and I'm the first to admit I touch a drop now and again.
But ever since that night I got me a firm belief in a hereafter. I
got me a belief in things the naked eye can't see. That fellow's
ghost was a sign from God all right. And I always stop just in
case whatever's out there waving from the dark is another one.
Another spirit I mean. Some folks is scared of such things but
not me. I always stop.

Well, it's lucky for me you do, Jimbo said.

I guess so, the old driver said and then after a long pause
said: Listen, I don't mean to seem the nosy sort, son, but could
you tell me why you're totin' that red box around?

It's a box of valentine candy.

I'll tell you that box sure looked peculiar when I picked you up in my headlights back there. All red and bloody looking. Like you was carrying some kind of bloody human organ or something. Or like one of them old kings going around carrying his cutoff head under his arm. I thought you was a spirit for sure. That's why I started sliding like I did. Got so excited I lost control. A box of valentine candy, you say.

Yeah, Jimbo said. It's for my mother.

For your mother, you say.

Yeah. She's in the hospital. She's got cancer.

That's real bad luck, son, the old driver said and took a sip from his mason jar, then solemnly passed it to Jimbo.

Jimbo's eyes watered when he sipped the bitter, licorice-tasting liquid. He passed it back to the old driver. They drove along in silence then, passing the mason jar back and forth, until they reached a closed gas station at the edge of town where Jimbo told the driver he would like to get out.

Well, boy, you take care of yourself, the old driver said as Jimbo opened the cardoor. And here, you go on and take this along, the old driver added, handing Jimbo the mason jar. It'll keep the chill out of your bones, boy.

Sure, Jimbo said. Thanks.

I hope the best for your ma, boy, the old driver said.

Thanks, Jimbo said. Thanks a lot. You know something, mister? Speaking of your basic signs from God. My mother gets signs from God all the time.

Really? the old driver said. Well I'll be damn.

Right, Jimbo said. She's a real religious person. She used to spend half her time visiting shut-ins. Before she became a shut-in herself. She's the most religious person I know. Gets signs from God right and left.

Well I'll be damn, the old driver said. Must be a real comfort for her at a time like this.

Right, Jimbo said, taking a sip from the mason jar.

Listen, son, the old driver said and put his hand on Jimbo's knee. I got me a couple of bucks here in my pocket.

No, Jimbo said, arching his eyebrows and wrinkling his forehead. No thanks, mister.

You sure, boy?

I'm sure, Jimbo said. He climbed out of the car.

Oh hell, boy, the old driver said, leaning across the seat. I don't mean to embarrass you or nothing. If you can use a couple of bucks go on and take them. No strings.

No, Jimbo said. No thanks. I'm all right. I only have a few blocks to go to get where I'm going.

Well, don't piss against the wind, boy.

Jimbo stood in the now lightly falling snow and watched the old Plymouth until its taillights disappeared into the distance. Old Captain Rebel Without a Cause On the Road has an adventure, Jimbo said aloud and laughed. Well, almost an adventure anyway. He took a long pull from the mason jar. Jesus Christ, Jimbo thought, old Captain done got himself about half shitfaced. They found old Captain that spring bobbing still shitfaced on the surface of the thawed glacier. Services pending depickling. Please, no flowers, no fuss. Jimbo laughed and took another long hit. Suddenly at the edge of his vision a polar bear moved. Or maybe it was a ghost. Who could tell for sure? Jimbo polished off the moonshine in a final big pull, then tossed the mason jar out into the dark hoping to hit a polar bear or ghost. To hit whatever was out there. To show whatever was out there beyond the edge of his vision that old Captain Rebel Without a Cause On the Road was still armed and dangerous.

Jimbo stood in the dark street looking up at Judy's house through the trees of the expansive frontyard. From the tall windows all along the house's front lights flared out brightly over the snow. Jimbo stood there in the dark street, wet, cold, totally exhausted, and he had never been happier. Well, my ass has done arrived, Jimbo thought, arching his eyebrows and wrinkling his forehead. Old Captain Polar Explorer has done found the Ice Palace of the true North. Jimbo laughed quietly.

The snow had stopped falling just as he had reached Judy's neighborhood. Talk about your basic signs from God! Old winter had just thrown in the towel, whipped. He had licked winter single-handed, by God! A thousand miles of snowflakes big as goddamn bats. Jimbo laughed out loud, his breath exploding like smoke in the cold air. Now if only I had me a goddamn dry cigarette, Jimbo thought. He could stand here at the edge of the yard in the dark smoking like a patient outlaw of love if he had a goddamn dry cigarette. And Judy, who was surely hovering behind one of those lit-up front windows sick with worry, would see the cigarette's glowing outlaw ember. Bursting coatless out of the front door, she would call for him. Shivering in bermuda shorts and a thin sleeveless summer blouse, she would rush across the front porch calling, calling for him. Shivering in short shorts and flimsy halter, she would plunge into the thigh-high snow. Falling often, sobbing, she would wade through the drifts toward him, her lovely bare arms outstretched. Finally, crawling the last yards on bloody hands and knees, her blond hair stiff with frost, snow white and naked, she would arrive at his feet. She would clutch his legs. She would beg his forgiveness. He would flip the cigarette out into the dark yard. He would pull her up from her bloody knees and hold her shivering snow-white naked body in his arms. He would forgive her anything.

Jimbo hunched in the shadows of the high hedges as he followed the winding driveway up to the house. Jesus! Jimbo thought as he rounded the house and spotted the Silver Ghost. It was parked in the widened flat area of the driveway in front of the garages. Jimbo was amazed it was not tucked away snug in a garage on a shitty night like this. No one should leave the Silver Ghost out on a shitty night like this. He hurried through the shadows to it. There was no snow on its top or hood and its engine was still warm. Someone had just been out in it. Right! Someone had been out in it and had just returned. And since they had not put it in a garage they meant to go back out. Judy! Jimbo thought with a pang. Judy out driving around searching for him. No. Probably Frankie was driving. Judy would be too upset to drive. Jimbo had a sudden picture of Frankie whipping the Silver Ghost around the dark, dangerous streets searching for him, sliding into snowdrifts, spinning his tires, while hit lovesongs blared on the radio and Judy, riding shotgun, wept and wept.

Jimbo bent over the Silver Ghost's hood and pressed his forehead against the warm metal. Warm, warm metal. Summer metal. Summer at last. Summernight dances at the Dreamland Pool. Judy still in her swimsuit. The firm, girlish muscles of her tanned legs flexing as she dances in the poolside torchlight. Jesus, Jimbo thought, jerking upright. For a moment he was confused. He blinked his eyes. It was snowing again. The back of his neck was wet and cold and snow was caked thickly in his hair. He had a sudden image of himself being shaken up in one of those old paperweight snow scene globes his grandmother collected. He shook his head. Damn, Jimbo thought, rubbing the cold back of his neck. Did the old Captain snooze or what? The old Captain just stretched right out on the old Silver Ghost and snoozed up. Jimbo raked his fingers through his wet, stiff hair and quietly laughed. He picked up the valentine box from the Silver Ghost's hood and gently brushed off the snow. Captain Cupid, Jimbo thought, turning the pitiful box about in his hands. Old Captain Crazy Cupid freezes his ass off hitchhiking hundreds of miles through a goddamn blizzard to hand his snow-white Queen of Hearts honey *this*. Jesus. Jesus. They found old Captain Crazy Cupid that spring bobbing still sound asleep on the surface of the thawed Silver Ghost. Services pending.

Jimbo waded through the deep snow along the darkened back of the house. When he reached the french doors that opened onto the snow-buried flagstone patio he stopped. Through a crack in the pulled drapes of the gameroom he could see the dim light of a teevee. It irritated him that anyone could be watching teevee tonight while he was out probably frozen to death by the road somewhere. Judy? he suddenly thought. Could it be Judy watching teevee at a time like this? Oh fuck, get serious, man! No way. No fucking way. Probably they were catching the weather report and someone forgot to turn it off. At a time like this who could remember to turn a goddamn teevee off? Well, so now what, Captain Cupid? Jimbo said quietly and then suddenly began to shiver again. Oh Jesus, it's cold. Jesus! Well, so now what? So here he was, the big hero on the scene with the beat-to-hell box of valentine candy, and so now what? He had not really made a plan beyond this. He had not *pictured* what he would do now. He had figured some Cool move to top the whole adventure off would just pop into his head as it usually did. So pop, Cool move, Jimbo thought. Pop, you sucker!

Well, he could toss the valentine out into the snow where it would not be found until spring. And he could just head back out on that dark, desolate, dangerous road where he would surely perish. Oh, lookie, Judy would say when she found the valentine. Lookie what I just found here in the melting snow. A heart. Someone's left-behind heart. And probably they would find his frozen stiff body the very day Judy found the left-behind heart in the melting snow. And when they told her about finding him she would know whose left-behind heart it was sure enough. And it would be *too late!* Oh fuck, boohoo, man, Jimbo said, laughing quietly. Not old Captain. Jimbo tried vainly to snap his stiff fingers.

No. No, man. Old Captain would just lean this here heart up against this here old door, then bang hell out of it and bolt like a low-down outlaw of love back into the dark, mysterious night from whence he came. Only not to perish but to *survive.* He would bolt on out back to the old gazebo above the river. He would hide out there. He would spread polar bear skins over those old gazebo bones and winter there invisible. Hibernate there in that warm gazebo belly and by firelight finish his poem. No, Jimbo smiled. No. That poem was as finished as it would ever be. No, he would just go hotwire the Silver Ghost and head for Hollywood. He would outlaw-roar over every shortcut backcountry road to California he could find. He would get discovered. Become a star overnight. Then let Judy eat *her* heart out for a change. Sure, Jimbo thought. Sure thing.

Jimbo was shivering now almost uncontrollably. With a shaking hand he took out his hip wallet and from its change pocket removed with difficulty the only ring in the whole wide world. Jimbo leaned the valentine against the middle french doors and placed the only ring in the whole wide world carefully in its cleft. No, Jimbo thought. That won't do. If the box gets knocked over Judy won't find the ring until spring. After a violent fit of giggling Jimbo opened the box and stuck the ring band-first into a piece of candy near the center. Candy blood, Jimbo said, scrutinizing the ooze on his fingertips. He licked it. Hmmmmmmmm, good! Cherry candy blood! Jimbo fell to his knees in the snow, choking back laughter. Cherries are so yummy! So yummy for the tummy! And they are *so* fun to eat! Jimbo stuffed his fist in his mouth and rocked back and forth. Oh Jesus, I have gone crazy at last, Jimbo sighed and wiped the tears from his eyes. He stood up stiffly and leaned the valentine back against the door. He arched his snow-filled eyebrows and wrinkled his numb forehead and for a few moments just stood there in the deep silence of the falling snow.

Shave and a haircut, two bits . . .

Jimbo banged with all of his strength against the door and swirled to run. This time when he slipped Jimbo bounced on his stomach and slid across the snowpacked patio headfirst into a drift at the edge of the yard. It's all just a cartoon, Jimbo thought, lying there with his face buried in snow. Just a fucking cartoon. The bright patio lawn lights flashed on. Jimbo pictured the box of valentine candy sailing like a strange red bird out into the dark yard when he heard the solid *whack* as the french doors were thrown open. Maybe I am buried deeper in this snow than I think, Jimbo hoped. Maybe they won't spot me. Then, just as he began to shiver violently again, and to whimper, whimper although he bit his lip until he tasted blood, Jimbo hoped that if they did have to spot him at least it would be sometime before spring.

2 ➤
walking wounded

The movie begins and you, James Dean, are lying drunk in a
gutter, your face framed in a closeup. Curled childlike about a
toy mechanical monkey, your sidekick, you are mooing, mooing, mocking the sirens that blare with anger and danger and
with fear from somewhere in the dark adult distance. Wherever I go everything is changed, you moo. At the police station
you slouch drunkenly yet Cool in a chair, still mooing, mooing:
All I ever wanted was compassion, understanding, love. All I
ever wanted was a real chance.

  In this movie it is Easter. Also at the police station on Easter
in this movie are your co-stars Sal Mineo and the beautiful
Natalie Wood. Sal Mineo's movierole Plato, confused, lonely,
frightened, is at the police station because he just celebrated
his sixteenth birthday by blowing out the brains of five pup-
pies. All he ever wanted also was compassion, understanding,
love: especially on his sixteenth birthday, especially on Easter.
Natalie Wood's beautiful movierole Judy is at the police station
because she was picked up walking the dark adult streets
alone. Her father had called her a tramp because of the ruby
red lipstick on her sweet teen lips. She had run out of the
house into the dangerous adult night to suffer, perhaps to die.
It is chilly in the police station on Easter and Natalie Wood's
movierole Judy looks cold so, wrinkling your forehead and
arching your eyebrows and letting your lower face collapse

into smiles, which is your most magic Cool look, as tender or tough as you need it to be, you tenderly offer her your sportcoat. She nervously refuses, her full, rich, ruby red lips trembling so childlike, breaking your heart. With her love I might make it after all, you think. Some movie, you think. Some co-star.

At last your folks show up, called from an Easter party, dressed to the gills. Immediately your dear old moviemom begins to moan that now the family will have to move once again, that they will have to leave this town just like the towns before when you got into trouble, when you fell into disgrace. It's the same old song and dance, your moviemom moans. Your moviedad, starring Jim Backus, offers a fat Havana to the tough but understanding cop who is in charge of your case. The boy just got a little loaded on Easter is all, your moviedad says, laughing nervously. Right, Jimbo? he says, still laughing. Just tied one on to celebrate Easter.

The tough but understanding cop takes you into his office for a little heart-to-heart. They're a circus, you tell him about your family. Why did you have to leave the last town? he asks you. I beat a kid up. I beat him up real bad, you say, wrinkling your forehead. Why, son? I had to, you tell him, arching your eyebrows. He called me chicken. The tough but understanding cop continues to ask you touchy questions. Finally, on cue, you take a swing at him. He ducks it easily, then shoves you into a chair and takes his coat off ready for your teenage action. He suggests that if you want to hit something and stay out of trouble why not take on his desk? Really? you ask, your lower face collapsing into smiles. Sure, he says, why not? In a closeup the tough but understanding cop's face flinches with pain and recognition and, most of all, with adult guilt as you beat your fists bloody against the desk. You moan. You moo. You moan. You were not born to survive. You will never grow old in America. In a closeup your face, wrinkled, arched, collapsed, is Cool perfectly in its pain.

On that mythic Friday night he first saw *Rebel Without a*

Cause, Jimbo Stark slouched out of the Palace Theatre as James Dean's moviedouble and was for the first time in his life Cool. But Jimbo soon discovered that it was not easy to stay Cool. He had to practice. He had to practice leaning Coolly against things for hours, hours. It took him months to master his Cool slouch. And in every reflecting surface he encountered, mirrors, plate-glass windows, hubcaps, Jimbo practiced his Cool expressions like piano: arching his eyebrows, wrinkling his forehead, letting his lower face collapse into smiles, until his flesh ached with the effort.

But more difficult than these things was the never-ending effort it took for Jimbo to be truly intense, to be sensitive, to be confused, to be misunderstood, and, most important, to suffer. Ultimately, Jimbo became the most intense, sensitive, confused, misunderstood, suffering James Dean moviedouble in his whole highschool. He resigned his positions as vice-president of the sophomore class and as treasurer of the science club. He was tossed off both the basketball and track teams for public drunkenness. He started cutting classes and smoking in the washrooms. He started keeping a pint of vodka in his hall locker. He got into fights.

Finally the principal of Central High called Jimbo into his office for a heart-to-heart. The principal was a kindly old gentleman who had years earlier taught Jimbo's old man highschool algebra. The kindly old principal had taken an interest in Jimbo and was truly distressed that Jimbo had started to go bad. He lectured Jimbo about how he could be a real credit to his family and his community and even his country someday, son, if only he applied himself like he once had. A lawyer perhaps, or a doctor or engineer. Who knows? The sky is the limit in America, son. Now, it is supposed to be confidential information but maybe you should know that according to our tests you have the third-highest IQ in the whole highschool, son, so there's absolutely no reason for your poor showing of late.

But there was a reason, Jimbo said, arching his eyebrows and wrinkling his forehead and slouching ever deeper in the chair in front of the principal's desk. I am, Jimbo explained patiently in his special quiet, faltering voice: confused, misunderstood. Then, to the kindly old principal's astonishment, Jimbo suddenly mooed like a wounded bull and began pounding his fists against the desk.

With actual tears in his kindly old eyes, the principal suspended Jimbo until such a time as he decided to sincerely shape up, son, and fly right. Jimbo spent the rest of that morning playing pinball machines in the greasy-spoon diner across the street from the highschool. At lunch hour he had his pal Pace give him a lift to the edge of town. Tell them you last saw me heading down the Mississippi on a raft with a runaway nigger, Jimbo said to Pace and winked. Jimbo slouched to the side of the road and stuck out his thumb.

Jimbo's old man had to drive over three hundred miles to pick Jimbo up after he was caught hitchhiking by a nosy sheriff. After picking Jimbo up at the county jail Jimbo's old man checked them into a local motel for a night's rest before the long trip home. Jimbo's old man was grim. Jimbo prepared himself for pain. The first thing Jimbo's old man did when they got into their motel room was click on the teevee. To hide the screams and pleas for mercy, Jimbo figured. But Jimbo's old man was strangely quiet and he just sat there on the end of the bed, not even taking his overcoat off, elbows on his knees, his huge hands flopped like fish between his legs. Old Popeye the Sailor cartoons were on the teevee, but Jimbo's old man didn't change channels or anything. Jimbo sat in a chair in the corner waiting for his old man to make his move. But his old man just sat there looking like a worn-out John Wayne after a roundup or something. That's who he was a deadringer for all right, Jimbo thought. John fucking Wayne. Everyone said so. After a time the teevee began to roll but Jimbo's old man didn't do anything about it. He just sat there on the end of the bed watching old Popeye and Olive Oyl rolling on the screen as though that was the way the cartoon was meant to be. More time passed. Jimbo did not know what to do. Finally, he got up to adjust the set himself. As Jimbo passed by suddenly his old man jumped up and grabbed him by the front of his shirt. Oh Jesus, this is it, Jimbo thought. Jimbo's old man pulled Jimbo's face so near his own Jimbo could smell his breath. It struck Jimbo that this was the closest he had been physically to his old man since he was a kid and for some reason he suddenly felt more embarrassed than frightened. His old man's breath smelled like whiskey and wintergreen mints. Jimbo could smell his old man's Old Spice after-shave. Images of the teevee screen were gathered like crazy moons in the centers of his old man's thick glasses and instead of his eyes Jimbo could see only those rolling cartoons. Finally, after what seemed hours, Jimbo's old man just shook his head slowly and let Jimbo's shirt front loose.

A little later they went out to a diner for sandwiches, then returned to the room where they spent the rest of the evening silently watching teevee. Jimbo kept thinking about that night years earlier when his old man had taken him for the first time to discover television, and how for a long time television had been a sort of hobby for them. It had been the only way they could usually talk. They would sit watching teevee, making jokes and comments about the shows, as though teevee were some strange medium they, ghosts from different dimensions, different channels, had to filter themselves through to talk. But even that had long ago ended. They had to sleep in the same bed together that night in the motel. Jimbo lay there on the edge of his side as still as death. He hardly breathed. He stared at the ceiling. He was afraid to close his eyes. He did not want to fall asleep. He was afraid that if he did fall asleep he might roll over somehow and touch his old man.

Jimbo's old man's nickname was *Captain*. He got it early in boyhood, when as the boldest and toughest and swiftest squirt in town he was always the leader, the Captain. He was prepared at any moment at any place to monster-fart, to ape a cripple, to fake a fit. He would take any dare, would water-balloon or snowball old ladies, teachers who might recognize him, copcars, the blind. He would howl insanely from bushes beside old maids' windows. He would ring their bells, then dash into the giggle-filled darkness, leaving against their doors leaning Coke bottles of steamy squirt piss. He would stuff three fingers down his throat and off any movie theatre balcony in town puke like a dog.

On the morning after the December 7, 1941, low-down Nip sneak attack on Pearl Harbor, Captain led a crew of his local buddies down to the recruitment office two hours before it opened. The enlistment line would begin behind them, by God. They waited there in a freezing rain. They stamped their feet and cursed and blew in their cupped hands. Some of them were drunk. Boomer, Captain's best friend and sidekick since childhood, was drunker than anyone. Boomer was the town's richest mortician's son and he had been a clown all his life. He was the town's most feeble twenty-year-old coughing drunk and no one took him seriously at all. It was a joke that he was standing right behind Captain waiting to sign up for the Second World War. Now and then Boomer would try to muster the boys in line into a patriotic song, but most everyone ignored him. Most everyone just stood there in the cold rain grimly. Captain did not sing along with Boomer either, but he was not grim. Captain was not even particularly cold. Captain had never been happier in his life.

Because he had attended a military school all through highschool and for two years of college Captain entered the army as a second lieutenant and after basic training and officers' school was sent to Fort Benning in Georgia as an instructor. After being stuck stateside until he almost despaired, until he felt almost as rejected by the Second World War as Boomer had been, Captain was shipped finally to the European Theatre, to France, to become a hero for the first time at the Battle of the Bulge. It had been near Christmas and presents and even fruitcakes from Mom had been flown to the troops and for weeks they had been capturing mere Nazi boys and old men. The Nazis were whipped, by God, and the Allies were confident in Christmas that year, confident it would be jolly and white and perhaps even star Bob Hope or Bing. Then, suddenly, in night assaults Nazis were coming down the chimney and Bastogne was surrounded and there were rumors of American prisoners being massacred, boys being taken by truckloads to lonely snowy fields and there machine-gunned down like dogs. Captain had been a hero in that Christmas battle all right. He had held his position and he had led a daring Christmas counterattack. And for the rest of his life Nazi panzers would push relentlessly through the winter woods of his Christmas dreams, emerging suddenly out of the swirling snow, emerging always silently in his Christmas dreams from the snow-white forests to roll across the frozen open field toward where he waits happily.

Captain was promoted to lieutenant.

All in all Captain's picture was in the town's local newspaper five times during the duration and twice it even made the front page of the state's biggest newspaper, making him truly famous. The picture the newspapers published was always the same one, the photo taken just before Captain was shipped overseas, in which he is in full uniform and is smiling a wide, toothy, confident smile. Captain's young bride dutifully saved a dozen clippings each time his picture appeared, even during the dark days of the strange laughter behind closed doors and the parade of new uncles for Jimbo. She kept them in her hope chest, along with the linens and monogrammed towels, the china and the silver settings, all the wedding gifts she hoarded for the time the world became real once again. How or exactly when Jimbo got to the clippings she did not know. One of those lonely, rainy afternoons she overnipped and napped perhaps. She wept when she first found them. But later, much later, years later in fact, she would come accidentally across them and laugh, enjoying them, enjoying the Captain's goofy crayoned face, the blacked-out teeth, the red mustaches and green beards, the pointy purple piggy ears, the crossed cartoon eyes.

Captain was at some point somehow promoted to Captain

of the Second World War and for years and years afterward this illuminated his life.

So Jimbo's old man, his daddy, is coming home a hero from France. France is across an ocean. Jimbo tries to imagine France. He tries to imagine an ocean. Who are you going to vote for when you grow up? big people ask Jimbo. Not that Harry Truman, Jimbo tells them cutely and they laugh and laugh. Where is your daddy? they ask him. In France shooting Hitler, Jimbo says cutely and they laugh and laugh. Jimbo tries to imagine Hitler and shooting and he tries to imagine his daddy with a tommy gun doing it. *Rat-a-tat-tat*, like in the movies, Jimbo imagines, and Hitler grabs his spilling guts and falls off a building *splat* into the gutter far below. Lots of people go to meet Jimbo's daddy at the train station. There is a band playing and later a parade. But does Jimbo really remember this? Does he really remember the station or band or parade? He *does* remember loud voices coming from somewhere in the house. But is he asleep? Perhaps he is dreaming. Should he be frightened? The room is suddenly so noisy and bright and Jimbo's eyes are so sleepy. He is being lifted up so high. The room is full of big people. He is being kissed and kissed and his neck is nuzzled and for the first time he smells his daddy. I have everything you sent me from the army, Jimbo tells his daddy. Jimbo sits in his daddy's lap and in one of his favorite books points out all the words he has somehow magically come to know. When he asks his daddy if he is going to live here now all the time his daddy laughs and hugs Jimbo tightly and tells Jimbo he will never leave them ever again.

A war hero. A beautiful waiting wife. A healthy chip-off-the-old-block baby boy. A world made safe. Nearly two thousand bucks won at poker on the ship home. A waiting job managing old Uncle Bob's appliance store, good enough for the time being, good enough for a start. Then the whole goddamn town turns out at the train station. A band, the mayor, a state senator, a parade. So pert and pretty, so sweet-smelling this waiting wife, this cute, slightly daffy June Allyson dreambride of his memory. But these signals she claims she gets from God. And this strange, quiet little kid who can read at three. Hell, I could hardly talk at three. But, hell, two thousand bucks, a shiny new Ford, some snazzy furniture, brand-new appliances, cute little house. Maybe later a shop in the basement and a big Lionel train set for the kid. Damn right. A shiny new Ford for drives on warm summer evenings with the little lady and the kid, slowly cruising through the swell sections of town, looking in the picture windows of the big brick homes, checking the fancy layouts for decoration ideas, or sometimes just cruising around town singing songs together, the kid even piping in, harmonizing on the old sweetheart torchtunes, picking up some vanilla icecream on the way home.

In the middle of this new life you return home from driving around town one warm summer evening, your boy sleepy in the backseat, your little lady humming softly along with a song on the radio, the vanilla icecream getting nice and melty the way you like it. You pull your new Ford, which you washed and waxed that afternoon, into your driveway. You click off the headlights and then for a few moments just sit there waiting for the song to end, just sit there enjoying the smell of the summer evening and of your wife and the new smell of the Ford's interior. Well, you say, turning off the radio and engine and patting your little lady's thigh, you tote the icecream and I'll tote the squirt. You get out of your new Ford and stretch. The glow of the streetlight is silvery on the leaves of the frontyard maples and over the old bricks of the street and the lawns shine like snow. You rub your eyes, yawning, then open the backseat door and gently shake your boy awake. You pick him up, enjoying as always the clean boysmell of his hair. Still half asleep, he wraps his arms around your neck. As you wait for your little lady you gaze about. You just can't get over how beautifully strange everything seems tonight, the rich smells, the way the neighborhood shines in the streetlight's glow,

grainy and mysterious somehow, like an old-timey photo-
graph, and you have this haunting feeling you somehow have
been here in this exact time and place before but just can't
quite remember when.

Captain, hey, Captain, someone huskily whispers from your
neighbor Bill Fox's front porch next door.

In that same instant you notice that your neighbor across
the street, Pat Massy, a one-armed drunken veteran you pity, is
sitting at the top of his front porch steps. By the glow of the
streetlight you see that he is sitting there in the dark holding in
his remaining hand, his right, a shiny, nickel-plated pistol.

He's already shot out in the yard twice, Bill Fox pants as he
emerges suddenly from the dark of his yard. He says he's
gonna shoot Mabel when she gets home. He's drunk as a
skunk. We already called the sheriff.

Then you realize that the porches all along the street are
buzzing with whispering neighbors.

Oh sweet Jesus, your little lady whispers.

Here, take the boy, you say calmly, handing him gently to
your little lady.

Then you, Captain, Captain, Captain, stroll slowly down your
driveway into the sweet, luminous street. You stop in its dead
center, a glowing bell of streetlight about you, and call calmly:
Pat. Pat, old boy, it's Captain.

Oh sweet Jesus, no, your little lady gasps behind you. Honey,
come on back here. Honey, she calls, come back.

Pat Massy jerks suddenly up to his feet and stands there
weaving on his porch's top step. He waves the pistol about, its
metal gleaming silvery in the streetlight. Who goes there? he
yells.

It's just me, Captain, you say, or someone says, for somehow
you are outside yourself. You feel as though you are outside
yourself looking at yourself. You are a neighbor in this moment seeing yourself from a neighbor's front porch and in this
sight suddenly your life has a clarity it has never had before.
You walk slowly on across the street and through Pat Massy's
frontyard up to his steps. In your ringing ears the intense

whispering of the neighbors is like wind of insects. You feel strangely light-headed, dizzy almost. Your mouth tastes like brass, but it is sweet. You have never been happier. Not even as a boy. Not even in your war.

Who goes there? Pat Massy says feebly, weaving, trying to focus his eyes on you, the pistol held limply now at his side, the stump of his left arm twitching randomly as though a thing independent of his thin body. Who goes there? he mumbles again and his gold front teeth gleam. He slumps back down to sit on the top step again.

It's just me, Captain, you say quietly, taking out and lighting a cigarette, then offering it to him.

What, with my stump? Pat Massy says, still trying to focus his wet, runny eyes on you. Vomit covers his shirt front and pants. Hold it with my stump. Is that how? I can't hold it with this hand, he says, shaking the pistol in the air. I got to hold my gun in this hand 'cause it's the only goddamn hand I got so fuck your cigarette, see!

Why don't you just put the gun away, Pat. You don't need it.

The shit I don't need it, he says, trying feebly to push himself to his feet again, then, failing, falling back to his seat. The shit I don't. I need this gun to stick up Mabel's whore pussy and pull the goddamn trigger. I'm gonna stick it up in there and blast away. I'm gonna blow Mabel's whore pussy to hell.

You don't mean that, Pat. That's just bad trouble is all, old buddy.

The sheriff's patrol car, siren off and lights out, glides slowly up in front of the house and stops. Sheriff Dipero and his deputy, Bob, get out. Both are carrying shotguns.

Is that Mabel, that cocksucking whore? Pat Massy mumbles, trying to focus his eyes on the sheriff and his deputy.

That's no one, don't worry, you tell him and calmly wave back the officers, old friends of yours who will be confident you have the situation well in hand.

Now, come on, Pat, old buddy. Let's put the pistol away. Put it down and let's have a drink. By God, I could use a good stiff shot. Let's tie one on and talk about it all. How's that, old buddy?

Gonna blow Mabel's pussy a new hole.

You don't mean that, Pat. You don't really want to do that.

Fuck I don't. Just 'cause you weren't man enough.

What, Pat? I didn't get you, old buddy.

Big hero. Just 'cause you didn't have the balls. Big hero.

I didn't have what?

Balls! Balls! Big hero. Some big shit hero.

What's that mean, Pat? I don't get you.

Balls! Buddy, you didn't have 'em plain and simple. Big hero didn't have 'em when it was his turn.

I just don't get you, Pat.

Balls, goddamn it! To shoot your own whore when she had it coming. Should of shot her stinking pussy off!

What the shit are you talking about?

Big hero's wife. Big hero's whore! Big hero off winning the war. Whore sucked off half the cocks in town.

Your first blow, a looping left hook, blasts into the dead center of Pat Massy's laughing face, arching him backward onto the porch where he thuds heavily. The pistol clatters across the boards. Pat Massy's legs twitch. Pat Massy vomits like a fountain. Pat Massy's face seems bird-frail beneath your raining blows, as it breaks up bleeding, its parts shifting strangely about, caving at last inward, until they pull you, Captain, the winner again, from him.

Your June Allyson dreambride dutifully clips the front-page article about how you saved the neighborhood and adds it to the other clippings in her collection. They use the same old photo they have always used, the full-uniform, toothy, confident one. As it turns out this is the end of your dream-bride's collection, the end of her longtime hobby, for you, Captain, will never get your picture in the papers again.

You got your Coke and candy handy, soldierboy? Captain asks. Jimbo nods yes. They are sitting on boxes in back of the appliance store. The only light is from a small lamp on a desk across the room and all about them are the darkened shapes of appliances humming like sleeping creatures. Everything else is quiet. Jimbo feels strangely like an intruder in some sort of sanctum. He thinks of the grave-robbing scene in the Wolfman movie and he shivers. At any moment he half expects to hear some floating, spooky radio voice like the one on Lights Out telling him to beware of the unknown, telling him there are things men were not meant to know. Beware of the unknown. Beware of the unknown. Go back. Go back before it is too late. Only the Shadow knows. Only the Shadow knows, Jimbo says to himself and shivers with excitement. He is sitting on boxes in the spooky near-darkness with his dad, and they are going to discover television together.

They almost did not get to go to discover television together, however. Jimbo's mother had been dead set against it.

What would your Uncle Bob think about you sneaking around the store at night like a low-down common nigger burglar? Jimbo's mother had said, standing at the kitchen sink washing dinner dishes, her back to them, her orange hair glowing in the bright overhead light like filament.

It won't do any harm, Captain had said. Uncle Bob doesn't have to know a thing about it. He never goes by the store at night. They're the first two television sets in town and we're displaying them starting tomorrow morning. It won't hurt a thing to let the boy see television ahead of his pals. It'll make him a big shot with his little pals to see television first.

Well, I'm dead set against it, Jimbo's mother had said and turned around from the sink to glare at Captain. For a few moments Jimbo's parents remained like that, eyes locked, and Jimbo's heart sank. In a sudden gulp Captain polished off his scotch and milk.

Nuts, Captain said.

Captain takes a long pull from his brown-bagged pint bottle of bourbon. Are you ready, soldierboy? Captain asks and lightly cuffs Jimbo's head. Jimbo nods yes, grinning so hard it hurts. Well, here she goes, Captain says and reaches forward to click on the strange machine before them, a small fishbowl embedded in a dark wooden box with knobs. They wait silently in the near-darkness. Each time Captain takes another pull from his pint, Jimbo drinks from his Coke. Finally, from the dark depths of the embedded fishbowl an asterisk of light flickers. What the hell, soldierboy, Captain says, laughing, why not sit on your old man's lap for this big event? Jimbo clutches his Mars bar and Coke as he is lifted suddenly through the air and plopped roughly on Captain's knee. Television, soldierboy! Captain says, laughing, and bounces Jimbo up and down on his knee. The Coke is Jimbo's third of the special evening and his bladder aches as Captain bounces him. Suddenly the asterisk explodes into a dazzling starburst of silver light. As the images, shapes, and finally faces begin to slowly form on the screen, Jimbo thinks of the bright aquariums at Murphy's Five-and-Dime. He thinks of the fish, usually angelfish and goldfish, darting like little pieces of light about the bright aquariums: aquariums whose sides' thick glass was like a lens which made everything inside seem slightly larger than it actually was and which rarefied the green of the flowing plants and the cool colors of the pebbles, and sometimes a fish would swim up close to one of the sides and hover there, pressing its face near the glass as though it wanted to get a real good look out.

The phone is ringing. The phone rings and rings. For a moment Jimbo does not know where he is. He has been dreaming that the back room of the appliance store is actually the inside of a set, a radio, or perhaps even a teevee set, and that the humming appliances are tubes and speaker coils and amplifiers and all those other mysterious electrical parts which magically weave the words, the pictures, out of the thin haunted air. In his dream Jimbo dreams himself a circuit, his bones thin and silvery as filament, the current of his blood electric with flowing images. The phone is ringing. Jimbo opens his eyes and blinks for a moment in confusion. The picture on the small teevee screen is rolling slowly. Jimbo realizes where he is and in the next moment realizes he is still sitting straddled on Captain's leg. Then, in the next moment, Jimbo realizes in horror that he has pissed his pants. He glances up at Captain's face. Captain's chin rests on his chest and his mouth hangs partly open. He is snoring loudly. Jimbo slides off Captain's leg. There is a large, dark, wet stain on Captain's pants. Oh no, Jimbo thinks and immediately begins shivering. He pounds his head with his fists. Oh no oh no please oh no please, Jimbo screams inside his head. The phone is ringing. Captain wakes suddenly with a start. What? Captain mumbles. What? He looks around. He puts his face in his hands and shakes his head. The phone is ringing. What the hell? Captain says and slowly pushes himself up. Who the hell? The ringing phone is over on the desk beneath the lamp. Captain nearly stumbles twice as he walks stiffly across the room.

Hello. Hello. Who? Oh. Oh yes. Uncle Bob. Yes. No, sir. Well, I had some stuff to do. I had . . . Well, Uncle Bob, I didn't see any harm. No, I'm not, sir. Not a drop. She did? Well, sir, that's not . . . What? No, I'm not. Not the least goddamn bit. Well, damn it, I didn't see any harm. Well, she had no goddamn right . . . What? Well, I'll have you know I'm going to buy the goddamn set! That's right. Tomorrow. Yes, by God. You damn right I can. Yes. OK. OK. Look, I'm sorry if . . . Yes, I realize . . . I said I'm sorry now . . . What? Yes, Uncle Bob. I said yes. Yes, sir. Good night, Uncle Bob. Yes. I will. Good night. Yes, sir. Yes, good night.

That two-bit goddamn bitch whore! Captain yells as he slams the receiver down. Jesus goddamn fucking Christ!

Jimbo has never heard Captain curse like this before. Not these words. Jimbo stands shivering in the near-darkness by the boxes, his legs spread wide apart as if he is straddling an invisible saddle, his hands gripping his wet crotch, gripping, pushing, as though he is trying to rub the awful fluid back into his awful flesh where it belongs.

Bracing himself often on boxes and appliances, Captain walks slowly back across the room. He is shaking his head and muttering. For a few moments, weaving slightly, he stands quietly looking at the rolling teevee. Then he looks suddenly at Jimbo and Jimbo jerks with a start. Jimbo can't stop shivering. Can you beat that? Captain says to Jimbo. She went and called Uncle Bob. She called Uncle Bob and leaked to him we were down here watching the new teevee set. Now why in the world? Why in the goddamn world? Captain shakes his head and looks back to the teevee set. Why in the world? he mumbles. Why in the world? For a few moments he just stands there in the near-darkness quietly shaking his head. Then, suddenly, he reaches out, roughing Jimbo's hair, and almost yelling says: Well, by God, soldierboy, we just bought ourselves a goddamn dandy teevee set! Now how's them apples!

Captain laughs and laughs until tears run down his face. He sits down on a box finally and holds his face in his hands. For a long time he just sits there like that. After a while he looks up slowly and gazes about. His eyes are wet and shining in the teevee's light. When his gaze falls on Jimbo he winks broadly. He burps and then begins to faintly hiccup. The paper-bagged pint bottle is lying on its side on a nearby boxtop. Captain picks it up and holding it before his face as though he expects to see through the paper bag shakes it. He puts the bottle to his lips and throwing back his head polishes off whatever is left. Where's the bottle cap? Captain mumbles, glancing about. Where's the cap? Jimbo doesn't say anything. You seen the bottle cap anywhere? Captain mumbles and awkwardly gets down on his hands and knees. He begins to slowly scoot about, running his hands over the dark floor. You seen the bottle cap anywhere, soldierboy? Captain mumbles vaguely several times as he crawls around the dark floor among the boxes and appliances searching. Jimbo doesn't say anything. Jimbo stands shivering in the light of the teevee, pressing his balled fists into his wet crotch.

Here it is! Captain says at last. Here it is, by God! Found the little bugger right here. The bugger was here by this box all the damn time. Captain stands up stiffly and with a flourish of gestures screws the cap on the bottle, then puts it in his suit-coat's side pocket. All set, Captain says, chuckling, and winks at

Jimbo. You and me and our own teevee! Brand-new teevee! Bound to be the first folks in this goddamn hick town to have one. Now you'll really be a big shot with your little pals. You'll be hero of the block. You'll be boss of teevee. Captain of teevee! Just wait till she gets a load of teevee. Talk about sin! Jesus H. Christ! Captain starts laughing again. He laughs until he chokes. He pulls his handkerchief from his back pocket and almost stuffs it in his mouth to smother the coughs. Whew, Captain says at last, wiping his face with the handkerchief. Whew, soldierboy. He puts the handkerchief away.

Then, at last, Captain makes the discovery. What in the world? he says and pats his wet pants leg. What in the world? He pats at the stain, then sniffs his fingers. He pats and pinches and tugs lightly at the stain and then sniffs his fingers again. Jimbo locks his eyes on the rolling teevee. A rippling American flag fills up the screen and the Star-Spangled Banner is being played. Oh say, can you see, Jimbo sings to himself, concentrating totally on the song's words, filling his mind with their images. By the dawn's early light. Bombs bursting in air. I must have spilled my bourbon all over myself, Captain says. Look at the mess I made on myself. Jimbo glances at him. Captain is pinching the wet cloth away from his skin with his thumb and forefinger. He is grinning broadly. Accidents will happen, right, soldierboy? he says, chuckling. Even to the best of soldierboys. Hey, there, you didn't spill any of your Coke, did you? he asks, still chuckling. Jimbo quickly looks back to the rippling flag on the teevee. Blood. That's what Jimbo has a sudden thought of, almost like a wish. That the dark stain was blood. Blood from a wound in Captain's leg. A war wound. Like the war wound Captain had told Jimbo about tonight for the first time and had even lifted his shirt to show Jimbo the jagged scar on his side. Shrapnel, Captain had said and asked Jimbo if he wanted to touch it. No, Jimbo had shaken his head shyly. Oh, go on, soldierboy, Captain had said, go on. For luck, he added. In the teevee's polar light Captain's flesh had looked as pale as a fish belly and the wide, slightly puffed scar line was purple. Here, for luck, Captain said. He took Jimbo's hand

and began tracing its forefinger along the thin, hard, crooked ridge of flesh. Jimbo tried to jerk away. Captain grabbed his hand and pressed it firmly palm flat against the war wound. For luck, soldierboy, Captain had said, laughing, then had launched into another war story. It seemed no matter what had been on the teevee set that night something would occur to remind Captain of an incident of his army days and he had told one war story after another, until at last his stories blurred, cross-faded strangely in Jimbo's sleepy mind with television.

No, not you, Captain says, lightly cuffing Jimbo's head. You wouldn't spill any of that good old Coke now, would you? No, I went and spilled my goddamn bourbon all over me, that's what happened. And you know, son, it's probably for the best, by God. If I'd have drunk it all I might have gotten right down shitfaced.

Captain laughs, then, noticing the teevee, says, Hey, soldierboy, that is the flag of the good old U.S. of A. on teevee. Captain tries to adjust the rolling picture but cannot. Damn, he mumbles. He turns the volume up full blast. He clicks his heels together, snapping to attention. He smartly salutes the teevee's rolling signoff. Hey there, soldierboy, attention! Captain calls out like an order over the blaring bombs bursting teevee signoff. Jimbo snaps to rigid attention and salutes just as he has been drilled to do. Drilled to do, drilled just as he has been drilled how to march correctly, how to left-face, right-face, how to about-face, so that when he does this for visitors perfectly, Captain barking the orders proudly, they always laugh and laugh and comment on what a smart and cute little soldierboy he is.

3 ➤
dreamland's deep end

For his tenth birthday Jimbo's parents gave him the best gift he had ever in his life received. His mother had been well enough to work again in her sister Garnet's beauty parlor and Captain had not only had a good year at the appliance store but had also done well on his moonlight job for the Paramount Collection Agency. They had splurged and bought Jimbo a small Sears, Roebuck movie projector, something he had dreamed about, requesting it each Christmas and birthday for years, years. Along with it came several short silent films, things like Woody Woodpecker cartoons and Hopalong Cassidy westerns. Jimbo played them again and again, projecting the magic light against the wall of his darkened bedroom for hours sometimes, often until the machine seemed almost to glow. The small bright rectangle became like a strange window for Jimbo, through which he could watch Hopalong Cassidy, dressed all in black, wearing two shining silvery guns, ride his huge white stallion silently across a luminous western world completely at Jimbo's will. Jimbo found that if he messed around with the projector he could slow the West down or speed it up. He could stop the West cold. He could make the West run backward, the strangest trick of all, with smoke returning like imploding ghosts to gun barrels and dead men falling upward alive into the movies again. Also, he found that if he became weary of the movie he could use the projected light to make hand shadows on the wall, heads of huge rabbits, big black birds, all sorts of strange creatures, who could eat their way across the western movie at their leisure. Over the years Jimbo had never forgotten how to use the projector correctly. He had never tired of it, ever. He got twenty bucks for the thing.

He got a half-dollar each for his twenty white mice and five for the two mousemazes he had built. He sold off his elaborate chemistry set, with all of its gleaming flasks and delicate glass tubing, which when arranged for an experiment looked like some strange miniature shining city of the future. He sold his microscope and his exotic collection of stained slides. He sold the radio he had built whose vacuum tubes he had so often sat softly fondling while thinking strangely of eggs. Finally the telescope. It was a four-inch reflector he had built alone, gently polishing the curved surface of its mirror for weeks, weeks, until it could reflect at last galaxies glowing from even deep space. From a clay plateau on a hilltop near his home Jimbo had often spent whole evenings with the telescope, dialing in the seas of the moon, Saturn's rings, the red moons of Mars: dialing in starry circles of the night sky like celestial teevee channels. Jimbo got thirty bucks for the thing. Still there wasn't enough money for the only ring in the whole wide world. Jimbo would lie awake at night in his dark bedroom trying to think of something else to forsake. But there was nothing else.

Now this was that summer of strange dreams when Jimbo had begun to make the silver cones, the magic transformers, after having read that story in *Fate* magazine (Jimbo's favorite magazine) about how this sensitive, misunderstood, fired L.A. highschool science teacher had stumbled onto a surefire, simple way to tap in on those fields and flows of ghost energies which haunt the world together. Silver cones, shaped from cardboard and covered carefully with tinfoil, which after removing the plastic model fighter planes Jimbo had hung from his bedroom ceiling, their points focused evenly upon his pillow, and had begun to dream the strange dreams for the first time.

One morning Jimbo woke up unusually refreshed from the strange dreams and he discovered that they had left him with a bright idea. The dreams that night had been dreams of gangsters, of jobs and shootouts and getaways and of gangster deaths. Gangsters take what they need, Jimbo thought, and while they live they live sleek. And gangsters blaze away at death not easily vanishing. Hell, why not become a gangster? Jimbo thought and yawned and laughed. An outlaw. A desperado. Just like in the movies. Jimbo had long before guessed he could live his life like a movie, and as its star he could become always just what he imagined he was. He didn't have much gangster experience though. Ever since he had become Cool he had been a wildass all right, but he had never been much of a thief. Of course he had shoplifted a little, like that beautiful yo-yo, glossy black with rhinestone stars on both sides. And he had thieved Trojans from his old man's dresser drawer, which he had carried in his wallet, their imprints clear through the smooth leather. Not much experience, but he was young and quite willing to learn the trade. From now on he would watch gangster movies sincerely. He would get all the gangster lingo down cold. From that moment on, Jimbo decided, grinning, yawning, stretching in the early morning sunlight, he would plan how to raise the rest of the four hundred bucks for the only ring in the whole wide world in terms of jobs.

So you don't have any idea about what happened to your movie projector? Captain asks Jimbo in one of his favorite Captain of the Second World War voices, the sort of tough but understanding one, a voice great for talking the frightened punk private out of going over the hill. Your mom and me have to make a lot of sacrifices, son, to get you a swell gift like that movie projector. Do you have any idea how long I have to moonlight to afford to get you things like that?

Well, I don't know where it is, Jimbo says, hating the whine in his voice. Anyway, you gave me that old thing over six years ago.

That, son, is not the goddamn point at hand, Captain says, his voice now one perfect for forced marches through winter woods.

Jimbo's family is sitting around the dinner table, eating, at his mother's insistence, by candlelight. Something they do often, for, as Jimbo's mother points out, just because they aren't as filthy rich as some folks doesn't mean they can't show some class. Tonight by candlelight they are eating waffles.

And your mom says that the projector isn't the only goddamn thing missing from around this house, Captain says, drinking from his water glass of scotch and milk and leveling his eyes on Jimbo's face. Jimbo averts his eyes from Captain's. He glances at his mother. In the soft candlelight the gauntness of her face isn't so apparent. Her face looks almost lovely again. She is smiling faintly as she studies her plate where she worries bits of waffle about in the syrup. Screw her, Jimbo thinks. Fucking snooping my room again. Like the last time when she had discovered his *Playboy* magazines. Un-Christian magazines, she had declared and burned them with great ceremony out back in the barbecue pit.

But Jimbo could remember her otherwise. Vaguely now. Always, it seemed, more and more vaguely. Memories of being rocked and sung to, of having his ears tickled with a bobby pin for hours it seemed; memories of sitting at the kitchen table together whole evenings sometimes, listening to their favorite radio shows, or sometimes she would just talk about their plans together of days-long train rides west to Hollywood where she would be discovered in a drugstore and break into showbiz and become overnight a star, and filthy rich beyond belief they would live in a hilltop mansion with walls of gleaming glass and a swimming pool, its water California sky blue and heated, and he could have a pony with a silver-trimmed saddle. But it never happened. They never train-rode west to Hollywood. Instead they moved in with Garnet, Jimbo's mom's older sister, to wait for Jimbo's old man to wrap up the war and return home like a parade. And then Jimbo's memories, still vague, were of his mom and Garnet and of Garnet's friends sitting around the kitchen table at night drinking from quart bottles of beer and laughing: memories of strange voices through closed doors and laughing and of streams of new uncles until that strange day of salvation.

It was on a cold rainy day in December and I had myself a case of the sniffles, Jimbo's mom would tell when remembering that distant afternoon of salvation at Ketchum's Funeral Home. Her sister Garnet's beauty parlor was contracted at that time by Ketchum's to fix the final hairdos of corpses being prettied for viewing and Jimbo's mom was there that afternoon alone working on old Miss Lawson's hair. I remember I was thinking about your dad, Jimbo's mom would tell, declaring she could remember it like yesterday. She hadn't received a letter from him in a couple of weeks and she knew from the papers that heavy fighting was going on in his theatre. She was worried that maybe he hadn't received the nice Christmas presents she had mailed. She was feeling sort of tired and blue while she worked slowly on old Miss Lawson's hair. I remember it perfectly, she would tell. I was just pinning a big curl by old Miss Lawson's right ear and Bing Crosby was singing I'm Dreaming of a White Christmas on the radio when suddenly she sat up. Old Miss Lawson just sat up as big as you please like she had totally forgotten she was dead. I mean I have heard of dead bodies floating up in water before but never in thin air. I must have hit my head on the table when I fainted for I went into sort of a coma or a trance or something and I didn't wake up until the next afternoon home safe in my own bed. But from the very moment she did wake up Jimbo's mom knew just as sure as breathing that she had had a religious experience, a signal from God. God wouldn't just go around terrifying a body like that for no good reason. Jimbo's mom just knew that God had picked her out special. She had been waiting her entire life to be picked out somehow, to be made special, and she had never lost faith in its eventually coming to pass. Now it had and she was saved by it. She was reborn. And don't ask me how I knew, Jimbo's mom would tell in her hushed, religious voice, but somehow deep in my heart I was sure that old Miss Lawson's corpse sitting up the way it did was a special signal direct from God to me that the Allies were destined to win the Second World War and that your dad would come home safe and sound and a hero to boot.

They went religiously then, Jimbo and his mom, every Saturday evening to the movies to witness the Second World War, the star of many films and of all the weekly newsreels, being won as surely as a serial. Outplotted again and again by the cunning and courage of Hollywood, German generals, cast as cartoons, goose-stomped their monocles in rage. With whole rising-sun battalions being beaten by handfuls of Seabees with bulldozers, Japs jabbered more and more hysterically and began dive-bombing their funny little yellow cartoon Zeros *splat* against the miraculous metal of American ships, vanishing to no avail.

Old Miss Lawson's rising corpse was but the first of many signals Jimbo's mom was to discover and identify over the years, including the most recent, when one morning just six months earlier Jimbo had trotted down for breakfast to find her sitting quietly alone at the kitchen table, an ashtray of smoldering stubs before her, the radio softly humming gospel songs. I don't think I'll get around to cooking up breakfast this morning, she had said, her voice hushed, a strange tight smile on her lips, and her eyes wide and bright. Terrific, Jimbo said and trotted over to the refrigerator. She started humming along with one of the hymns, then after a few moments said: You know, I had wonderful, wonderful dreams all night long that our Lord Jesus came back to earth and walked among us again making miracles right and left. Here we go, Jimbo thought, scanning the refrigerator shelves, amen city. Yes indeedy, Jimbo's mom said, Jesus touched all the lame and the blind and all the sick and He cured them. There was no pain nor misery anymore. Nobody had to die anymore. And I just know deep in my heart it's going to come to pass soon. Because I got me a signal, Jimbo's mom said, turning her face toward him, its creamed skin glistening in the bright overhead light. You know, this morning when I took my bath I discovered a lump.

Well, what about it, son? Captain asks, and except for the low drone from the teevee in the living room, everything falls silent. Things just don't vanish into thin air. You best come up with some answers.

Jimbo looks at Captain's huge hands, at the thick fingers enfolding the water glass of scotch and milk. He remembers having heard somewhere that big fingers meant big dicks and for a moment, in spite of himself, he wonders. Jesus, but he is a big bastard, Jimbo thinks, sizing his old man up, as he does at least once every single day of his life. And goddamn if he isn't just like everyone says a deadringer for fucking John Wayne.

Well, son, answers, Captain says in his firm but polite Captain of the Second World War interrogating a Nazi officer voice.

I don't have any answers, Jimbo says. Things just get lost sometimes. But they always turn up. Anyway, why do I always get blamed for things vanishing around here?

Jimbo's mother's fork, spearing minced waffle, clinks china. Pitched battle noises flare up from the teevee in the living room: shouts, exploding shells, machine gun fire, screams. From where Jimbo is sitting he can see the image of the teevee screen reflected like some strange low moon in the left bottom corner of the living room's picture window, the battle raging across its ghostly surface. Captain carefully forks another waffle from the platter and butters it slowly, the movements of his huge hands precise. Jimbo is fascinated, as always, by the strange grace, the delicate touch, of Captain's powerful, frightening hands. Jimbo thinks of Captain's hobby, his miniature armies of tiny toy soldiers, with all the small features of the faces, all the details of the uniforms, so exact: all the bright colors so cleanly painted, so painstakingly perfect. Those huge hands, Jimbo thinks. Big dicks. Big dicks.

The candlelight glistens like liquid on the butter knife, its motions, and on Captain's wide gold wedding band. Small moons of candle flame are gathered in the thick centers of Captain's glasses and Jimbo worries. He always worries when he can't see Captain's eyes. Carefully Captain covers the waffle with syrup, the liquid spreading thickly, evenly, to the waffle's edges, stopping there, a perfect puddle. Captain is smiling faintly. He is smiling his tightly grim smile, the most dangerous of all. Jimbo's stomach knots with fear. He has a sudden urge to swirl from the table and run. *Run for his life.* He remembers suddenly that long-ago day he failed at fishing. That fearful day he could not touch the silvery form flopping to death in the deep grass. You have to snap its neck, Captain had told him. So it won't suffer too much. So it won't have to drown in the air. *Could not.* Could not meet the eyes, the fisheyes, Captain's. Captain had had nothing but contempt for him, had even hated him at that moment, Jimbo had more than suspected as he watched Captain pick up the still twitching trout and walk grimly toward him.

It can't hurt you, Captain had said. It's just a fish. Here, do it. Goddamn, I said do it! Goddamn girl!

Jimbo swirled to run but Captain caught him by the back of his shirt. Captain cupped the back of Jimbo's head and neck in one of his huge hands and with the other slowly rubbed the trout over Jimbo's face, until at last the fish hung limp and dripping.

Jimbo is being held up like a fish. His mouth feels torn. A thumb stuffs a gill. Fingers burn scales. Perhaps he is dreaming. Should he be frightened? Actually, he is numb and more sees these things than feels them. No, he *only* sees them. He does not feel them at all. It is a dream. It is the old fish dream, a dream he has had often since that day he failed at fishing. The pressure is gentle, a gentle squeezing. But this is not the fish dream. It is his foot, his right foot. But is he asleep? His right foot is being held, squeezed gently. Jimbo awakes slowly. His right foot is warm in a huge hand. Jimbo blinks his eyes in the darkness. The dark form sitting on the bed beside him is framed in the hall light coming through the open door. Soldierboy, the dark form whispers. Jimbo can smell whiskey. The warm hand holding his foot is damp. Soldierboy, you awake? Yes, sir, Jimbo nods in the darkness. You want to camp out tonight, soldierboy? the form whispers. Yes, yes, sir, Jimbo says and sits up.

Jimbo rubs his eyes in the bright hall light as he follows the slightly weaving Captain toward the kitchen. *Camping out!* Hot dog! It had been a long time since Captain had asked him to camp out. Maybe everything was all right now. Maybe it didn't matter that he had failed again. Failed today at the Dreamland Swimming Pool. Failed this time at swimming. Maybe it was all right now. Captain had gotten him up, *right?* And Captain had asked him to camp out again, *right?* Maybe he would not have to go to summer camp after all. Maybe swimming would not matter now.

Uncle Boomer is sitting at the kitchen table. His face is very pale in the bright overhead light and there are deep shadows under his eyes and in the hollows of his cheeks. He is wearing his old, battered gray fedora tilted back on his head as always and as always a cigarette dangles from the corner of his mouth. With his fedora and his thin black mustache, Boomer looks, to Jimbo, like that teevee detective, Boston Blackie. Jimbo wishes he had a fedora and a thin black mustache. Jimbo wishes he was a teevee detective. He will be someday all right. Someday. Anyway, Boomer sure doesn't look like an undertaker, which is what he is. Worm pies, Boomer always says, that's my business. Worm pies.

Hello, squirt, Boomer says to Jimbo in his deep, froggy voice, the source of his nickname. Jimbo grins at him. Uncle Boomer is his best buddy. Jimbo sits down at the kitchen table. Jimbo blinks, then rubs his eyes. Jimbo stares at the snow-piled tabletop. No, it's not snow, Jimbo realizes, squinting his eyes. No, it's sugar, he realizes, spotting the opened sugar canister at the table's edge. *Sugar?* Two, maybe three pounds of sugar, white and sparkling in the bright light, spread out over the tabletop, shaped into little rolling hills with finger tracks traced like small roads through them.

Damn, Captain says.

Jimbo glances up at Captain's looming, weaving form at the end of the table.

I went to wake up my soldierboy and I clean forgot to relieve myself, Captain says.

You forgot to go potty? Boomer says and pours a water glass nearly full from a bottle in a paper bag.

Yes. Yes, I did. I clean forgot to drain my hog, Captain says and walks unsteadily back toward the hallway.

Boomer chuckles and takes a long drink from the water glass.

Jimbo touches the nearest hill of sugar, then puts his finger in his mouth.

How does it taste, squirt? Boomer asks and winks one of his droopy-lidded, always sleepy-looking eyes.

Sweet. Like sugar, squirt *yourself*, Jimbo says.

Like sugar! You're kidding, squirt, Boomer says, taking another drink. It should taste like cheese. It should taste like the moon. That's a lunar landscape you're nibbling at, squirt. The man-in-the-moon's cheeks.

What's that mean, squirt yourself? Jimbo says, tracing a finger around the sugar's edge.

Doesn't mean a thing, squirt, Boomer says and winks again. I don't mean to confuse you. I'm pulling your leg actually. Actually that's the Second World War you're tasting there, squirt. Actually that's your basic Battle of the Bulge you're calling sweet.

What's that mean? You're just talking silly. 'Cause you're drunk. And Daddy's drunk too.

Why you're not quite as dumb as everyone says you are, Boomer says and chuckles.

Sometimes you're the one that's dumb, Jimbo says.

Captain walks back into the kitchen and turning a chair

around from the table straddles it. His thick glasses are steamy about their edges and tufts of hair are plastered against his damp forehead. He rolls a toothpick about in his mouth and for a time just sits there staring at the sugar on the tabletop. Jimbo stares at the sugar also. The moon, Jimbo thinks. The man-in-the-moon. A sugar moon. A sugar man-in-the-moon.

Do I look like a worried man, Boomerboy? Captain finally says, squinting his eyes at Boomer. Just because I piss bright red.

Are you a worried man? Boomer says, polishing off his drink and pouring another.

Not me, Boomerboy. Just because I piss blood. Why would pissing blood bother an old warhorse like me, Boomerboy?

You're right. It shouldn't. Just a goddamn leaking war wound probably.

Right, Boomerboy. And by God, red's a patriotic color. Red, white, and blue, Boomerboy. When I piss it's like a goddamn salute.

No, Boomer says. Sorry but you're wrong there, Cap. Red's a commie color. You piss commie.

Smile when you say that, Captain says.

Boomer flashes his small yellow teeth.

Check, Captain says and holds up his glass.

Check, Boomer says and clinks his glass against Captain's and they both toss their drinks down.

Boomer pours them both another drink and for a time they just sit there silently sipping and staring at the table. Captain, almost absently, begins smoothing the small hills of sugar and retracing the little roads, the sugar dimpling faintly in the wake of his moving finger. Jimbo intently watches the slow movement of Captain's huge, hairy hands as they gently shape and reshape the sugar. A wooden kitchen match is stuck blue tip up like a small flagless pole near the sugar's center, and it occurs to Jimbo, as he watches Captain's hands, that Captain is shaping everything, all the little hills, the roads, around this match, that the match is the center of it all. It occurs to Jimbo that the match is the Captain, and he has a sudden crazy picture of the Captain standing knee-deep in sugar wearing a strange blue helmet.

Yes, sir, Captain says, they thought they were being smart when they split the goddamn column. Captain takes the toothpick from his mouth and flicks it toward the garbage pail under the sink. With his forefingers Captain carefully traces two lines that circle the bottom of a sugar hill toward the match. Suddenly he flicks little sprays of sugar like small explosions. They thought they were cute until we nailed their asses. Captain laughs and takes the match from the sugar and puts it between his teeth.

Right, soldierboy? Captain says and covers the top of Jimbo's head with his huge hand like a helmet. They thought they were cute, didn't they? Captain says and shakes Jimbo's head. Hey, soldierboy, did you tell your old Uncle Boomerboy about summer camp? Yes, siree! Old soldierboy here's heading for old Camp Six Nations a week from Saturday. Get him ready for old Greenbrier Military someday. Got your heart set on it, right, soldierboy?

Yes, sir, Jimbo says.

Yes, siree. Old soldierboy here's been getting all set for old Camp Six Nations. We've been getting ready for weeks. Getting in shape. Practicing everything. Got him batting and fielding like a Cincinnati Red. Like old Gus Bell or Ted the K. Even been going out to the driving range a few evenings a week. Listen, the kid just might make another Slammin' Sammy someday. Had a little trouble with the swimming over at the Dreamland Pool today though. But we'll get it licked. He'll be swimming like a fish by the time he heads for camp. Right, soldierboy?

Yes, sir, Jimbo says.

Swimming like a fish you say, Boomer says.

Like a goddamn fish, Captain says. Right, soldierboy?

Yes, sir, Jimbo says. Yes, siree.

Soldierboy, how's about I go get things set up? Captain says and polishes off his drink. He rises heavily to his feet. Boomer, you stick around, buddy. I'm just going down to the shelter and get old soldierboy's cot ready. While I can still crawl, Captain says and laughs and walks unsteadily over to the basement door. He stomps heavily down the basement steps.

Swim like a fish, eh? Boomer says and chuckles.

I'll probably drown first, Jimbo says and flicks at the sugar with a finger.

Then you'll be one of my customers, squirt. A soaked squirt worm pie.

Who cares? Jimbo says.

Is this a private party? Jimbo's mother says. She is standing in the hall doorway. Her blond hair is rolled up in curlers and her face is shiny with cold cream.

No, come on in, my dear, Boomer says. You don't need a ticket for this party.

What the dickens are you doing up, little man? she asks Jimbo. As she walks toward the table she clutches the top of her blue quilted robe together tightly with both hands. Do you have any blessed idea what time of night it is, little man?

Dad got me up, Jimbo says and flicks at the sugar. We're going to camp out together. He's down in the shelter fixing my cot.

Oh, that's peachy. Oh my word, what in heaven's name is this mess? she says and bends over the table squinting her eyes at the sugar.

That mess is your basic Second World War, Boomer says. You remember. Boom boom. Bang bang. Don't you recognize a basic Battle of the Bulge mess when you see one, my dear?

I don't believe it. I just don't believe it, she says, shaking her head slowly. The sad, tired look comes over her face, the lines around her mouth deepen, and her eyes get wide and watery. Well, this is just peachy, she says. Well, just how far gone is our Captain tonight?

No more than half, Boomer says. About like me.

Thanks for getting him home anyway.

A pleasure, my dear.

Jimbo's mother holds the sugar canister under the edge of

the table and begins to scrape the sugar into it. Boomer stands up and helps her. Jimbo scoots his chair away from the table and just watches as the little sugar hills and roads disappear. He feels vaguely sad.

Well, so how have you been, Bob? It's been a spell since you've been around here, Jimbo's mother says.

Can't complain. Business is brisk, Boomer says. He carefully scrapes the last of the sugar off the table into the canister which Jimbo's mother now holds with both hands. Worm pies forever, he says and sits back down. How's it been with you, June?

I stay busy with my church work, she says. She puts the canister on a shelf over the sink, then returns to the table with a washrag and begins to slowly wipe the grainy surface.

Still Jesus, eh? Boomer says and raises his glass toward her. Well, here's to you two.

You never did understand, she says. She stops wiping the table and stands there staring at Boomer. You never really tried, did you, Bob?

Wrong, Boomer says and drains his glass. You're the party who never tried.

When Captain calls for him Jimbo jumps up from the table. His mother glares at him and he looks away. He walks eyes downcast slowly over to the basement door. He noisily hops down the basement stairs two at a time.

Such a nice full basement, warm enough in winter, cool enough in summer. But no shelves of jellies and jams, no rows and rows of mason jars of green beans will you find in this basement; and no boxes or barrels or trunks or old furniture will you find stored along its walls or stacked in its corners. There is room only for Captain's battle tables, tables Captain has built all around the walls of the basement and then in exact, miniature detail has lovingly landscaped with chicken wire, with papier mâché, with earth and stone, the terrains of famous battlefields. There is a Battle of Hastings table, a Waterloo table, a Gettysburg table, and along with three other

Second World War tables, a large Battle of the Bulge table.

This is Captain's hobby.

Night after night, scotch and milk in hand, Captain descends into his basement to drink alone and play war games on his battle tables with his tiny toy soldiers for hours, hours: recharging the great charges, reretreating the great tactical retreats; companies, legions, whole armies of tiny toy soldiers Captain cast himself, then painstakingly painted and each night breathed battlelife into, whole armies of tiny toy soldiers rising and falling and rising once again, all by Captain's command. He could save Napoleon at Waterloo with an unexpected daring charge of confederate cavalry. He could crush the Normans at Hastings with a surprise Roman ghost legion and pluck that fateful arrow from Harold's eye just as he pleased. Then there was the one toy soldier Captain had made special, had cast him larger than the others and had fashioned him in an elaborate, princely uniform of his own design. It was this special toy soldier of the Captain's who always led the victors to their glory, no matter what battle of what armies of what age. For years, night after night, for hours sometimes, hidden in the dark beneath the basement steps, Jimbo would watch Captain's intense face as he fought.

I'll turn the teevee on, soldierboy, Captain says. You can watch the late show until I get back, how's that?

Why don't you stay now? Jimbo asks. He sits cross-legged on the army cot Captain has spread over with a sleeping bag.

Well, fellow, I'll be right back. I just want to say goodnight to old Uncle Boomer is all. I'll come directly back. Listen, there's a good late show on I bet.

I want you to stay down here. It's no fun being down here by myself.

Why, you're not afraid, are you? A tough old soldierboy like you? Afraid of the buggerman? I'll leave the lights on.

No! I'm not afraid! I just want you to stay here, that's all. Why can't you stay here anyway?

Now don't you start any of that damn whining.

Yes, sir.

Oh hell, soldierboy. Listen, I'll open you a Coke. How's that? Only don't tell your mom, all right?

Mom's up.

She is?

She's up with Uncle Boomer in the kitchen.

She is.

She and Uncle Boomer cleaned your sugar off the table.

Well, listen, soldierboy, I'll be right back.

Can we use the ham radio tonight?

Sure. Damn right. We'll call all over the goddamn place. We'll call Cincinnati. We'll call Hollywood, California. Hell, we'll call the goddamn moon!

Will you tell me some monster stories like you used to when we camped out when I was a little kid?

Damn right, Captain says. He gets a Coke out of the refrigerator which he opens and gives to Jimbo. I'll scare holy hell out of both of us. I'll tell you about the time old Count Dracula and the Wolfman teamed up to fight Frankenstein to the death in this spooky old castle.

And some spook stories? And some spaceman stories?

Damn right, soldierboy. I'll tell you about the time some moon spook tried to invade town.

And some army stories?

Army stories? Army stories! Hey, soldierboy, just who the hell do you think fought off the moon spooks? The good old U.S.A. Army, that's who.

Do I have to go swimming anymore, Dad?

Captain walks over and clicks on the teevee. He stands there beside it until its screen lights up, then he adjusts the picture until it is steady and clear.

How's that picture? Captain asks.

It's all right.

Looks like a cowboy movie.

Yeah.

I'm sorry, soldierboy.

Captain has to duck slightly as he passes through the shelter's low door into the basement.

Jimbo listens to Captain walk across the basement, then stomp up the stairs to the kitchen. Shit, Jimbo thinks. Shit, shit, fart, puke, damn, hell, fuck. Fuck. Double fuck. Double shit fart fuck. I won't go to sleep, Jimbo thinks. He shakes his head to clear it. I won't go to sleep before he comes back no matter what. Jimbo looks around the room. He hasn't been down here for a long time. This was Captain's room and you did not come down here unless he asked you. Captain had spent almost a year digging the room off the basement, then cinder-blocking its sides and finishing it up inside with knotty-pine walls. There was a small refrigerator in one corner and a teevee set in another. There were floor-to-ceiling shelves along one wall which were stacked high with cans and jars of food and with rows of gallon jugs of spring water. On a long table along another wall Captain had set up his ham radio outfit and on wooden racks above the table were his four favorite rifles and two shotguns. On another wall were colorful maps of the town and county and state all stuck with small red pins showing the area civil defense locations. On another wall were framed photos of General Patton and General MacArthur and of President Ike. This was the only bomb shelter in the whole county. Those commies won't catch me with my Pearl Harbor hog hanging out, Captain would say when he was showing someone around the basement and shelter. Captain was fully prepared for World War Three and for a long time he had been sleeping nightly down in the shelter on a rollaway bed.

Jimbo hears loud voices from the kitchen, his mother's voice, Captain's voice. This means Uncle Boomer has left. This means Captain won't be back down for a while. Jimbo hears shouts from the kitchen. Shit, he thinks. This means Captain might not be back down until morning. Or tomorrow night. Or next week. Shit, Jimbo thinks. Shit fart fuck. Well, I won't go to sleep, Jimbo thinks. I don't care how long it takes. I don't care if it takes until Christmas. Until Easter. Jimbo opens his eyes wide and stares intently at the teevee.

The shouting from the kitchen suddenly stops. Jimbo tiptoes from the shelter across the basement to the bottom of the stairs. The kitchen door is shut. Jimbo can hear his mom crying. She cries for a long time and no one says anything. Suddenly she shouts something and Captain shouts back. They start shouting and shouting again and someone smashes something glass. Jimbo runs back to the shelter. He slams its door and locks it from the inside, something he has been ordered never, never to do. Let him whip me, Jimbo says out loud. Who cares? Who cares? No, he can't whip me anyway, Jimbo thinks. Even if he wants to he can't. He can't get in. The shelter door was closed and locked and Jimbo would never open it again. Never. Never. They could beg him but he wouldn't open it. Please, please, they could call to him. Shit fart fuck, he would call back. Even if World War Three started up and commies were dropping bombs all over town. Even if moon spooks invaded town. Jimbo still wouldn't let them in. It was his room now. There were Cokes in the refrigerator. He had a teevee set. He could camp out in the shelter forever. And he wouldn't have to go to summer camp. And he wouldn't have to worry about the deep end ever again.

The shouting from the kitchen gets louder and louder. Even through the closed shelter door. Jimbo puts his hands over his ears. He shakes his head. Nothing helps. He pulls the cot over directly in front of the teevee set and turns its sound up full blast. He takes the four remaining Cokes from the refrigerator and opens them, then sets them in a line on top of the teevee. He checks to make certain the shelter door is really locked, then sits on the cot with his face only inches from the blaring teevee screen so that its picture fills up all he can see. He can feel the teevee's heat on his face. There is a faint crackling on his flesh. He squints his eyes until they water, until the cowboy forms fade, dissolve, become shadowy fish shapes his skin can feel. Captain took him for the first time to discover teevee. A night long ago. A hundred years ago. Jimbo shakes his head.

He doesn't want to remember things outside the shelter. He doesn't want to remember Captain at all. He wants to dissolve in the teevee's light, to be a shadowy fish form in teevee's deep end.

Let's head for the deep end, Captain had said. You can swim like a fish, soldierboy, Captain had said. Just jump in and swim to me, son. I'm right here, soldierboy. Jimbo curled his toes over the pool's edge. The deep end. He could smell chlorine. The choppy, faintly green water shivered with light. Squeals of laughter, screams, splashing, loud music blasting from the clubhouse filled the air. Jimbo shivered. He wanted more than anything to be with Captain in the deep end. Come on now, Jimbo, Captain called. I'm right here. You're not going to drown, damn it! Jimbo gazed at the blue, onion-shaped domes of the dressing rooms at the far end of the long pool. He wished with all of his heart that the day was over and that he was in that dressing room right now. Jimbo knew he would not drown. He knew that. He knew that. Damn it, jump! Jump! Captain shouted and slapped the water with a cupped hand. It sounded like a shot. Jimbo flinched. He stared at his toes, at the deep end only inches beyond them. He felt dizzy. Jump, damn it! *Slap.* Jump! *Slap.*

Why don't you go on and jump, chicken? someone from behind Jimbo said and laughed. You ain't gonna drown, chicken. Others laughed. They were all around him. Boys. Girls. Giggles. Laughter.

Jump! *Slap.* Jump! *Slap.*

Jump, jump, jump, they began to chant along with Captain.

It was not really much of a shove. More a touch, a mere pressure of fingers from someone behind him. The deep end's water strangled into Jimbo's throat. He chopped desperately to the deep end's surface. He chopped choking, half blind, toward Captain. That's it! That's it! Captain called as he paddled backward in the deep end away from Jimbo.

From where Jimbo is sitting he can see the image of the

teevee screen reflected like some strange low moon in the left bottom corner of the living room's picture window.

Well, answer me, son, Captain says. Where is your movie projector? Where are the radios and that telescope you built? Things don't just vanish into thin air.

They're all my things, Jimbo says, sliding bits of waffle about on his plate, wishing those moons of candle flame were not gathered in Captain's glasses hiding his eyes, wishing that tight, dangerous smile was not on Captain's lips. They're my personal business. She has no right nosing around in my room.

I beg to differ, Jimbo's mother says, tapping her lips lightly with a napkin. I have every right. I am your mother, after all. And I worry about you day and night. Here I am sick and all and I have to worry and worry about you. Honey, I don't like those crazy books you read. I've told you and told you. And then I find all those dirty poems you wrote about that little Catholic girl. And now all your nice toys have up and disappeared. I just worry myself sick. And I am already sick enough.

Bullshit! Jimbo yells. Stay the fuck out of my room!

For a backhand it is a good blow, quick, solid, and Captain's middle knuckle catches Jimbo high on his forehead cleanly. Jimbo falls over backward in his chair. It all seems strangely like slow motion. A series of freezeframes. A slow-motion cartoon backward fall. In less than two seconds the back of Jimbo's head will strike the baseboard and he will be knocked cold for nearly five minutes. It is in that slow-motion moment before Jimbo's head strikes the baseboard knocking him silly that he plans fully the last job he will need to pull to purchase the only ring in the whole wide world. Yes, Jimbo gets the bright idea to steal the Second World War and to sell it off soldier by goddamn soldier.

4 ➤
wolfman moon

Sandy Dee and Troy Donahue are frenchkissing behind a large
rock on a secluded beach when several guys come trotting past
and slow up to make wisecracks about Troy getting some.
Troy jumps up and chases after them but they run, laughing,
on down the beach. When Troy returns and flops back down
beside her Sandy sees he is embarrassed. She takes his hand.
After a few moments of silence Sandy shyly asks Troy if he has
ever been bad with a girl. No, Troy says, I guess not.

As soon as Sandy calls him with the bad news Troy runs
away from prep school and hitchhikes to her side. They will
need money, lots of it. Sandy gives Troy her mink coat, a
Christmas present from her father, to hock, and with the
money Troy buys an old Plymouth for their getaway. It is their
first home, they joke. They will make the perfect getaway in it
all right. No one will ever find them. They have their truelove,
and they will have their baby, and they will be happy forever
and ever. But things just do not work out for them that way.
They find themselves hiding out under bridges as copcars wail
through the dangerous adult night. They decide to face the
music. They will confess to their parents. Troy's father is a sad
old drunk who blew his inheritance. Sandy's mother is a bitch
obsessed with the evil of sex. Troy's mother is married cur-
rently to Sandy's father. Hand in hand the stepbrother and
stepsister confront their mutual parents. Their mutual parents

receive the news with understanding and forgiveness. People in glass houses shouldn't throw stones, Sandy's father, Troy's stepfather, starring Richard Egan, says and they all embrace.

Sandy and Troy will live on the beautiful island in the lovely old rambling Victorian mansion among the pines. In the fadeout they stand arm in arm on a cliff above the blue summer sea. The music is by Percy Faith. There are a lot of strings. Theme from a Summer Place will remain high on the charts for over a year and thereafter it will remain a favorite oldie-but-goodie.

As they walked up the crowded aisle out of the theatre Judy pressed tightly against Jimbo and squeezed his hand. Jimbo looked down at her and he saw she was smiling at him and that her eyes were bright and glistening. Perfect, Jimbo thought as he kissed her forehead. The movie had been perfect, perfect. For Judy to see this movie right now was perfect timing. The young and in truelove teenagers who can't help but go all the way and who get into trouble but everything works out wonderfully for them in the end. Jimbo couldn't have asked for anything more perfect. He kissed Judy's forehead again, then whispered to her that the movie was just like them. It was their own special movie.

When they reached the lobby they found Penny and Pace waiting for them by the water fountain. Judy and Penny immediately pranced off to the little girls' room whispering excitedly. Jimbo and Pace fired up Camels and slouched against the wall. Although Pace had a face shaped like a wolf, thick lips, kinky blond hair, and about the worst case of acne in the whole highschool, he was the first of Jimbo's crowd to get pussy. Indeed, he and Penny had been going all the way for over a year and because they both enjoyed talking about it everyone in town but their parents knew. Because Penny had perhaps the second worst case of acne in the whole high-school, she and Pace were even more certain than Jimbo and Judy that their love would last until the end of time.

Like, what's shaking, man? Pace said, nodding his head and looking sheepishly at Jimbo.

Not much, Jimbo said, wrinkling his forehead and arching his eyebrows.

You still cut off, man? Pace asked and frenchinhaled deeply.

Yeah, Jimbo said. I'm still cut off cold. Got the blue balls.

Tough titty, Pace said. Tough titty.

Right, Jimbo said.

Well, this might help you remember how sweet it was, Pace said and waved his right hand's middle finger under Jimbo's nose.

Thanks a lot, man, Jimbo said. You want me to cream in my jeans or something?

Not bad, is it? Pace said and sniffed the finger himself. Yes, sir, that was a good year.

What's this test shit about? Jimbo asked. Judy said Penny's married cousin told Penny about it.

The old puffed pussy test, Pace said. It's a bunch of crap, man. Penny's cousin is a real turdhead. We do that test every month. Hell, I ain't about to knock old Penny up. I always pull the hog out, man. Always. Willpower, daddy. Willpower. The only thing I'm going to ever knock up is old Penny's belly button, man. But every goddamn month old Penny gets the sweats.

I figured it was a bunch of crap, Jimbo said.

Right, man. It doesn't prove nothing, man. Except maybe that Penny's got a nice wet pussy. Fuck, man, if I ever felt anything hard in Penny's box I'd figure some cat lost his watch up there or some shit.

What would you do if you ever did knock Penny up?

Never happen, man. Like I said I pull the hog out.

An accident. What would you do?

Operation Summerplace, man.

What's that?

Like the movie tonight. You know something, old Penny has seen this goddamn movie eight times. Eight goddamn times! Well, like the movie, man. We'd run off and get everyone all excited. We'd let everyone get used to the idea. Then we'd come back and get forgiven. Penny's old man would put me through law school. We'd live happy ever after. Operation Summerplace, man.

So you'd do it? You'd marry her and everything?

Sure, man. Hey, I love old Penny. Like with all of my heart, man. We'd be happy. We got a lot in common. And I mean a lot more than just liking to screw and our pimples. Dig it? Well, what about you, daddy? What happens if sweet Judy is knocked up? Besides Frankie putting you in the hospital.

Frankie ain't putting me in any hospital, man, Jimbo said and arching his eyebrows dropped his Camel's butt on the lobby's carpet where he ground it in slowly.

Well, what would you do? Seriously?

Who knows? Jimbo said and shrugged. Probably the same thing you'd do. Your basic Operation Summerplace.

It was called Snake Road and it had been falling apart for years, its narrow, chuckhole-pocked pavement twisting up through the wooded hills south of town seeming to go nowhere at all, just circling through the hills turning back and back on itself. According to the local legend, the road had been started many years before by work gangs of prisoners from the state penitentiary. Later on in the 1930s it had been worked on by federal WPA laborers. Why it was started in the first place and just where it was supposed to go, no one seemed really to remember for sure, at least no one Jimbo ever talked to about it. For many years this road had been the town's main lovers' lane, where several generations of high-school kids had gone up to knead their love in parked cars at night. It was also the place where the even younger kids of the town went to learn their own early lessons about love: went to hide behind trees and bushes beside the road, hoping to catch a glimpse of the mystery through fogged-up car windows. It was also the place where during the past spring and early summer someone else had taken up hiding behind trees and bushes beside the road. Someone who had been only glimpsed but who looked like your basic dirty old man, everyone who had spotted him agreed; whose leering phantom face would appear suddenly at a car window, then vanish just as quickly into the darkness; a phantom face no one could recognize, for through the fogged windows it was like a mask. The Peeker, everyone called him. The crazy, perverted Snake Road Peeker creep.

Jimbo pulled the goddamn BozoBoat into his and Judy's special parking spot and stopped. He switched the key in the ignition onto auxiliary so they could leave the radio playing. At least the goddamn BozoBoat had a goddamn radio. The *BozoBoat:* that described it perfectly all right. An old, fire-engine red Plymouth station wagon with *Paramount Collection Agency* painted in large silver letters on its doors: and instead of a regular horn, a regular beep-beep white man's horn, it had a huge Clarabelle-the-Clown horn bolted onto its left front fender; a horn as loud as a siren which Captain would turn on and leave blaring when he pulled up in front of a deadbeat's house to make a collection. You ought to see the neighbors hit the windows, Captain would tell, laughing, when I pull up and blast that goddamn horn. I know how to nail a deadbeat all right. Shame 'em. Shame 'em in front of their neighbors. Jesus, Jimbo thought. He seldom drove the BozoBoat anywhere, much less on a date with Judy. Not that Captain ever offered it anyway. But who the fuck cared? Jimbo seldom even got near the goddamn BozoBoat if he could help it, except sometimes when he came rolling home late at night and figured it was time for a BozoBoat bath: late at night, in the dark, after holding it sometimes for hours, saving up until he thought he would pop, he would piss all over the goddamn BozoBoat.

Tonight, the night of the big *test* of all nights, Judy had not been able to score one of her family's cars and since Captain was away Jimbo had hotwired the BozoBoat. Slumped as low in the seat as he could get, Jimbo had driven back streets to pick Judy up and after the show he had refused to take her to the Beacon Drive-In. They had come directly parking and Judy was pouting about it but *shit man* no way was he going to cruise the BozoBoat around the Beacon. Besides, Captain might get wind of it. But fuck, who cares? Old Captain. Pecker tracks, Jimbo thought. Now if only he could leave pecker tracks all over the goddamn seats. Old Captain would shit a brick. Old Captain was going to shit a brick anyway. Old Captain was on the first vacation he had taken in ten years, a two-week fishing trip with a couple of old army buddies, and man, did he have a surprise or two waiting for him at home. Things had sure been easier with Captain gone all right. Stealing the Second World War right out from under Captain's big nose would have been one hell of a job.

Do you think we ought to roll up the windows and lock the doors? Judy asked. She had her shoes off and she was sitting with her legs tucked up in the seat under her. Her cotton dress was pulled high on her thighs and Jimbo could see the dark lower edge of her hose. She had not let him touch her since she missed her period a month ago. Not even her breasts. They had not even frenchkissed.

Afraid of the Peeker? Jimbo said. He fired up a Camel and frenchinhaled deeply.

I'm just nervous.

Don't you think I can take care of you? Where's all that old-time confidence in the kid?

Don't make a federal case out of it.

Sorry, Jimbo said.

He rolled up his window and locked the door.

I'm not really afraid, Judy said, smiling shyly. The edges of her teeth were very white in her tanned face. Not when I'm with you.

Jimbo took her hand and squeezed it. For a time they sat silently listening to the radio and looking out at the view from their special parking place of the town's lights and of the lighted bridge over the dark river to Ohio. The red lights of a radio tower on the next hilltop blinked in lazy sequence. Lightning bugs blinked like small hot eyes from the dark. Judy's perfume filled the car.

Well, honey, Jimbo said, what about this test business?

Judy folded her hands in her lap and gazed down at them.

Well, she said, using her cute inhaling husky voice, it's so embarrassing.

Honey, what could possibly be embarrassing between us? We're too close for that. We've been as close as two people can be. Like, our love has made us close.

Well, Penny's married cousin told her about it. You have to do it with me. The test that is. Oh, this is *so* embarrassing!

Judy put her hands over her eyes and shook her head.

Honey, for Christ's sake.

I can't help it if I'm embarrassed, Judy said, a slight break in her voice. I'm *so* sorry. I'm *sorry* I'm the way I am but I just can't help it.

Hey, sweetheart, Jimbo said. He took Judy's hand and kissed it. I understand. Really. It's not your fault. You just take your time, honey, and tell me about this test the best way you can. Just do it your own way, honey.

Judy smiled and kissed Jimbo's hand. He could feel her tongue between her lips on his skin. Her eyes were shining with tears.

Well, she began with a sigh, one part of the test is to feel my breasts and see if they seem to be getting larger. I tried but I can't really tell if they are or not. Getting larger I mean.

Judy put Jimbo's hand to her lips again and for a few moments was silent.

Well, honey, Jimbo said, what's the rest of it? I mean, what's it supposed to show and all?

Well, Judy said with another small sigh, according to Penny's married cousin the other part is to touch me. Down there. To see if that little thing is hard or not. That's it. That's the whole test.

I still don't get it, Jimbo said. He turned down the radio. I mean, exactly what's the test supposed to prove?

According to Penny's married cousin, if my breasts seem to be getting larger and if the little thing is hard too, then probably I'm going to have a baby. I don't know if it's true or not but that's what Penny's married cousin told her.

Oh, yeah. Right, Jimbo said. I've heard about that test before. I read about it somewhere I think.

Did you really?

Yeah, I'm sure I did. Like, in the *Reader's Digest* I think.

Well, maybe we can tell about it then. Maybe we can find out for sure.

Right. At least it's worth a try.

Yes, I guess it is.

Right. We'd better be finding out for sure as soon as possible. So we can make plans and everything if we have to.

Yes, I just have to know. I've been sick all month from worrying. This is the first time in my whole life I've been so late. I've prayed for I don't know how many hours. I just hope God forgives me and I'm not pregnant. I even thought about telling it in confession.

For Christ's sake, don't do that! I mean, honey, a priest would run right to your parents. I mean, he'd make you tell them. And, like, that would sure be the end of us.

I'm just so worried and confused about everything.

Look, honey, don't sweat it. I'll take care of everything. Things will work out.

Jimbo opened Judy's hand and kissed its palm. He kissed her wrist.

Penny says she doesn't care if she is pregnant, Judy said. She says she loves Pace and that they can work something out no matter what just as long as they're together.

That's the way I feel about us, Jimbo said. He kissed the inside of Judy's elbow and then her shoulder.

Penny says that they'll run away if they have to. They've even been making plans and things in case. They're going to leave clues that they ran off to Florida but really they're going to run off to California. There are lots of jobs in California. Pace has even been getting California papers and checking the want ads.

If you're pregnant would you want to run off with me to California? Do you still love me enough?

Of course I love you, silly. I love you more than anything in the whole wide world.

Jimbo kissed Judy's neck.

Well, honey, you sure haven't shown it much lately. Like, it's been a long time since you proved how much you love me.

Please! Judy said, pushing away from him. Please! Please don't start that. Not now. Please.

Start what? What the hell have I done wrong now?

Oh, you know what I mean all right. Don't play dumb. I can't help the way I feel. Why make it harder for me? I feel so guilty about everything. About my family and my faith. And all you do is make it harder for me.

Look, I know, honey, Jimbo said. He hugged Judy to him and kissed her hair. I feel the same way a lot of the time myself. I mean, you're not the only one who has let God down. But like, we talked about all of that before we ever went all the way in the first place. Like, God isn't going to leap on someone's chest for being in love. God understands if anyone does. He's on our side if anyone is. I mean, God is supposed to be love itself and everything, honey. Sweetheart, like, we love each other and that's all that matters. A stupid piece of paper isn't going to make our love any more real or deep than it is right now.

I'm sorry, Jim, but I can't think of it as a stupid piece of paper.

You're right. You're right, honey. It's not stupid. I didn't mean exactly that. It's right to be married in the eyes of the church and all. I know that. Like, it's being respectful to God for what He has given us. It's like a covenant with Him. You know what I mean. All I'm saying is that God isn't going to come down on us for being young and in love. Especially since we're going to get married for sure and everything.

Do you really think God understands?

Sure He does. Like, God is no idiot.

I really do love you, Jim.

And I love you, honey. And if you are going to have our child then we'll work something out. We'll go to California like Pace and Penny. I know everyone will be upset and everything but after we get married and settled somewhere and have the baby, then they'll come around. Just like in the movie tonight. They were young and in love and they made mistakes just like us. But everything worked out for them in the end. And it will for us, sweetheart. I promise.

I really do love you, Jim. I want to spend the rest of my life making you happy.

And I want to make you happy, babe. And I could make you happy right now if only you'd let me. We could really make each other happy. If you'd let things be like they were.

Oh for God's sake! Judy cried. You just won't quit! You just won't!

Jimbo flopped back in his seat. He quickly fired up a Camel. Judy covered her face with her hands and began to cry. Fuck this bullshit, Jimbo thought and turned up the radio. He was a goddamn human being, wasn't he? How was he supposed to handle this sort of bullshit?

I need some air, Jimbo said and got out of the car. He slammed the door. He suddenly thought of the Peeker creep who was supposed to be prowling around Snake Road spying on parked cars. He shivered and looked over his shoulder. Well, at least someone is getting his jollies, Jimbo thought and spit out into the darkness. But not if he was spying on the old BozoBoat. If the Peeker creep was spying on the old BozoBoat he was wasting his time. That was a goddamn fact of life.

Jimbo walked around to the front of the BozoBoat and sat up on the hood. By the dashboard light he could see Judy was still crying. Fuck it. He flicked his half-smoked Camel out into the dark, then immediately fired up another. He watched the distant lights of the cars coming across the bridge from Ohio. A warm breeze stirred the fat summer leaves on the trees around the small clearing and he shivered again. Fuck it, he thought and lay back on the still warm hood and slowly blew a series of smoke rings into the night air. The sky, cloudy earlier in the evening, had begun to clear, and as the dark clouds shifted Jimbo could see several pale stars and the bright, full moon. Wolfman moon, Jimbo thought and shivered again. Jesus Christ, what's wrong with me? Old Captain Nerves of Steel with a case of the shivers. Jimbo laughed quietly. He looked over at the radio tower on the next hilltop and began blinking his eyes in sequence with its flashing lights.

Jimbo slid off the hood and walked around to the back of the BozoBoat and pissed along its bumper. When he finished he ducked low and sneaked around the car. Judy had her head resting back on the seat, her face turned away from the door window. Jimbo pressed his face against the window, smudging his features on the glass. He twisted his mouth into a wide leering grin, then gently tapped on the window. Peek peek peek, he called when Judy turned to look. Judy screamed and ducked down in the seat.

Honey! Honey! Jimbo called, trying to open her door. I'm sorry! Honey, I'm sorry! Jimbo ran around the car to his door. Baby, I'm sorry! I was just playing a dumb joke, he said and pulled Judy to him. She shivered and pressed her face into his neck. Hey, honey, come on now. Hey, there, sweetie. Settle down. Settle down now. I'm sorry. Really, baby. I was being dumb. Jesus, I'm sorry.

You scared me silly, Judy said. I didn't know *who* you were.

Hey, there, Jimbo said. He lifted Judy's chin. Hey, there. Forgive me? Please? Pretty please?

You can be such a brat, Judy said in her cute husky inhaling voice.

I can be a bad boy, I know it well, Jimbo said and kissed her eyes. Hey, honey, listen there! Jimbo turned up the radio. Listen to those sounds. Theme from a Summer Place. Our song coming right over the radio just like the doctor ordered. Our song.

Judy kissed Jimbo's hand. Her eyes were bright.

May I have this here dance, ma'am? Jimbo said in his John Wayne voice. He opened his cardoor.

Oh, silly.

No, ma'am, I reckon I insist. I reckon this here is our dance, ma'am, Jimbo said and clicked on the headlights. Come on now, ma'am, don't tarry. Let us shake a foot while the band is cooking.

Silly, I'm barefoot, Judy said and pulled back. I'll ruin my new hose. You are such a nut.

Nonsense, my dear, Jimbo said in his cartoon Donald Duck voice and slid out of the car. He tugged playfully at Judy's hands. Like, it's all soft grass, my dear. Soft as your basic baby's ass, my little chickadee.

Jimbo led Judy around to the front of the BozoBoat and they began to slowdance in the headlights. Jimbo clasped his hands in the small of Judy's back just above the swell of her hips and Judy clasped her hands behind Jimbo's neck and began playing gently with his hair. Jimbo pressed his face into Judy's freshly washed fragrant hair. Jimbo could feel Judy's breasts and thighs as she pressed tightly against him and they swayed slowly together to the song, their song, their summerplace song, on the car radio, their feet nearly motionless in the deep grass. In the headlights they were a moviecouple, incandescent and romantic perfectly. And somewhere beyond the edges of the shimmering light, somewhere out in the darkness where lightning bugs blinked like tiny flashbulbs, an ice cupid melted slowly bluegreen. Jimbo shut his eyes. They were in the backseat of Pace's planed and decked and lowered midnight blue '49 Ford: the imaginary mass of blue Hawaii glowed like a dim curved dream through the steamed windshield: from the speaker hooked onto the steamed left front window the ghostwave voice of Elvis Presley whispered soft truelove surfsongs: Do you really and truly love me, Judy whispered as Jimbo slowly slid down her pedal pushers: really and truly really and truly? she whispered as they went *all the way* for the first time: they were stars slowdancing on Happy Hop with everyone as their witnesses: the small red light on the gliding camera glowed like grace upon them and their love was its own program on teevee, its signals pulsing out like light into space, becoming real in some new set forever. Yes, sir, Bebop Billy had said, our little Judy is Sweet Sixteen today. And Jimbo here has a very, very special surprise for you, sweetheart. Right, Jimbo? And he wants to give it to you right here live on camera so you two lovebirds can share this happy moment with everyone out there in teeveeland. Right, Jimbo? Right, Jimbo said, his lower face collapsing into smiles, and he took the only ring in the whole wide world from his sportcoat's side pocket and taking Judy's left hand slid it quickly onto her ring finger. Judy's blue eyes popped wide and her mouth popped open. She held her hand up, letting the only ring in the whole wide world glitter in the bright studio lights. Judy squealed and covered her face with her hands and jumped up and down. Suddenly she threw her arms around Jimbo's neck, knocking him off balance, and they staggered backward across the slick dance floor until Jimbo regained his footing. He frantically arched his eyebrows and wrinkled his forehead. Judy covered his face with kisses. Everyone laughed and applauded. Hey, gang, Bebop Billy said, let's dedicate this next slow number to the lovebirds and let them have the floor to themselves, OK? The studio lights dimmed and the platter Sixteen Candles began playing. Jimbo pressed his face into Judy's hair, his breath thick with more blondness than he had ever known. Blond was Judy's essence. Soft blond down on her arms. Her skin. Her blond smell. Her blond ponytail, which bounced relentlessly when they bopped. Because Jimbo was tall Judy danced on tiptoe. See Judy press against Jimbo. See Judy play with Jimbo's hair. Everyone witnessing Jimbo and Judy's slowdance smiled. Thunder sounded far off in the hills across the river and a warm breeze stirred the fat summer leaves on the trees around the small clearing. Jimbo opened his eyes. The song, their special summerplace song, was ending.

Ugh! Judy cried, jumping back away from Jimbo.

What? Jimbo cried. What's wrong? What'd I do?

Ugh! Ugh! Judy cried, pointing at the grass and hopping up and down.

What? What?

I stepped on something! Something slimy! A snake! I think it was a slimy snake!

Snake! Jimbo cried and hopped backward himself. Snake? What goddamn snake?

Ugh ugh ugh! Judy cried. She ran toward the BozoBoat.

Snake? Jimbo said. Snakes aren't slimy, Judy.

Squinting his eyes in the bright headlights, Jimbo bent over to peer into the deep grass. When Judy hit the BozoBoat's siren Jimbo jumped straight up in the air, then stumbled backward falling into the grass. He scrambled to his feet and ran to the BozoBoat.

What the hell do you think you're doing? Jimbo yelled as he jumped into the frontseat.

Judy had both hands clasped over her mouth and was laughing too hard to speak.

That's really funny as shit, Jimbo said, arching his eyebrows and firing up a Camel. Really goddamn funny, Judy.

It was, Judy said, gasping. The way you jumped up and fell down. You jumped so high. You looked like a frog or something. Judy clasped her hands over her mouth again and started laughing.

Oh yeah, Judy. Really goddamn funny. A million goddamn laughs. You're a real card, Judy. Real cute, Judy. Jimbo said and frenchinhaled deeply. He clicked off the headlights.

Well, you scared me first. What's the matter anyway? Afraid of a little biddy snake or something?

Me? Me? Me afraid of snakes? Are you kidding, girl? Are you crazy? Of course I'm afraid of snakes, lamebrain. I'm scared shitless of them, the horrible creatures, Jimbo said and grinned. Did I really jump like a frog?

Just exactly like a frog, Judy said, laughing.

Old Captain Rebel Without a Cause hopping like a frog, Jimbo said, grinning, and slowly shook his head. Well, hey, little Miss Wiseass, did you really step on something in the grass?

Yes, now I really and truly did step on *something* ugh ugh,

Judy said in her cute inhaling husky voice. I cross my heart and hope to die I really and truly did step on *something*.

Probably just a used rubber, Jimbo said.

What? A what?

Nothing, Jimbo said. Nothing. Whatever it was I scared it off no doubt. It knew better than to tangle with old Captain Badass. It crawled off in the grass to save its ass.

My hero, Judy said.

Damn right, Jimbo said and in several poses flexed his muscles.

Judy chuckled and taking Jimbo's hand kissed it. To Know Him Is to Love Him began playing on the radio and Judy turned it up. Judy ran her tongue slowly over Jimbo's knuckles.

When the record was over Jimbo quietly said: Well, honey, what should we do? About the test I mean.

I want to do the test, Judy said, almost whispering. I just have to know for sure.

Right, honey, Jimbo said. We should find out. So we can make plans and all if we have to.

For a few moments Judy just sat there looking down at her hands in her lap. Slowly Judy began to unbutton the front of her dress. In the dashboard's faint light the down of her bare tanned arms glowed golden. The only ring in the whole wide world's diamond and heart of small perfect pearls glowed on Judy's engagement finger. Operation Summerplace, Jimbo thought. If Judy is knocked up then it's Operation Summerplace. And they would find their summerplace too, by God. Jimbo scooted over beside Judy and casually slid his arm around the back of her seat. Judy sat there looking down at her hands in her lap, the front of her dress open. Jimbo put his arm around her shoulders and gently drew her to him and kissed her forehead.

Whatever happens, honey, Jimbo said, remember I love you. And I'll always take care of you. Always. We'll be together no matter what. And as long as we're together nothing can hurt us. I love you so much.

I love you too, Jim, Judy said and smiled shyly.

The moment Jimbo's fingertips touched the smooth skin of her stomach Judy shivered. Jimbo jerked his hand away.

Did I hurt you, honey? Did I scratch you or something?

No, Judy said quietly. No, I'm OK. Go ahead.

Jimbo lifted Judy's bra and gently took her small right breast in his hand. In the evening air Judy's breast felt cool at first but warmed quickly as Jimbo caressed it. Besides her delicate perfume a faint scent of sweet soap lifted from Judy's skin. After a time Jimbo took her left breast in his hand. Judy closed her eyes and leaned her head back on the seat.

Can you tell yet? Judy said, in her cute inhaling husky voice. Are they getting larger?

I can't tell yet, Jimbo said and moved his hand back to her right breast. Her nipples had stiffened under his fingers. Jimbo kissed her ear.

Can you tell anything at all yet? Judy asked. She opened her eyes.

Not yet, Jimbo said.

Well, it shouldn't be all that hard to tell, Judy said. Her voice quivered. She placed a hand over the back of Jimbo's hand and held it in place.

Well, honey, Jimbo said and removed his hand and sat back in the seat, actually I think they are getting larger. Now I could be wrong but I really think they are.

Oh no, Judy whispered. She slowly pulled her bra down and straightened it. She started to rebutton the front of her dress but stopped and just sat there staring at her lap.

Honey, please don't worry, Jimbo said and lifted her chin. He brushed her lips with a kiss. Please don't worry. We'll get married and we'll have our squirt and everything will work out fine in the end. You'll see. Just remember God is on our side. God is love itself. And since we're in love that means what we have is a part of God Himself. We should thank God for what we have. He's been so good to us.

We can thank God by raising this child for the church, Judy said. Her eyes were bright.

Dig it, Jimbo said and kissed the palm of Judy's hand.

Yes, Judy said, if it's a girl we'll raise her up to be a nun. And if it's a boy we'll raise him up to be a priest.

A priest would be great, Jimbo said and kissed Judy's shoulder.

He might even be a missionary someday, Judy said.

Dig it, Jimbo said and softly kissed Judy's neck. Why, who knows, he might even go on to get himself martyred. Boiled in the Congo. Eaten by savage niggers. Then someday get voted in as a big-shot saint.

A bishop, Judy said. He might be a bishop. Or even someday a cardinal.

Dig it, Jimbo said and slowly ran his tongue along the edge of Judy's jaw. Any squirt of ours is bound to get his name up in lights. Hell, the kid might turn out to be the first pope in history who ain't a goddamn spaghetti sucker.

Oh, Jim, please, please don't talk like that! Judy said and pulled away from him.

Hey, honey! I'm sorry, Jimbo said. He gently drew Judy back to him. I didn't mean anything by it. I only meant that any rug rat of ours will turn out to be a star no matter what he does.

Well, sometimes you really worry me, Judy said in her pout voice. Sometimes I think you don't mean to convert at all. Like you promised. Sometimes I think you intend to go on believing in all that crazy, sinful reincarnation stuff forever and burn in hell for it. And Jim Stark, if you intend to burn in hell, well, then I just don't intend to marry you at all. Even if I'm pregnant.

Oh, honey, come on. Don't sweat it. I promise I won't burn in hell. I just told you how thankful we should be to God for our love. And I think raising a squirt for the church is a great idea. And let me tell you, babe, I intend to be one gung-ho, mackerel-snapping, bead-squeezing demon. No kidding, babe.

Why do you talk like that then? Like you're making fun of everything?

I don't mean anything by it, honey. Listen, I'm serious when

I say we should thank God. We should trust God. Do you trust God, honey?

I trust God, Judy said.

Trust me too, honey. Please.

I trust you.

Well, honey, Jimbo said, I guess we best get on with the test.

I guess so, Judy said.

I love you, babe.

I love you too. I really do.

Jimbo put his hand on Judy's knee, then moved it slowly up under her dress, his fingertips gently scraping her hose. When his hand reached the soft flesh of her upper thigh above her hose Judy parted her legs slightly. Jimbo worked his middle finger under the damp crotch of Judy's panties and after briefly brushing her pubic hair slipped the finger into her pussy.

Can you tell anything yet? Judy asked immediately.

Not yet, for Christ's sake! I just got it in. I mean, like, relax, sweetheart. Relax. I love you, sweetheart.

I love you too, Judy said and put her head back on the seat. She shut her eyes and licked her slightly parted lips. Her breath was uneven.

We're so lucky, Jimbo whispered and kissed Judy's ear. So lucky to have each other and our love. The love God has given us. I love you so much. So much. So much. Jimbo kissed Judy's eyes, then ran his tongue along the hollows of her throat. He began using two fingers.

Do you really and truly love me? Judy whispered.

You bet, Jimbo said.

Everything *will* work out. I just know it will. I know it. I almost hope I am pregnant.

Dig it, Jimbo said and began using three fingers.

Judy wet Jimbo's ear with her tongue. When Jimbo kissed her lips Judy opened her mouth and sucked his tongue into it. Judy arched her hips up slightly and squeezed Jimbo's hand with her thighs. She put a hand over Jimbo's hand and pressed it and frenchkissing deeply they slid slowly down in the seat. Jimbo lifted Judy's bra and sucked her right nipple gently into his mouth. When Judy screamed Jimbo rolled off her onto the floor.

What? Jimbo yelled. My God, what?

The window! Judy screamed. A face! A face was at the window!

Face! Jimbo cried. He arched quickly up and around off the floor and seeing a face at the window fell backward onto Judy.

My nose! Judy cried. Your elbow's on my nose!

Jimbo scrambled up off her and seeing the face again froze until he realized it was his own reflection in the glass.

There's no face, Jimbo said. What goddamn face?

There was too! Judy cried. She pushed frantically at Jimbo trying to get her legs out from under him. There was too! There was! Oh, my nose. You broke my nose.

I didn't see any goddamn face, Jimbo said, arching upward to let Judy slide from under him and sit up behind the steering wheel. Jimbo reached across her and clicked on the headlights.

It was God, Judy said and began to cry.

God? God? What the hell does that mean? God! Jesus Christ!

God made it happen. To stop us. We were getting carried away again. And God made that horrible crazy man peek in our car to stop us from sinning again. Oh, my nose. I just know my nose is broken.

Oh bullshit, Judy! Fucking bullshit!

I almost let God down again, Judy said, crying. But He saved me. And He taught me a lesson. He punished me. He had you break my nose.

Fuck it! Fuck it! Jimbo yelled and opened the cardoor.

What are you doing? Close that door! He might still be out there!

I hope he is! I'm going to get that creep son of a bitch!

Jimbo jumped out and slammed the door.

Judy quickly slid across the seat and rolled down the window. What are you doing? Are you crazy? Get back in this car!

I'm going to hunt down that creep, Jimbo said, arching his

eyebrows and wrinkling his forehead. Someone has to do it. I guess that someone's me.

Oh, Jim, don't be so silly. You always try to act so big.

Jimbo walked slowly out around the front of the car into the headlights. He stopped and stood legs spread wide apart and looked intently into the dark trees around the small clearing. Dark clouds moved swiftly across the full moon and the wind blew into the trees, twisting their fat leaves in the headlights' glow. Jimbo arched his eyebrows and wrinkled his forehead and took his switchblade from his windbreaker's pocket. With an elaborate flick of his wrist he clicked the switchblade open and held it up in the headlights.

Oh, creepo. Oh, creepo baby, Jimbo called out. He waved the switchblade before him. Oh, creepo baby, I got something here all for you. Come and get it, creepo baby.

Jim, quit acting silly! Judy called. Get back in this car right now!

Jimbo began flipping the switchblade into the air and catching it by its handle. He began flipping it higher and higher, light flickering like quicksilver on its metal, until it began disappearing for moments into the darkness above the carlights. Jimbo felt light-headed, dizzy almost. Jimbo felt his eyes go away. They went away and then looked back at himself flipping the switchblade in the carlights. They looked back from the trees. When Judy hit the BozoBoat's siren Jimbo jumped and then for a moment froze, forgetting the switchblade spinning down from the darkness above the carlights until it hit him on the head.

Jesus fucking Christ! Jimbo yelled. He clutched his head and hopped around in the grass. He could hear Judy laughing from the BozoBoat. He looked at his hands. Sure enough, there were traces of blood on his fingers. He held his fingers up in the carlights for Judy to see. You think this is funny! he yelled. I'm bleeding like a stuck pig and you think it's funny!

Get back in the car! Judy called.

Jimbo pulled out a handkerchief and held it to his head. He began kicking about in the deep grass searching for his switchblade. Jesus, he thought, what if it had been the fucking blade instead of the handle that drilled him. He had a sudden picture of a quivering switchblade sticking out of his bloody head. Jesus, Jimbo thought, what a joke. What a fucking cartoon. Just as Jimbo spotted his switchblade in the deep grass and reached for it Judy clicked off the carlights.

Goddamn it, Judy! Jimbo yelled. Turn those goddamn lights on! Jimbo bent over and began feeling around in the grass where he had dropped the switchblade. *Snake*, he suddenly thought and jerked his hand back. Fuck it! Fuck it! Fuck it!

Judy, turn those goddamn lights on! I mean it, Judy!

Get back in the car!

Fuck her, Jimbo thought. He began kicking lightly about in the grass. He could not afford to lose another switchblade. It was the third switchblade he had bought in six months and he had shelled out ten bucks for the thing. The other two switchblades his dear old mom had discovered while searching his room for dirty poems and had tossed away. The dark clouds over the full moon suddenly parted and in the bright moonlight Jimbo spotted a gleam in the grass. He snatched the switchblade from the grass and held it up in the moonlight, looking it over carefully. He waved it *screw you, sweetie* in Judy's direction, then closed it and put it back safe in his windbreaker's pocket. Jimbo dabbed lightly at his head with the handkerchief, then looked at it closely. He was bleeding all right, no mistake about that.

Please, please get back in this car! Judy called, clicking the carlights on and off, on and off.

Hey! Jimbo yelled. He pointed to the trees down the slight slope in front of the car. I see him! Over there! The Peeker creep! Right over there!

Quit that! Judy called. Please, honey, get back in the car.

I got the old Peeker creep spotted, by jove! And he's all hairy like an ape, by jove! Look, Judy! Over there. Right over there. His face is all hairy, by jove!

You're not being funny one bit! Judy called and clicked the carlights back on. I want to leave, Jim. Please.

He's there, by jove! He's right over there and he's a hairy devil, what. Great scot, the bloke's a wolfman!

You're so dumb! You're acting like a dumb little kid.

Duty calls, my pet. Duty! God and country. A man has to do what a man has to do! Jimbo called and saluted the moon. He whipped the switchblade out of his windbreaker's pocket and with a flourish clicked it open and held it high in the carlights. Sing, O Singing Sword! O Singing Switchblade! Hi-ho, Silver, away! Jimbo shouted and jumped out of the carlights and ran yelling *charge, charge* down the slope toward the dark trees.

Jim! Jim! Jim, please! Please!

Jimbo ducked under the low branches of a spruce at the edge of the clearing and skidded to a stop in the underbrush. He crawled on hands and knees back up the slope to a slight depression under the spruce and flopped there on the soft needle loam and watched the BozoBoat intently. Blood pounded small explosions behind his eyes and in the hollows of his ears. OK, Judy Judy Judy, it's your turn, baby, Jimbo thought and laughed softly. The carlights' beams shone brightly into the trees above him. He scraped away a small patch of fallen needles and then while still watching the BozoBoat dug absently at the moist earth with the switch-blade. The rich smell of the turned needles and of the moist earth filled his nose. He sniffed the tips of the three middle fingers of his left hand, then ran each finger under his nose slowly in turn and inhaled deeply. Ah yes, he said and grinned, that was a good year all right. Jimbo stabbed the switchblade into the loose earth to its handle.

The wind blew suddenly up and thunder clapped overhead and Jimbo could hear rain hitting higher in the trees. He suddenly snatched the switchblade from the earth and swirled about. What the fuck was that? Jimbo stared intently into the darkness behind him. He crouched and thrust the switchblade before him. Maybe Judy really had seen a face, he thought and shuddered. Hey, man, just cool it. Captain Nerves of Steel, man. Jimbo arched his eyebrows and wrinkled his forehead and spit out into the darkness. Well, come on, creepo, make your move, Jimbo said aloud. Come on and get your cold bite of old Captain's singing switchblade, creepo baby. *Again.* Jimbo jumped backward and fell down. He heard it again. He lay on his back and laughed. He stabbed the switchblade back into the earth. The wind. Branches in the wind and old Captain Nerves of Steel about shits his pants. Jimbo laughed again. Who's afraid of the big bad wolf, the big bad wolf? he chanted quietly.

Jim. Jim.

Jimbo rolled quickly onto his stomach. Judy was standing behind the BozoBoat's driver's side door. Leaving the door open, she slowly rounded it and gazed intently about. Jimbo could hear faint radio music.

Jim. Jim, honey. Please, Jim.

Judy slowly crept toward the front of the BozoBoat, tiptoeing almost, running her hand along its fender. When she reached the front she bent near the carlights and stared out their beams into the trees. Rain flicked out of the dark across the carlights and in their glow Judy's wet face was pale.

Please, honey. Are you all right? Honey, are you OK?

When Jimbo screamed so did Judy. Jimbo screamed and screamed and thrashed wildly about in the brush. Judy screamed and tumbled backward against the cardoor, slamming it shut. Jimbo began to howl like a wolf at a full moon and Judy frantically jerked open the cardoor and scrambled into the BozoBoat. Jimbo rolled over and lay there on his back under the tree alternately laughing and howling, howling like an outlaw wolf at a full moon, imagining himself transformed in moonlight, a face of growing hair, fangs, nails for ripping: howling, howling his ancient beastheart out, a beastheart he could almost imagine remembering. When Judy hit the BozoBoat's siren Jimbo as always jumped. Jesus fucking Christ! Jimbo shouted. I swear to God I'm going to bust hell out of that goddamn horn! Then Jimbo began to alternately laugh and moo, moo like a cow. Jimbo arched his eyebrows and wrinkled his forehead and mooed like James Dean did at the sirens blaring with anger and danger and with fear from somewhere in the dark adult distance. Finally Jimbo rolled onto his stomach laughing, laughing so hard he was almost choking. He bit his fist. He pounded the ground. Then he looked up and through his tears saw Judy and was suddenly as sad as he would ever be.

What's going to happen anyway? Jimbo said quietly to himself.

Judy had turned on the BozoBoat's interior light and was sitting far forward with her weeping face pressed almost against the now rain-streaked windshield, and seeing her weeping face like that, so strangely shadowed, pale and dissolving, staring through water, Jimbo suddenly imagined her, imagined himself, imagined everything, submerged in some deep end, drowned.

5 ➤
breaking up is hard to do

Say your life breaks down. You are only seventeen and already your life breaks down. After wearing it for only three days your girl returns the only ring in the whole wide world: a ring you have gone into a life of crime to buy for her, a life of pulling jobs—shoplifting, stealing spinner hubcaps, knocking over parking meters—a ring you stole the Second World War for, a job you are now going to pay for dearly.

Keep the goddamn ring, Jimbo had told Judy.

Judy had cried, cried softly. She still loved him, Judy told Jimbo. It wasn't that at all. And she still wanted more than anything in the world for them to someday marry and to have their twelve children, their six boys and six girls. But they had to be realistic about their love. God had answered her prayers. She was not pregnant after all. God had given her another chance to be good. And she was just being realistic. She knew that if they continued going steady, being together and so intense all the time, they could not keep from going all the way again and she could not let that happen ever again until they were married. God had forgiven her and she would not let God down again. She would not be bad again until she was married and that was final. So it was best they did not let themselves get into tempting situations if you know what I mean. From now on they would always double date with couples who were not themselves going all the way. And they would go only to shows, no drive-ins, and to dances and they would never go parking. And to be really safe they would not even frenchkiss. And what's more they should both date other people.

Oh, that's cute, Jimbo said.

Well, if our love is real it will last until we can get married someday.

Who do you have in mind anyway? What old flame is waiting in the wings, Judy?

I don't have anyone in mind. I love you. I really do. We have to be careful, that's all.

Is it good old Hutch? My old pal old buddy Hutch Bodine? Old college joe himself? Is that who it is, Judy?

I don't have Hutch or anyone in mind. God has given me another chance, that's all. If I was really thankful I'd become a nun.

Oh Jesus fucking Christ!

Don't you talk like that!

Well, hell, keep the damn ring anyway.

No. I don't think I should. That's not fair to you. You might find someone else you want to give it to, Judy said and put the only ring in the whole wide world in Jimbo's hand.

Well, suit yourself, babe, Jimbo said, arching his eyebrows. And by the by, babe, just to keep the old record straight, I never intended for a fucking minute to join up with your goddamn bead-squeezing, mackerel-snapping church, dig? I still believe in that crazy, sinful reincarnation stuff and I always will, dig? And, babe, if you ask me the goddamn pope is queer as a three-buck bill, dig?

Say your life breaks down. You are only seventeen, it is summer before your senior year, and your life is coming down around your ears. Your old man, old Captain himself, returned over an hour ago from the first vacation he has taken in ten years, a two-week fishing trip with a couple of old army buddies, and he must have had swell luck for you could hear him happy and hooting around downstairs about all the wonderful trout he caught: We're going to be gobbling trout around this old house the rest of the goddamn summer, he hooted. Gosh old Captain sure is a great fisherman. Gosh he sure is a great sport. Old Captain can take his stinking trout and stick them up his ass. Old Captain is not really lucky at all. Old Captain sure has a homecoming surprise or two waiting for him all right: just as soon as he goes down into his basement and spots his almost empty battle tables, especially his absolutely empty Battle of the Bulge table.

So Jimbo lay there on his bed smoking and waiting and now and then examining the only ring in the whole wide world squeezed on his thumb tip and he was sick to his stomach. It was only a matter of time. It was only a matter of time. Jimbo smoked and waited. He looked up at the silver cones hanging from the ceiling, hanging in place of all those plastic fighter planes he once had strung up there in some strange freeze-frame dogfight. Jimbo smoked and waited and stared up at the silver cones and wished with all of his heart he was safely deep within one of their strange gangster dreams.

Jimbo felt around under his pillow for the one soldier he had kept: Captain's special soldier, the one who always led the victors to their glory, no matter what battle of what army of what age. Jimbo held it up and examined its elaborate, bright blue and red, silver-trimmed uniform, its silver, high-pointed, plumed helmet. Jimbo had not sold it with the rest. He could have scored a few bucks off the bozo thing all right but he did not. Maybe if he gave Captain back his special bozo soldier Captain would only break his arms and legs. Sure. Hell, Jimbo thought, he might as well keep the thing as a goddamn souvenir. His very own personal Second World War bozo hero souvenir. Jimbo stuffed the bozo soldier back under his pillow. And all for this, he thought, holding up the only ring in the whole wide world. In the dim light from his desk lamp across the room the ring's diamond and surrounding heart of small perfect pearls glittered faintly. It's not fair to you blah blah, she had said. You might find someone else you want to give it to blah blah blah. Fuck her. He should have stuffed it up her ass. Stuffed it up her precious pussy. Knocked her up with the only ring in the whole wide world. Puffed her pussy with pearls. Tears suddenly flooded Jimbo's eyes and he threw the only ring in the whole wide world against the far wall. He listened with pain as it bounced about.

Well, hell, she is a fine girl, Jimbo thought. Goddamn it anyway. And he was a jerk. An asshole. That's for sure. To give her all that punk grief. Jesus Christ. Jesus fucking Christ. Oh, well. Hell, what old Captain Boohoo needs right now is a little distraction. A little entertainment is just what old Captain needs. Damn right. Like a good old whack-off. That's what old Captain Boohoo needs all right: your good old basic whack-off. One last mythic whack-off in honor of Judy-poo's pussypie, by God. Jimbo stubbed out his Camel, then rolled onto his stomach and felt around under the bed for the sock. Well, here goes your basic terminal case of the hairy palms and pimples, Jimbo thought and laughed. He rolled onto his back and unzipped his jeans. It was an old athletic sock with blue and green stripes around its top and it was stiff as a corpse. Jimbo crunched it gently in his hands until it softened. Jimbo shut his eyes. Jimbo opened his eyes. The hell with this, he thought and tossed the sock back under the bed. He zipped up his jeans quickly. Jesus. What if Captain happened to come marching in about right now. Captain comes stomping in to square off with Jimbo and there Jimbo is flopping his dork. That would be cute all right. About as bad as that time old Captain nearly stared a hole through Jimbo's dork. How old had he been? Thirteen, fourteen maybe. Seventh grade, anyway. When on a dare he had put an unwrapped cherry popsicle in his homeroom teacher's top desk drawer to melt. What a neat mess it had made. Sticky cherry juice all over everything, even gluing the grade book's pages together. Old bitch Scott had really shit a brick all right. She'd stomped and hooted around like crazy. And old bitch Scott had suspected Jimbo right away, of course, for although he had the highest grades of anyone in the homeroom she had his number as a trouble-maker. He would never help clean the erasers and he was always squeezing his hands together making obscene fart sounds and whenever it was his turn to lead the class in either the Lord's Prayer or the Pledge of Allegiance to the Flag he would quack them like his favorite cartoon character Donald Duck. A troublemaker for sure. So when some fink squealed that Jimbo had, indeed, put the popsicle in her desk drawer old bitch Scott had cackled and jabbered with hateful joy as she jerked him down the hall to the principal's office. Jimbo had been immediately suspended for three days and sent home where he went directly to the bathroom and sat on the commode to wait. Somehow he felt that if he was sitting on the commode Captain would not immediately break his arms and legs when he got home. After all, no one walks in on someone taking a shit, Jimbo figured. Then maybe Captain would have a chance to calm down. It did not work. Captain had thrown open the bathroom door and charged in yelling and slapping at Jimbo who was in turn crying, I'm on the commode! I'm on the commode! Jimbo jumped up and with his pants down around his ankles tried vainly to hop to safety. I'm on the commode! Jimbo kept crying as he hopped about trying to duck under Captain's slaps. Then suddenly Captain stopped slapping and Jimbo peeked up through his guarding arms and he saw that Captain was staring a hole through his dork. Only then did Jimbo realize with amazement he had a hard-on. His eyes met Captain's and they both flushed and looked quickly away. Captain turned abruptly and stalked from the bathroom. Jimbo flopped back down on the commode. He sat there on the commode and held his face in his hands.

Jimmy.

Jimbo jumped up off the bed. His mother was standing in the doorway. She was clutching her bathrobe to her throat.

Why don't you ever knock?

Jimmy, what in the world have you done this time? she asked. Her eyes were wide and bright.

Done? I haven't done anything. Why don't you ever knock anyway? This is my room you know.

Well, your dad wants to see you. He says for you to come down to the shelter. What in the world did you do this time, honey? I've never seen him so . . . Well, I've never seen him like this.

I didn't do anything I said. And I'm not going down to his damn shelter.

Well, he says for you to come down. I've never seen him like this before.

I'm not going down there I said. I'm busy.

You best do what he says, honey.

I'm busy I said.

I don't know. I just don't know what to think. I've never seen him like this. Honey, you better go down.

No, damn it! I'm busy!

I just don't know what to think. I try and try and it doesn't do a bit of good. I pray for you all the time. And I pray for your dad. I'm so sickly and all and you give me nothing but more worries. The both of you. Well, I'll tell your dad you won't come down I guess. I've never seen him like this before, Jimbo's mother said, shaking her head and turning away slowly.

Hey, close that door too. And how's about knocking for a change?

Oh Jesus fucking Christ, Jimbo said aloud. He thought he was going to be sick. He felt dizzy. He had a sudden urge to crawl under the bed. He could not believe it. He held his hands up in front of his face. They were actually trembling. He shut his eyes and leaned back against the wall. Well, big bad boy, this is it, Jimbo thought. The big squareoff. Because by God, he was not going to let Captain just pound around on him this time. This time he would fight back, by God. If Captain came in swinging he would swing back. Goddamn right, Jimbo thought, arching his eyebrows and wrinkling his forehead. The big squareoff. The big showdown. Jimbo suddenly pictured Captain's huge, hairy hands, his thick, powerful fingers. More like the *last* showdown, Jimbo thought and smiled grimly. He leaned there against the wall with his eyes shut, feeling weak, and he thought of the ending of *Red River*, a movie ending he had thought about a lot lately, an ending he had rerun in his mind again and again. He reran John Wayne, big as a barn, stalking through scattering cattle toward where Montgomery Clift waited in the dusty cow-town street for their big showdown. John Wayne had been like a father to Montgomery Clift, had taught him how to ride and rope and shoot and how to quickdraw with the best. John Wayne had taught Montgomery Clift everything and they had loved each other like father and son and now they were going to gun each other down like dogs in the street. Wayne thought Clift had stolen his herd of Texas longhorns but Clift had not really and when it came down to it Clift could not quickdraw against Wayne. Wayne tried to force Clift's hand. Wayne quickdrew and scattered hot lead all about Clift, once even grazing his cheek, but Clift just would not go for his big iron. What's it take to make you act like a man? Wayne said and stalked right up to Clift and punched his face. Wayne punched Clift again and again, belting him bloody all about the dusty cow-town street, until at last Clift had had enough and let fly. Clift let fly with a roundhouse haymaker right and caught big John flush on the jaw. Wayne went down like a ton of bricks with a look of surprise and, more important, pride spread on his kisser. A good one! A haymaker right smack in the kisser. And John Wayne, *John Wayne*, big as a barn, big as all outdoors, went down on his ass. And of course John Wayne forgave Montgomery Clift and they loved each other like father and son once again. And to prove his love John Wayne drew the ranch's new brand in the sand with a stick: a brand using both their names' initials. *Blam*, a roundhouse haymaker smack on John Wayne's kisser. Jimbo kept rerunning the surprised but proud look on John Wayne's face as he sat on his ass in the dusty cow-town street looking up at Clift. *Blam. Blam. Pow. Socko.* Jimbo danced around the room tossing lefts and rights, tossing jabs, uppercuts, crosses. Then he heard Captain's heavy steps on the stairs and he quickly backed to the wall farthest from the door and held his breath.

Jimbo listened as Captain walked heavily down the hallway

to the bedroom door. Jimbo could hear Captain's heavy smoker's rattle as he then just stood there outside the door. What the fuck is he waiting for? Jimbo thought. Make your fucking move, cowboy. At last Captain slowly opened the door and Jimbo thought he would piss his pants. Captain just stood there framed in the hall light, his big-as-a-barn, big-as-all-outdoors body a massive shadow filling the doorway, blocking all hope of escape.

I want to talk to you, soldierboy, Captain, after what seemed to Jimbo minutes, at last said in a quiet voice not of the Second World War at all.

Yes, sir.

Captain clicked on the overhead light and Jimbo blinked in the brightness. Then Captain just stood there not speaking again. He was weaving slightly and he lightly pressed the backs of his hands against the doorframe to steady himself. Behind the thick lenses of his slightly fogged glasses his eyes looked swollen and watery and he blinked them often. Fisheyes, Jimbo suddenly thought. They made him think of bulging, filmy fisheyes staring out through the thick glass sides of some aquarium. And there was no glint, no *look*, in those strange fisheyes Captain could not seem to focus on Jimbo's face: they seemed not even to reflect light, but to absorb it, suck it in, flat, lifeless.

Did you have a good trip, sir? Jimbo said at last.

Where are they? Captain said.

What, sir?

Where are they?

Where's what, sir?

Where are they, soldierboy?

I took them and sold them.

You took them and sold them?

Yes, sir.

You sold them? Where?

Well, I sold some down at Bob's Hobby Shop. But most of them I just sold around to kids. You know, just around the neighborhood.

You sold them?

Yes, sir.

Why?

I had to buy something.

You had to buy something?

Yes, sir.

What?

A ring.

A what?

A ring, sir.

A ring?

A ring for Judy.

A ring for Judy? Captain said and stepped on into the room. He shut the door behind him.

Yeah, a ring for Judy, Jimbo said. It cost four hundred buckeroos.

Four hundred what?

Buckeroos. Bucks. Dollars.

A four-hundred-dollar ring for Judy, Captain said and walked slowly toward Jimbo.

Right, Jimbo said. He clenched his fists at his sides.

Captain's head bumped a silver cone and he stopped and stared at it. He blinked his eyes. As though in slow motion Captain reached up and touched the silver cone. He stopped its spinning and then just held it still and stared at it. He squinted his wet eyes. With a slight tug he pulled the cone's string loose from the ceiling. Captain turned the silver cone over and over in his huge hands, examining it intently with his wet, blinking eyes.

But he's seen them before, Jimbo thought, remembering all the hell Captain had raised when Jimbo had first taken the plastic fighter planes down and put up the silver cones. There's nothing new about those things. They were the same old silver cones. A *fish*, Jimbo suddenly thought. The silver cone looked like a small silver fish in Captain's huge hands. As though Captain had just landed it and was getting all set to gut it. Jimbo pictured Captain carrying the still twitching silver cone grimly toward him. Jimbo pictured Captain slowly rubbing the still twitching silver cone over his face, until at last it hung limp and dead.

Captain tossed the silver cone onto Jimbo's bed. He looked back at Jimbo, still blinking his wet eyes as though trying to focus them. In the bright overhead light his face looked lined and old and his shoulders were slumped like Jimbo had never seen them before. *Attention!* Jimbo suddenly had an urge to yell. *Shoulders back! Belly in! Left-face right-face about-face!*

So you sold them? Captain said. Except for what's left down on the battle tables. You sold all the rest?

Yes, sir.

How much money did you get for everything, Jimbo?

I don't remember exactly.

You don't remember exactly?

No, sir. I didn't exactly keep count.

You didn't exactly keep count, Captain said and rubbed his lined forehead with his hand like some strange, slow salute.

Here's the ring I bought, Jimbo said and bent to pick up the only ring in the whole wide world from where he had spotted it glittering faintly on the floor. He held it up in the light. Two of its small perfect pearls were missing. Judy gave it back to me. It's almost as good as new. Except a couple of its pearls are gone. You want it, Dad?

What, Jimbo?

The ring. You want the ring, Dad? You can have it, Jimbo said and held the ring out. You can sell it and maybe get your things back. I'm sorry, Dad.

I'm going to call your Grandma Carver, Jimbo, Captain said quietly and ran his fingers back through his hair. I'm going to call her tonight and see if you can live with her down in Hundred Mines next year. You can finish up highschool down there.

Here, Dad, why don't you go on and take it?

I'll pay your expenses and she's got plenty of room in that

old house so it will probably be all right with her. She can probably use some help around there. And I'll send you some allowance I guess.

Here, Dad, please take the ring. Please. You can sell it. I don't want to live with Grandma, Dad.

I don't want you to live here anymore, Jimbo.

Hey, Dad, here's the ring. Please, Dad.

I don't want your goddamn ring, soldierboy, Captain said and turned and walked from the room, closing the door quietly behind him.

It was the night of the big sendoff. Jimbo was to take the bus the next morning to Hundred Mines to live with his grandmother. His dear old mom had spent two days washing and ironing his clothes and now he was all packed and ready to blow this burg. Here he had stolen the whole Second World War from his old man and he had gotten off scot-free. His old man had not laid a hand on him. His old man had only tossed him out on his ass but who in the fuck cared anyway? Jimbo was bored with this burg anyway. In Hundred Mines he'd be a big frog in a punk pond. He'd screw every halfway clean coal miner's daughter he could find. Jimbo was going to celebrate his last night in this burg by cruising around town with his best buddies Boots and Pace in Pace's planed and decked and lowered midnight blue '49 Ford and by getting drunk as a skunk on orange-flavored sloe gin and by at long last kicking the shit out of Hutch Bodine.

Jimbo, sitting at his desk, checked his watch: another hour before Pace was to pick him up. He fired up a Camel and glanced through his notebook of poems once again. Now and then he stopped to read a poem through, trying as he did to imagine Judy reading it, to imagine her sorrow, her heartache, as she realized what she had done. Jimbo put the notebook and the letter in a large already addressed envelope and sealed it. Well, that's that, he thought and smiled. He had destroyed all other copies he had of his poems. Judy would have the only copy in the whole wide world to do with as she wished. And he did not give a damn what she did with it. She could throw it in the river for all he cared. He was through with that sort of sissy shit. He would never again write another poem.

There was a light knock at the door.

Yeah, Jimbo said. He pushed his chair back and swung his feet up on the desk.

It's just me, Jimmy, his mother said as she opened the door and came in. I got some hankies here I forgot to pack for you.

That's what I need all right, Jimbo said, frenchinhaling deeply. Your basic snot-rags.

Jimbo's mother arranged the handkerchiefs in the open suitcase on the bed. There, that ought to hold you for a while, she said. She retied the belt of her bathrobe and then, humming softly, she walked slowly, aimlessly, around the room touching things. You know, this is a nice room. It gets that nice morning sun and all.

I know, Jimbo said.

Jimbo's mother walked over to the bedroom's front window and pulled back the curtains: *cowboy curtains*, she had called them when years earlier she had made them special for Jimbo's bedroom, made them from cloth decorated with horses' heads. She stood there humming and staring out into the frontyard and street. God's ways are ways of mystery, she said after a time and absently patted her cheek with long, fluttering fingers. So maybe it's all for the best right now. What with me being ill and all. Maybe you staying with your grandma is what God thinks is best right now. I don't know. Maybe so. Maybe. We aren't what you'd call a happy family right now I guess. I wish we were a happy family. Maybe when I get cured things will be happier around here. I pray for it every night.

Right, Jimbo said, stubbing out his Camel and immediately lighting another. Happy, happy. Just like on teevee. Like the Nelsons. Like Father Knows Best.

I used to be so happy when I was a girl. And pretty too I'll tell you. And I was always so gay. So lighthearted. I was always singing and laughing. You remember the laughs we used to have? When you were little? You remember how we'd sit out in the kitchen after supper and listen to all our favorite radio shows? You remember that, Jimmy?

I remember.

Didn't we have some laughs back then? We had more fun than a barrel of monkeys. And I'd make up stories for us about riding a train all the way to Hollywood where I'd get discovered and we'd be filthy rich and buy us a big fancy house with a big old swimming pool.

And I'd get a pony with a silver-trimmed saddle.

And I was pretty enough too. Everyone used to say so. We sure had some fun, you and me.

Yeah, Jimbo said. We had some fun.

Oh, well. Oh, well. God's ways are ways of mystery. I guess everything is just a test. Life is just one big test. You know I'll miss you, you stinker. I know we fuss a lot around here but I'll miss you.

Yeah. I'll miss you too, Mom. Really.

Well, I'll be down to visit you and Mom whenever I feel up to it. And your dad didn't say anything about you not visiting here.

Forget it.

Well, your dad's just upset right now. He'll cool down.

I don't give a damn what he does, dig?

I pray every night for things to get happier around here. And I have faith they will. Just as soon as I'm cured. You'll see. I think I'll say a little prayer for us right now, Jimbo's mother said and shut her eyes and began moving her lips silently.

Jimbo watched her. He squinted his eyes and stared at her. Although she was only feet from him she seemed strangely far away, as though he was observing an image of her that had been in some way magnified from far away: as though she was not *happening* here and now with the room at all. The more intently Jimbo stared the more rarefied with clarity and sharpness her features became, yet always with that sense of magnified distance. Then her image seemed to slowly recede. Past the window she went, out into the evening yard into the darkening trees, then beyond. Jimbo squinted his eyes at her slow going away. The praying woman fading out through the window into the evening shadows. Who is she? Jimbo wondered. Who is she? Who is she?

God's ways are ways of mystery, Jimbo's mother said aloud and turned from the window to look at him.

Jimbo shook his head slightly and blinked his eyes, trying to focus on her *here and now* evening-shadowed face. Streetlight coming through the window behind her trimmed her hair like a thin encircling flame.

Yeah, sure, Jimbo said. Like, amen.

Yeah, sure, she repeated, imitating his voice. Like, amen. Honestly, Jimmy, what's going to come of you? I swan to gracious I don't know.

Suddenly she laughed, giving her head a slight toss, and in the desk lamp's light her white teeth flashed and the electric glow about her hair shimmered in the dark. In the soft light laughing she looked almost young and beautiful again. Smiling, she walked over to the bed and fussed briefly with the packed clothes in the suitcase.

Well, if you do come visit I promise I won't be so gloomy all the time, she said, still smiling.

Amen, Jimbo said.

Amen is right. Yes, indeedy, I will be downright lighthearted. We'll have us some laughs like the old days. Anyway, I have what you might call a little bon voyage surprise for you.

Gee, you shouldn't have, Jimbo said.

Oh, it's not much. Just a trifle. Just an old book actually. An old book someone gave me once.

Your basic Gideon Bible.

Now, don't you be cute, young man. No, it's not a Bible although that's not a bad idea at all. Anyhow, it's packed in here under your socks.

I hope it has pictures.

Oh, you, Jimbo's mother said and walked over beside him. Well, I guess I better get some supper for your dad. You sure you won't come on down and eat a bite with us on your last night? It'd be all right I just know. I bet your dad would even like it.

Forget it. I'm going out with the guys anyway.

Oh, please don't get in any trouble. Please behave.

Sure. I promise I won't do anything you wouldn't do.

You stinker you, she said and roughed Jimbo's hair and winked. You sure are a handsome devil, I'll say that. I just hope you'll turn out a good boy. Well, I'd actually settle for a *pretty* good boy. I'd be happy with that I guess. And be lighthearted. You can be lighthearted and good too. You don't have to turn out gloomy like me just because you're good.

Well, I promise I won't turn out gloomy anyway.

What about being good?

Don't I get any credit around here? Didn't I tell you that my dirty-poem-writing days are over? I've turned in my dirty quill for good. How's them apples?

Oh, I don't know if that's so good or not after all. I don't know. I used to know someone who sure liked poems. I think I was just being gloomy about those poems. I don't know. Sometimes I think I've just been going around here like a wicked old stepmother or something.

What if I told you I was taking up praying instead of poeming for a hobby?

You stinker you. I'd say you'd best watch your nose doesn't start growing right off your silly face. That's what you get for fibbing. That's what I'd say. Well, I just have to get busy on supper. Please behave tonight, you hear now?

As soon as his mother had left the room Jimbo rummaged through the suitcase on the bed. Well I'll be damn, he thought when he found the book. Your old basic *Sonnets from the Portuguese*. Your old basic How do I love thee syndrome. Jimbo turned the thin leather-bound book around in his hands, looking it over carefully. I'll be damn, he said aloud and laughed quietly. Let me count the basic ways blah blah. I love thee to the depth and breadth and blah blah my soul can reach blah blah blah. So someone once laid old love sonnet city on old Mom. Love sonnet city. Damn. Jimbo looked for an inscription. The title page had been carefully cut out. Jimbo smiled and put the book back in the suitcase under his socks.

Well, boy, this is the night of the big sendoff, Jimbo thought and checked his watch. He shadowboxed for a few minutes in front of the full-length mirror on the back of his bedroom door. *Blam blam pow socko. Blam blam* Hutch Bodine. *Blam* your ass is grass tonight, baby! Jimbo laughed and flopped on his bed. He was going to kiss this two-bit burg good-bye in style, by God. Shit yes, man. Hell, he wasn't being run out of this two-bit burg like a goddamn dog with his tail tucked. Hell, he was making the perfect getaway. Scot-free, by God! He was going to kiss this two-bit burg good-fucking-bye in *style*, man. But first, Jimbo thought and checked his watch again, how about taking a little time out for a final whack-off. Yes, siree. Now that just might hit the old spot. A little old whack-off for old time's sake. It would probably be the last whack-off this old bed would ever see. This bedroom. It was on August 15 in the Lord's year of 1959 that our hero Captain Rebel Without No Cause last took dork in hand and for a final time puffed his imaginary honey's pussypie with pearls. Yes, siree, Jimbo said and unzipped his jeans. He rolled over onto his stomach and felt around under the bed for the sock. He didn't know what to think when he found the sock. He rolled over onto his back and held the soft, limp, laundered sock up before his eyes. Jimbo just didn't know what to think.

6 ➤
a star is born

The movie continues.

The students of Dawson High School, on a field trip, sit in the L.A. Planetarium's darkened auditorium, a projection of the universe glowing on the dome above them like a giant expanding movie, on whose curved screen the lecturer may at will expose stars, inflate galaxies, collapse constellations, or just spin them near for a closeup.

For many days before the end of our earth, the lecturer drones, people will look into the night sky and notice a new star, an increasingly bright and increasingly near new star.

New at Dawson High School and arriving late for the field trip to the planetarium, James Dean, perfectly on cue, enters the darkened auditorium. When in a stage whisper he announces his name to the teacher checking names at the door the lecturer hesitates and all of the students turn in unison to stare at James Dean. Letting his lower face collapse into smiles, James Dean slouches to a seat.

As this star approaches us the weather will change, the lecturer drones on. The great polar fields of the north and south will rot and divide, and the seas will turn warmer.

Whew, James Dean sighs, leaning back in his seat and looking up at the projected stars. Once you've been up there, you really know you've been someplace, he says quietly to no one in particular.

As the lecture on the nature of the universe continues, the lecturer points out constellations and describes them and tells the students their myths.

And this is the crab constellation, Cancer, the lecturer says.

Hey, I'm a crab, Buzz, the leader of the pack, says and walks his fingers across Natalie Wood's breasts and pinches Goon's nose. The other pack members giggle. James Dean, sitting several rows behind them, lets his lower face collapse into smiles.

And this is Taurus, the bull, the lecturer drones.

Moo, James Dean moos. Moooooooo.

The members of the pack turn around and stare at James Dean. Nobody laughs.

Yeah, moo, Crunch says.

Moo. That's real cute. Moo, Buzz says.

Hey, he's real tough, Goon says.

I bet he fights with cows, Crunch says.

Moo, Buzz says.

James Dean slumps back in his seat.

You shouldn't monkey with Buzz, Sal Mineo whispers from where he is sitting in his movierole Plato behind James Dean.

What?

Buzz is a wheel. So's Judy. It's hard to make friends without them.

I don't want to make friends, James Dean says.

Later, outside the planetarium in the dazzling L.A. sunlight, Crunch asks Buzz what they can do now for kicks. What about Moo? Goon suggests. OK, Buzz says. OK. Moo.

James Dean, sitting on a parapet outside the planetarium, watches the pack circle his raked black Mercury parked in the driveway below. Dancelike, Buzz swings Natalie Wood around beside the raked Mercury's right front fender and she hops up on it and dangles her beautiful nylon-stockinged leg beside the right front whitewall. Taking out his switchblade, Buzz kneels slowly and clicks the knife open. Only inches from Natalie Wood's beautiful ankle Buzz presses the knife's tip against the tire. He hesitates a moment, then plunges the switchblade deep into the whitewall. They all stare up at James Dean.

James Dean lets out a slow painful breath of air and slides from the parapet and slouches slowly down the winding driveway to where the pack waits patiently around the wounded raked Mercury.

You know something? James Dean says wearily as he walks past Buzz.

What? Buzz asks, grinning.

You read too many comic books, James Dean says and opens his Mercury's trunklid and takes out a tireiron.

Hey, Buzz says to the pack. Moo is real abstract.

I'm cute, too, James Dean says, taking off his sportcoat and tossing it onto the trunklid. He slouches slowly around the Mercury to the stabbed whitewall.

Suddenly Goon begins clucking softly like a chicken. One by one the other pack members pick it up. Buzz, the last, crows loudly.

Does that mean me? James Dean yells and draws back the tireiron.

What? Buzz asks, grinning and rolling his tongue in his cheek.

Chicken!

When on cue James Dean has finally been egged into picking up the switchblade someone tossed to his feet to knife-fight Buzz says: Remember, no cutting, just sticking. Jab real cool.

I thought only punks fought with knives, James Dean says.

Who's fighting? Buzz says. This is the test, man. It's only a crazy game.

James Dean and Buzz circle each other, their switchblades flashing in the dazzling L.A. sunlight. Buzz snarls, grins, rolls his tongue in his cheek. James Dean is hesitant, awkward. The L.A. sunlight is fierce. Things seem to steam in the heat. The heat presses James Dean's shoulders and back. It begins to scorch his cheeks and beads of sweat gather in his eyebrows. He thinks suddenly of the horrible heat at his mother's funeral that day long ago in the Midwest. Veins seem to be bursting through the skin of his forehead. It strikes James Dean that all he would have to do is turn and walk away from this scene and think no more about it. Go back to the Midwest maybe and think no more about movies. Suddenly a shaft of light shoots upward from Buzz's knife and James Dean feels it as if a long, thin blade has transfixed his forehead. Sweat from his eyebrows splashes down, covering his eyes, and beneath the veil of brine and tears he is almost blind. Buzz is a blurred dark form dancing in the heat haze. James Dean is aware only of the keen blade of light flashing up from Buzz's knife. Everything begins to reel. James Dean lunges at Buzz who steps easily aside. Oh, that was cute, Moo, Buzz says and laughs. The other pack members laugh, laugh. James Dean makes another quick, awkward lunge and Buzz deftly jabs Dean's stomach with his switchblade. A spot of blood blossoms on James Dean's shirt.

Cut! Cut! Nick Ray, the director, yells when he spots the blood. He calls frantically for a first-aid man.

What the hell are you doing? James Dean screams at Nick Ray. Can't you see I'm having a goddamn *real* moment? Don't you ever cut a scene while I'm having a goddamn real moment! What the fuck do you think I'm here for?

the perfect punch

Sha da da da
Sha da da da da
Yip yip yip yip
Yip yip yip yip
Mum mum mum mum
Mum mum
Get a job
Sha da da da

The radio blares full blast from Pace's planed and decked and lowered midnight blue '49 Ford: Sha da da da da. They are parked up on Snake Road in what was once Jimbo and Judy's special spot overlooking the city's lights, radio blaring, the midnight blue '49 Ford's doors wide open, the headlights on. This is the third time they have checked the special spot this evening. They have driven slowly past Judy's house five times and past Hutch Bodine's house four. They have cruised the town's main downtown drag and through the Beacon Drive-In's parking lot a dozen times each. No sign yet of Judy and Hutch Bodine. Jimbo and Pace are sitting up on the Ford's warm hood with their backs pressed against the cool windshield passing a pint of sloe gin between them. Boots, at sixteen a year younger and sort of Jimbo's sidekick, is bopping about in the carlights in time to the blaring rock and roll while he slashes and stabs at invisible foes with his brand-new switchblade.

Hutch Bodine is going to fall, man, Jimbo says and takes a pull from the pint, then passes it to Pace.

Hutch Bodine is bad news, Pace says.

He is going to fall, Jimbo says, arching his eyebrows. His ass is grass and I am a power mower, dig?

Well, man, like, I ain't poor-mouthing your fistic abilities, dig? I mean, like, I've seen your action, right? You're no pussy, man. But *Hutch Bodine*, man. *Hutch Bodine*.

Listen, man, Jimbo says, I got one fist of iron and the other of steel and if the right one don't get him then the left one will.

But *Hutch Bodine*, man. Hell, he's three years older than you and at least twenty pounds heavier, man. Like, he's in *college*, man.

Pass that pint, asshole. That's my in-training drink. I'm in training, man. Some asshole trainer you are. You're fired, man. I'm going to get a new trainer. A trainer who has faith in me. Damn it! I'm telling you Captain College is going to fall, Jimbo says and smacks his sock-covered right fist into his left palm.

What the fuck are you wearing that sock on your hand for anyway, man? You're getting crazy as batshit.

This is your basic clean and well-laundered sock, man, Jimbo says and holds his sock-covered fist up like a hand puppet, his fingers and thumb its mouth. Its name is Plato, Say hello to Uncle Pace, Plato.

Hello, Uncle Pace, you cocksucker, Plato the puppet quacks.

Plato sounds like fucking Donald Duck, man, Pace says and takes a hit of gin.

Yeah, well, old Plato may sound like Donald Duck but he knows some shit. He knows that Captain College is going to fall tonight. Plato has faith in me. Faith.

That figures, Pace says. Fucking Donald Duck.

Plato is my new trainer, man. Because Plato has faith.

Yes, I'm Jimbo's new trainer, Plato quacks. And in my

expert trainer's opinion Jimbo needs another hit off that pint so pass it, Uncle Pace, you cocksucker.

Quack, quack, Pace says and passes the pint.

Yes, old Plato knows all right. Plato knows I'll kick shit out of Hutch Bodine, man, because Plato knows God is with me. Destiny is on my side, man. Fate, man. We heroes know who we are. The stars, man. The stars are with me.

Quackshit, Pace says and takes a hit of gin. Let's talk about something important. Let's talk about pussy.

Pussyquack, Jimbo says and scratches his suddenly itching balls with Plato's mouth.

Ah, pussy, Pace says. What the fuck am I doing driving you around town so you can find Hutch Bodine and get your ass kicked when my sweet Penny and her pussyquack are at home all alone? All alone and unfulfilled.

Yeah, pussy, Jimbo says and shuts his eyes tightly. Pass that fucking pint, man.

My baby loves the western movies.

The radio blares from the planed and decked and lowered midnight blue '49 Ford: My baby loves the western movies. Boots still bops about in the carlights slashing imaginary monsters with his brand-new switchblade.

Don't slice your quack ass off, Jimbo calls to him.

Hey, man, I'm a cool cat, Boots calls back and snapping his fingers bops over to the car. Cool cats don't get cut, man. Hey, you really gonna lay this blade on me? For keeps?

It's all yours, Jimbo says. For quack keeps. It's your very own singing switchblade, man. And you take good care of it, man. It's special. I had to pull that sucker out of a magic stone to get it. I was the only cat in the realm who could do it. Everyone had tried to pull it out. All the big shots. Knights, princes, the king, the goddamn Duke of Earl. But I was the only one who could pull the sucker out.

Dig it, Boots says.

Quackshit, Pace says.

Let's roll, Jimbo says and takes Plato off his hand and stuffs it in his red windbreaker's pocket along with Captain's bozo toy soldier. Jimbo slides down off the hood and bounces around in the carlights flicking punches.

Well, man, I don't see Bodine anywhere, Pace says, as he slowly cruises his midnight blue '49 Ford down the town's main drag. Why don't you just forget it, man? Fuck it. Quack it, man. It ain't worth it.

Boring, man, Boots says, as he raps on the dashboard with his forefingers in time to the rock and roll on the blaring radio. Jimbo's gonna kick some badass tonight, man. Action, man. Action.

Stick it in your fucking ear, Boots, Pace says. That's you, Boots, all right. Punk. Just love that action as long as your ass ain't in it. Love to watch that action.

What you gettin' so hot about, man? Boots says.

Cool it, Jimbo says. He takes a swallow of warm beer from a bottle. He is lying in the backseat, his feet sticking out the left window. Try the Beacon again, Pace.

It's your ass, Pace says and peels out.

Jimbo takes another swallow of warm beer and through his squinted eyes watches the lush neon lights along the drag as they gather like schools of small, bright tropical fish in the curved rear window, then flow and fade dreamlike. It had been in this very backseat. Jimbo and Judy had gone all the way for the very first time in this very backseat. Jimbo polishes off the warm beer with a final big pull and tosses the empty bottle onto the floor.

One more dead soldier, Jimbo says. Pop me another brew, Boots.

Well, man, Pace says, as he deftly left-turns off the busy drag into the Beacon's parking lot, you finally bought it. Bodine's here, man.

Hot shit! Boots yells. Action, man. Stark is gonna bring that asshole down, man.

Is Judy with him? Jimbo asks.

No, man, Pace says. Bodine's sitting on his hood shooting the shit with some of his flunky cronies. They're all parked at the end of the lot. So what's the script, man?

Just pull in somewhere. I want to kill this goddamn beer.

Hey, man, Pace says, as he slides his bomb into a vacant slot, I actually think you can take Bodine. I was just jiving you about him kicking your ass, man. But, fuck, man, it's going to be a bad news brawl. And you've been boozing all night. You've been boozing like it's going out of style, man. You're half shitfaced.

Half, my ass, Jimbo says, laughing. Total, man. I'm wrecked.

Dig it, man, Pace says. Listen, why don't you fight the cocksucker sometime when you're straight? Then you can really kick his ass proper, man.

I'm pretty shitfaced all right, Jimbo says.

Right, Pace says. And from here Bodine looks sober as a goddamn judge. I'd love to see you kick his ass, man. Take the punk on when you're straight, man.

Boring, Boots says. Fuck, man, Stark can take Bodine anytime. Drunk as a skunk, man. Don't matter, man. Stark is a mean man.

Shut your fucking mouth, man, Pace says.

Hey, you assholes, cool it, Jimbo says. You guys are supposed to be my seconds, dig? We're a team, dig? Anyway, Boots is right. I'm a real mean man.

You're a jerk, Pace says. Quack you, man. Get your ass quacked, man. It's not my ass.

Hey, Pace, old pal, Jimbo says and sitting up in the seat pats Pace's shoulder. The stars, man. The stars are right, remember?

Quack the stars, toughboy.

I don't have a choice.

The fuck you don't, man. You got a choice.

No, I don't, man.

Action, Boots laughs. Gonna have some action tonight.

Action, Jimbo says quietly and opens the cardoor.

You sure you don't want your blade back? Boots says.

Knife-fighting is for punks, man, Jimbo says. He zips his red windbreaker up to his throat and pulls its collar up in back. Besides, man, I got one fist of iron and the other of steel and if the right one don't get him then the left one will.

I can dig it, man. Boots laughs.

Quackshit, Pace says.

I don't reckon one of you seconds would like to double for me, Jimbo says, letting his lower face collapse into smiles.

Double for you my ass, Pace says. I'll dub in your quack screams for you though.

Hey, pal, thanks, Jimbo says and pats Pace's shoulder.

Action, Boots says. Let's rumble.

Right, man, Jimbo says and fires up a Camel. Action. Lights. Scene one. Take one. Camera. Roll 'em.

Jimbo polishes off his beer, drops the dead soldier onto the backseat floor with the others, and climbs slowly out of the car. Whew, he thinks, leaning back against the door. Fuck, I am shitfaced. Whew. Jimbo squints his eyes in the strange bluegreen light, light in which he feels submerged, light he can almost imagine as water. Jimbo shakes his head to clear it.

You OK, man? Pace asks as he climbs out of the car.

Fine as wine, Jimbo says, arching his eyebrows and wrinkling his forehead. He takes the Camel from his lips with his left hand and flicks its ash. He stuffs his right hand into his windbreaker's pocket and squeezes Captain's bozo toy soldier. He squeezes it until he feels pain. Jesus, he thinks. Steady, boy. Jimbo puts the Camel back in his lips and shakes his head again. He rubs his eyes and gazes slowly around the packed parking lot. Everything looks so goddamn strange, all the cars, the people, as though they are all slightly out of proportion somehow, slightly larger or smaller than they should be, as though he is, actually, seeing them through water. And in the strange, submerged bluegreen light the colors seem so intensely technicolor they burn his eyes. Jimbo tightens his grip on the toy soldier in his pocket and tries to push erect from the cardoor: but suddenly dizzy, almost sick to his stomach, he slumps back. Got to stay in contact, boy, Jimbo thinks to himself, shutting his eyes. Can't lose it. Got to stay in touch.

Hey, man, just fuck it, Pace says. You're in no fucking shape to tangle with anyone, man. Much less Hutch Bodine. You can hardly stand up, man. Let's take a drive and get some air. Then come back later. Dig, man?

I didn't know I was getting so fucked up, man, Jimbo says, rubbing his closed, aching eyes.

Come on, man, Pace says. Let's cruise for a while.

Maybe you're right, Jimbo says. Let me think a minute, man. Jimbo takes a deep breath and leans his head back on the cartop. He watches the beams from the two huge search-lights on the Beacon's roof as they sweep across the gather-ing summery rainclouds like swift, ghostly moons. Opening night, Jimbo thinks as he watches the searchlights. Your basic Hollywood premiere. The premiere of Captain Rebel Without a Cause getting his ass kicked at the Beacon Drive-In. Pace was right. Captain Rebel Without a Cause was going to be the star at his own asskicking. Well, at least he was going to be the star of something. There's just no fucking way I can beat Hutch Bodine, Jimbo thinks, closing his aching eyes and rubbing them.

Hey, daddy, Boots says, lightly rapping Jimbo's shoulder. Get a load of who just made the scene.

Jimbo opens his eyes and blinks them, trying to focus. *Judy*. Driving a load of giggling girlfriends in one of her old man's fancy black Lincolns. Jimbo and Judy's eyes meet and Judy glances away. Laughing and waving often to friends in other cars, Judy idles the Lincoln along in the bumper-to-bumper cruising drive-in traffic. Finally, she pulls into a vacant slot only three cars away from Hutch Bodine's Mean Green Machine, a 1958 green Impala with long chrome lakes and glass-pac mufflers, a bomb almost as famous far and wide as the Silver Ghost.

See, man? Pace says. Judy's not even out with Bodine to-night, man. Like I told you, Penny just saw them out at the country club together today. She didn't know if they had a date or anything.

They were hanging out together all afternoon, Jimbo says. You said so, man. You said Penny saw Bodine carrying Judy around in the pool.

Forget it, man, Pace says. It's no big thing. I should of kept my fucking trap shut.

The scene is set, Jimbo says, arching his eyebrows and wrinkling his forehead. Action, man. Camera. Roll 'em. *R-O-L-L,* roll 'em, man.

Jimbo flicks his cigarette away. He pushes erect from the cardoor and stuffs both hands into his windbreaker's pockets. He shuts his eyes and squeezes the toy soldier tightly in his right hand until the dizziness passes. Got to stay in touch, he thinks and takes several unsteady steps. Fuck this, man. Just fuck this. Jimbo stops and takes a deep breath. Captain Rebel Without a Cause ain't gonna stagger-ass like a goddamn drunk nigger across this fucking parking lot, man. No way, man. No fucking way. Imagining with each heavy, self-conscious step that he is walking through some giant aquarium's deep end, Jimbo, flanked by Pace and Boots, slouches slowly but steadily across the parking lot toward the Mean Green Machine. When Jimbo reaches the edge of Bodine's circle of flunkies Bodine looks up at him and grins broadly. Trying to stand without weaving, Jimbo puts a Camel to his mouth, and after successfully striking a match with one hand, a trick it took him two weeks to master, he lights the cigarette's center. Jesus Christ, Jimbo screams inside himself and tosses the burned Camel to the pavement in disgust. In spite of himself, Jimbo glances toward Judy's car only to discover that she is, indeed, laughing.

Like, I mean, Bodine will fuck anything that crawls, man, Bob Tweel, one of Bodine's flunkies, says, and all Bodine's other flunkies laugh. Tweel is bopping about in the center of the circle of flunkies telling Hutch Bodine stories while Bodine sits on the hood of the Mean Green Machine grinning.

I mean Bodine will fuck anything that even scoots, man, Tweel squeals. And, man, I mean the chick we picked up that night was really a dog. Really ugly. I mean *ugly*. So I say to Bodine, man, I wouldn't fuck this dog with your dick, and so Bodine says to me, man, you turn cunts upside down and they all look just the same, then Bodine says to the dog, honey, for my good deed of the month I'm gonna mercy-fuck your brains out your ears.

Well, boy, like I always say, pussy is pussy, Hutch says and laughs and all his flunkies laugh and nudge each other. Ain't that right, Jimbo baby? Pussy is pussy.

Nudging each other and grinning like crazy, all Bodine's flunkies turn to look at Jimbo. Jimbo arches his eyebrows and wrinkles his forehead and tries frantically to clear his mind, to *focus* on this scene, to smack that shit-eating superior smirk off Hutch Bodine's handsome, tanned, country club kisser with a devastatingly clever right-cross roundhouse reply. But he can't. He just can't think, can't focus. Sweat pops out on his forehead and runs in thin, cold streams from under his arms. He just can't think. Dumbfuck. Dumbfuck. And there is smart-ass Hutch Bodine, big college jock, neat Princeton haircut, country club cool and summery in bright plaid bermudas and a blue boat-neck shirt, sitting so superior on the hood of his Mean Green Machine grinning at Jimbo the jerk. On this sweet, sweet summer night, Jimbo the jerk, in his scuffed motorcycle boots, his jakey jeans, his ratty red windbreaker: Jimbo the jerk, with his long hair swept back hopelessly un-summery on the sides, swept back almost like a low-down punkboy Presley DA, hopelessly uncountry-clubby, unsummery, unbright and neat, hopelessly low-down and greasy. *Greasy*. Greasy is the word all right, Jimbo thinks, imagining bluegreen beads of punkboy grease sliding slowly from his hairline, sliding over his sweaty forehead, sliding in thin, bluegreen, snail-track streams down his face and neck. Jimbo arches his eyebrows and wrinkles his forehead and lets his lower face collapse into a sappy grin.

Yeah, Hutch says, my experience has been that pussy is pussy. You agree, Jimbo boy?

You read too many comic books, Jimbo says, his grin feeling sappier by the second.

Hutch laughs. He drops his arm around a flunky sitting on the carhood beside him and whispers something to him. Hutch holds the middle finger of his left hand up and runs it slowly under his nose, sniffing it. Hutch laughs, then runs the finger slowly under the flunky's nose who sniffs it loudly and rolls his eyes.

Come over here, Tweel, Hutch says. Let me get another opinion on this.

Tweel bops over to the car and Hutch slowly runs the finger under his nose.

Oh, la la! Tweel squeals and bops about snapping his fingers. Yum yum yum for the tum!

Yeah, I guess I'll have to amend what I said about pussy, Hutch says, sniffing at his finger. Some pussy is sure sweeter than other pussy. Some pussy is downright finger-licking good. Yum yum.

Hutch licks his finger, then runs it slowly in and out of his mouth.

Right, Jimbo boy? Hutch says. Finger-licking good.

Fuck you, Bodine, Jimbo says.

Hutch laughs and slides down off the carhood. Jimbo stares at Hutch's muscular, college-fullback arms. Jimbo's own arms feel like noodles. He tries to imagine throwing a punch at Hutch's face. Hutch blocks the punch easily and Jimbo pictures his noodle arm wrapping helplessly around Hutch's thick wrist. Jimbo's legs suddenly also feel like noodles. He grips the toy soldier in his pocket until pain shoots up his noodle arm, shoots up his neck, and spreads like a blush on his right cheek. Please, God, Jimbo thinks. Please. Please, at least don't let me puke. Or, Jesus, Jesus, piss myself.

You want a whiff, Jimbo boy? Hutch says as he walks slowly toward Jimbo sniffing and licking the finger. Hell, boy, you can even have a lick if you want it. For old time's sake, kid. Hell, I ain't greedy. Yum yum.

Fuck you, Bodine, Jimbo says.

My, my, Hutch says and stops a couple of steps in front of Jimbo. Now what kind of language is that, son? You never did learn your lessons good, did you, boy? You just haven't got any manners at all. When a party offers to share a sniff of the sweet stuff, son, you ought to accept. Now that's good manners, see? Otherwise a party might take offense. Then, boy, you might find that your ass is grass and some party is the mower, see?

F-U-C-K, fuck you, boy, Jimbo says.

Well, Jimbo boy, Hutch says, laughing, you got a choice. I like to be fair. So if you take a great big whiff of this sweet stuff on my finger, and maybe even give my finger a little lick or two, or maybe just suck on the tip a bit, just the tip mind you, I might not kick the shit out of you. See?

Why not let me have a little whiff? someone says from the edge of the gathering crowd. Everyone turns to look. The crowd parts as Frankie walks through it toward Hutch. Although he is short, Frankie slouches slump shouldered, and except for his arms, more muscular even than Hutch's, he looks almost frail. A cigarette dangles from his mouth and his heavy-lidded eyes look almost shut. He walks slowly through the parting crowd right up to Hutch and tilts his head back to gaze up into Hutch's face through squinted eyes.

Me too, Bodine? Frankie says, almost in a whisper. He smiles and runs both hands back through blond hair almost as long as Jimbo's. Yum yum, Bodine?

Hey there, Frankie, Hutch says, smiling weakly. What's shaking, man? Long time, man.

What's shaking, Bodine? What's shaking? Hey, gosh, I want a little sniff, Bodine, Frankie says, still smiling. I want a little sniff. Or maybe a lick, Bodine. Yum yum, Bodine.

Hey, man, Hutch says, laughing faintly. We're just fooling around, man.

Oh, Frankie says. Oh. Fooling around. Oh.

Yeah, man, Hutch says and shrugs his shoulders. Just jiving old Jimbo here, man.

Oh. Just jiving old Jimbo here, Frankie says. Hey there, old Jimbo.

Hey, Frankie, Jimbo says.

How you doing, old Jimbo? Frankie says.

Hanging in there, Frankie. Hanging, man.

Well, what's new, old Jimbo? Frankie says, still smiling and squinting his eyes at Hutch's face.

Not much, man, Jimbo says. I've been drunk a lot.

Oh. Drunk a lot, Frankie says. Well, you seen any good movies lately, old Jimbo?

Fuck no, Jimbo says. I been drunk a lot lately.

Oh. Well, check out *Thunder Road*, man, Frankie says and takes the cigarette from his lips. He holds it up between his thumb and forefinger and blows lightly on its ember. It's playing out at the StarLite Drive-In. Great flick, old Jimbo. Starring badass Robert Mitchum. And starring his kid too. Co-starring Mitchum's real-life kid. Only, Mitchum's real-life kid plays his kid brother in the flick. Hey, you seen that flick, Bodine?

Yeah, Frankie, Hutch says. Sure, I saw it, man. You're right, man. Great fucking flick.

Yeah, man, Tweel squeals, snapping his fingers. Great fucking flickeroo.

Please don't do that, Frankie says quietly and squints his eyes at Tweel. Please don't talk so loud. You don't have to shout around all the time. Or snap your fingers all the time. It gives me a headache, friend.

Sure, Frankie, Tweel says. Sure, Frankie. Sure.

Hey, Hutch, Frankie says and squints his eyes up at Hutch's face. He smiles. You remember that wonderful, wild scene where this moonshining gangster cat is trying to run Mitchum off the road? Remember that scene, Bodine?

Right, Hutch says. Great fucking scene, man.

Yes, it was. Yes, it was a great fucking scene, Frankie says. He blows on his cigarette's ember. And remember how old badass Mitchum and the moonshining gangster cat pull up even while they're roaring over them twisty backcountry roads smashing shit out of each other's bombs and then old Mitchum suddenly flicks his fag through the cat's open car-window and it fucking hits the cat in the cheek? Crazy, man. Fucking sparks everywhere, man. Crazy. And the cat loses control of his bomb and runs the fuck off the road and *boom* it blows the fuck up and the cat fries. Crazy, man. Great fucking scene. Great scene.

Yeah, man, Hutch says. Great scene.

Gee, Bodine, Frankie says and winks at Hutch, why won't you let me sniff your finger? I never smelled my sister's pussy before, Bodine. Pretty please, Bodine.

Hey, Frankie, Hutch says, I was just shooting the shit, man. Honest, man. Just jiving Jimbo around, man.

Oh, Frankie says, smiling. Oh.

Frankie flicks his glowing cigarette at Hutch's face. Hutch flinches and the cigarette splatters against his throat in a shower of sparks and falls down the front of his boat-neck shirt.

Jesus Christ, Frankie! Hutch yells, slapping the front of his shirt like crazy and hopping around. Jesus fucking Christ, man! Shit, man!

His hand heavy with the metal toy soldier, Jimbo swings a roundhouse right at the center of Hutch's face. Hutch's eyes pop cartoon wide with shock as Jimbo's weighted fist slams into his upper lip and nose. Jimbo's knuckles crunch against collapsing teeth and bone and blood splurts. Hutch screams and tumbles crazily backward, bouncing against the Mean Green Machine. He staggers forward two steps, then falls to his knees, holding his dripping face in his hands. He slowly rolls over onto his side and draws his knees up to his chest, moaning.

Staggered several steps backward by the force of the blow himself, Jimbo, dizzy, tingling, stares at the fallen Hutch in stunned disbelief. No one in the pressing crowd moves or speaks. Jimbo holds his right hand up before his eyes and looks it slowly over as though it is a thing not his own. His middle three knuckles are bloody and misshapen and pushed back on his hand but he feels no pain at all. He opens his hand and examines with interest how several parts of the toy metal soldier are actually embedded in his bloody palm.

Beautiful, Frankie says quietly, breaking the spell. Beautiful punch. The perfect punch.

Jesus Christ! someone in the crowd says. Goddamn! someone else says. Motherfuck! several say.

Suddenly Boots runs past Jimbo to where Hutch is lying, leans down over him, and waving a finger in the air begins to count: one two three four five six seven eight nine ten you're out, you cocksucker!

Boots runs over to Jimbo and raises his battered right hand in the air. Winner by a fucking *KO* in one second of the first round! Boots shouts. The new champ, Jimbo Stark!

Fuck that! Tweel squeals. Stark suckerpunched him. He suckerpunched Hutch and he's got something in his goddamn hand too! That's not fair, goddamn it!

No, Frankie says quietly, squinting his eyes at Tweel. But it's over.

Fuck that! Tweel squeals. Stark suckerpunched Hutch!

Yeah, Stark suckerpunched Hutch! another flunky yells.

Yeah! Tweel squeals. That's not fair! That's chickenshit as hell.

Yeah, chickenshit! another flunky yells.

Chickenshit! others yell. Chickenshit! Chickenshit!

You goddamn chickenshit! Tweel yells and runs toward Jimbo.

In a quick move, Frankie steps in front of Jimbo and catches Tweel rushing in with a looping left hook to the gut. Tweel squeals and doubles over and starts staggering about grunting for breath.

Anyone else want a piece of my heart? Frankie says, smiling.

Hey, man! Jimbo says, pushing Frankie aside. This is my movie, man! I'm no chickenshit, goddamn it! I'll fight any one of these punk cocksuckers, goddamn it! Come on, you punk cocksuckers! Let's rumble! Jimbo yells and stalks toward the flunkies crowded around the fallen Hutch.

Pace grabs Jimbo's arms from behind.

Come on, man, Pace says. It's over, man.'You won. Let's get the fuck out of here, man.

I'm gonna kick ass all night! Jimbo yells, trying to shake loose.

Your buddy is right, Frankie says and steps in front of Jimbo. It's done, kid. You ought to cut out. The fuzz are going to appear. Cut out, old Jimbo.

Shit! Boots yells. Jimbo Stark can kick ass all night! Jimbo Stark hasn't even started to kick ass!

Be quiet, Frankie says to Boots.

Yes, sir, Boots says.

Jimbo sees Judy emerge from the crowd. Her eyes are wide and bright and she is clutching her throat. She looks at Jimbo and starts quickly toward him. Then she spots the fallen Hutch and stops dead in her tracks. She looks back and forth between the fallen Hutch and Jimbo, her mouth open wide with astonishment. Jimbo arches his eyebrows and smiles. Suddenly Judy swirls and runs to the fallen Hutch. She falls to her bare knees beside him and making sympathetic cooing sounds takes his head onto her lap. She runs her fingers through Hutch's hair. She is wearing short shorts and her brown bare legs become smeared with Hutch's blood.

You hoodlum! Judy cries at Jimbo, glaring at him, her eyes filling with tears. You gangster!

What? Jimbo shouts, trying to break free from Pace's grip. No! That's not fair! I won!

Let's get him out of here, Frankie says to Pace, and together they muscle Jimbo backward across the parking lot.

I did it for you, Judy! Jimbo shouts. I love you, Judy! I love you!

Just as Frankie and Pace shove Jimbo into the backseat of Pace's Ford the fuzz arrive, the black and white patrol car swinging into the parking lot with red bubble flashing.

Can you handle him? Frankie asks Pace.

No sweat, Pace says and hops into the frontseat.

Wait for me, man, Boots calls, running up to the car.

Vanish, punk, Frankie tells Boots.

Yes, sir, Boots says and walks quickly away.

Firing up a cigarette, Frankie strolls slowly across the lot to where the Silver Ghost is parked.

You stay the fuck down in the fucking seat, champ, Pace says to Jimbo and starts up the engine quietly, with no revving, no muffler popping. Pace drives off the parking lot slowly.

So where to, champ? Pace says.

I love her, Jimbo says. She did me dirt.

Come on, champ, where to? Pace says. Home, man?

Home? Home? Are you shitting me, man? Jimbo says. I don't have a home. I don't have shit, man.

Jesus Christ! Pace says and shifts into low, peeling out. Don't start blubbering on me, man. Come on, Jimbo, where to?

Boomer's, Jimbo says.

Where's Boomer at, man? Out at his summer camp?

Yeah, Jimbo says. Hey, Pace, do me one last favor.

Name it, champ.

The big envelope I brought with me tonight. Give it to Judy for me, man. Tell her she can do anything she wants with it. Tell her I dropped her ring in it and that she can do anything she wants with it too. And tell her I loved her.

Sure, champ. Sure.

8 ➤
the unknown soldier

The old cemetery at the edge of town had not been used in twenty years, ever since old man Ketchum, Boomer's father and the richest mortician in town, had closed it and incorporated the rolling slopes of several farms south of town into burial lots whose reasonable rates marked them from the beginning as good investments. The old cemetery was mostly overgrown now, with many toppled tombstones and sunken graves. The old, one-story stone caretaker's house, its front rooms gutted by fire years earlier, stood at the top of steep, narrow stone steps that wound up around the hill at the town-side edge of the old cemetery. Each year at the first sign of warm weather Boomer would move from his small apartment above the mortuary to the back unburned rooms of this old caretaker's house for the summer. The old stone house was cool inside and private and the overgrown graveyard had almost returned to forest. It made a dandy summer camp, Boomer always explained. And every red-blooded American boy ought to get to go off to summer camp.

Jimbo watches Pace peel out in the spraying roadside gravel. He watches the Ford's taillights until they disappear toward town. He turns and begins stumbling up the steep stairs. Panting, he sits down on the top step and awkwardly with his left hand fires up a cigarette. His right hand is swollen now and aching. With his left hand's fingertips he lightly brushes the smashed knuckles and winces at the shooting pain. Oh Jesus, he says aloud and blows on the knuckles. He takes the sock out of his windbreaker's pocket and carefully slips it over the battered hand. The old soldier tends his bloody war wounds, Jimbo thinks and smiles. The perfect punch. Jimbo cradles the hand close to his chest and gazes out over the lights of the town and the headlights and taillights of the cars coming and going across the new bridge to Ohio. The old bridge, a half-mile south and closed for years, is dark except for small, red, blinking lights scattered about its piers to warn riverboats. He could buy that old bridge for a lousy buck. That was the rumor anyway. You could buy the whole shebang for a lousy buck. Then of course you had to tear it down yourself and apparently the salvage was not supposed to be enough to make it pay. But for a lousy buck. A whole goddamn bridge for your own. He ought to buy the sucker and refuse to tear it down. Buy it and live on it. Live right in the middle of it. Like the mean old troll, Jimbo thinks, looking at the blood spots spreading on the sock. No one fucks with mean old trolls.

Wind rises up in the trees behind him and Jimbo looks back over his shoulder. Summer rainclouds have covered the earlier clear sky and the old caretaker's house is just a large shadow higher on the hill. Here and there on the hillside among the trees Jimbo can see the dark shapes of tombstones. He shivers. He used to run through these tombstones at night when he was a squirt: run with his pals playing insane spook, hooting and screeching and sometimes toppling over tombstones. And there was that one Halloween night when they had carried off several small stones to leave on people's porches: small stones with little lambs perched on their tops or carved on their surfaces. For a long time after that Halloween night Jimbo had had horrible dreams of rotting babies rising from their graves for revenge, their little bald heads pushing up out of the earth like mushroom caps after a rain: dreams of rotting babies dragging him screaming and kicking back to be buried with them in the old cemetery. Jimbo shivers again and stands up.

The old cemetery, he thinks, looking around the dark, silent hillside. The last, the ultimate boondocks. The boondocks of death. For a moment Jimbo thinks of running down the stone stairs like a bat out of hell. Jesus, he thinks. I need another goddamn drink, Jimbo says aloud and laughs.

The shades are drawn in the windows of the back room Boomer uses but Jimbo can see a dim glow of light behind them and he hears low music coming from inside. Jimbo walks across the small back porch and raps lightly on the door. Immediately someone inside begins to moan horribly and to boo like a ghost. For years the town squirts have been deliciously titillating their terror by skulking around the old haunted caretaker's house at night. Jimbo smiles. He can remember running crazily down the hill as a squirt himself, pop-eyed with delightful fear.

Oh ooooooooooooooh oooooooooooooooh, the haunter moans. Boooooo boooooooooooo, the haunter boos.

Moooooooooooooo moooooooooooo, yourself, Jimbo moos.

Hey, squirt, come on in, Boomer calls, in his deep, froggy voice.

Boomer is sitting at the old kitchen table in the center of the small room. The only light in the room is from a portable teevee sitting on a chair in one corner. The teevee's sound is turned off and the music, a country tune, is coming from an old Silvertone radio placed on top of the teevee set.

Get yourself a brew, squirt, Boomer says.

Thanks, Jimbo says and gets a beer out of the refrigerator, then pulls a chair up to the table across from Boomer and sits down.

I was wondering if you'd get around to saying bye-bye to your poor old Uncle Boomer, Boomer says, the cigarette dangling from the corner of his mouth jerking little perfect clouds as he talks. He pushes his old, battered gray fedora even farther back on his head with a thumb, then carefully fills the shot glass on the table in front of him to its brim from a quart bottle of bourbon. He refills a half-full water glass with beer, then freely sprinkles its top from a large-sized circular Morton's Salt container.

I've been saying a lot of bye-byes tonight, Jimbo says, staring at the sinking salt crystals as they dissolve in effervescent bubbles in Boomer's beer. Jimbo takes a long pull from his own bottle of beer.

What time does your bus depart tomorrow, squirt?

Fuck the bus.

Now that couldn't be a great deal of fun. That's sure a cute glove you're wearing there, squirt.

That's my sidekick Plato, Jimbo says, laying his sock-covered bloody hand out on the table in front of him. He's bleeding.

So I see.

War wounds, Jimbo says. With his left forefinger and thumb he picks at the blood-soaked sock. I kicked shit out of Hutch Bodine tonight. That was a bye-bye I wish you could have seen.

Not me, squirt. The sight of blood makes me burp. But congratulations anyway, Boomer says. He drinks half the bourbon from the shot glass, chases it with half the beer from the water glass, then carefully refills them both.

What a goddamn mess. I'm only seventeen and already everything's broken down, Jimbo says, shaking his head. He holds the nearly empty bottle up before him and rotates it slowly, watching the small image of the teevee move like a tiny moon over the curved dark surface of the glass. Across the room, on floor-to-ceiling shelves, glass jars reflect hundreds of tiny teevee screens: rows upon rows of glass jars full of dead little creatures floating in alcohol. And they were only a small selection of Boomer's Grand Scientific Specimen Collection, a collection he had worked on steadily for years. *Eyes*, Jimbo suddenly thinks. The tiny teevee screens reflected in the glass jars are like hundreds of eyes: bright, unblinking, busy little eyes, as though all the little creatures in the jars are suddenly alive and staring at him. Jimbo reaches for Boomer's quart bottle of bourbon.

I'm going to miss you, you old weird duck, Jimbo says. You're about the only friend I have. You and old Pace.

Well, I suppose I'll miss you too, squirt. You're about the only witness I have. An old weird duck needs a young weird duck around for a witness.

Dig it, Jimbo says and takes a drink.

Listen, squirt, Boomer says, as rain suddenly gusts against the windows. Sounds like a nice night out. For spooks and weird ducks anyway.

Dig it, Jimbo says. He picks up the Morton's Salt container and studies the little blond girl with the umbrella who spills salt behind her as she walks along in the rain. When it rains it pours, Jimbo reads. He pours a small mound of salt out on the tabletop.

Profound, Boomer says. Profound.

Fuck, man, Jimbo says. He puts his head on the table. I'm only seventeen and everything is already fucked up.

Now, now, squirt, don't get my tabletop all teary, Boomer says. He drains the shot glass. He puts the empty quart bourbon bottle in the middle of the table.

One more dead soldier, squirt, Boomer says. Maybe our last dead soldier together for a spell.

Yeah, I guess so, Jimbo says. He holds the empty bourbon bottle up in the light and shakes it, then puts it back on the table. He takes the toy metal soldier from his windbreaker's pocket and places it beside the empty bottle.

Now, here's your basic dead soldier, Boomer. What do you think of this basic dead soldier, Boomer?

Boomer picks it up and turns it around slowly in his hands, carefully examining its elaborate, bright blue and red, silver-trimmed uniform, its silver, high-pointed, plumed helmet. When Boomer puts the toy soldier back on the table beside the bottle Jimbo picks it up and begins marching it around the tabletop.

Forward, march, Jimbo says. Your left, your right, your left, your right, your left. Marches pretty good for an unknown soldier, right, Boomer? Pretty goddamn good. Hup, hup, hup.

Not bad at all, Boomer says.

Marching the fuck over hill and hup hup dale, Jimbo says and marches the toy soldier through the small mound of salt. Marching, marching, marching bravely through the goddamn snowy dead of winter. Marching the fuck all over the goddamn snowy Second World War's dead of winter. Left-fucking-face. Right-fucking-face. About-fucking-face.

Right-fucking-face, Boomer says. He begins marching the empty bourbon bottle about the tabletop too.

You're in the goddamn army now! Jimbo yells and jumps up from the table, knocking his chair over. You're in the goddamn army now, Jimbo sings at the top of his lungs and begins to stomp around the table. You'll never get rich, you son of a bitch, you're in the army now!

You're in the army now! Boomer croaks, pounding the bottle on the table. You're in the army now!

Onward Christian soldiers! Onward Christian soldiers! Jimbo sings, stomping and waving his bloody, sock-covered hand in the air. Onward as to war! With the cross of Jesus going on before!

The cross of Jesus! Boomer croaks and pounds the table.

Jimbo flops down onto Boomer's cot near the door and lies there laughing. Finally, catching his breath, he just lies there listening to the rain and staring up at the strange shadows the teevee light flickers over the ceiling.

Coughing, Boomer gets up slowly and walks unsteadily over to an old chest of drawers against the wall opposite the door. From its top drawer he takes an unopened quart bottle of bourbon. Back sitting at the table, still coughing, Boomer carefully refills the shot glass to its brim.

That cocksucker is the one, Jimbo says. He's the one who taught me to march. Drilled my ass off. Left-fucking-face. Right-fucking-face. About-fucking-face.

Jimbo swings his legs over the cot's side and sits there holding his face in his hands. He's the one I should have given the big good-bye to. The cocksucker. The big good-bye in the sky. Banished his ass to the big boondocks in the sky. He's the one I should have drilled with the perfect punch, Jimbo says, standing up wearily. He picks up his knocked-over chair and sits down at the table. He stretches his bloody, sock-covered hand out on the tabletop. *Rat-a-tat-tat-tat-tat,* Jimbo says and flicks the toy soldier's face with Plato's stiff upper lip, knocking it over. He picks up the Morton's container and slowly covers the fallen toy soldier with salt.

Dead as a doornail, Jimbo says. The unknown cocksucker. Amen.

Don't get salt in your wounds, squirt, Boomer says and sips his bourbon.

Amen, Jimbo says.

Amen, squirt, Boomer says.

How could you love him? Jimbo asks. How could you ever love him?

It was supposed to be the grandest Fourth of July celebration the town had ever witnessed. The mayor at that time, who happened to be Boomer's father, spent months planning the whole shebang. Planned a grand parade. Grand patriotic floats. Every highschool band in the county. A crack army reserve drill team. The parade paraded all over town. It did not miss a main street. Boomer's father was its grand marshal and, carrying an American flag, he marched out in front of the grand parade all over town. The parade ended up on the old bridge late in the afternoon where they were going to shoot off the grandest fireworks show of all time. But first the crack army reserve drill team was to shoot off a grand twenty-one-gun salute from the center of the bridge.

I can still see all those shiny spent shells bouncing all over the bridge in the late afternoon sunlight, Boomer says. I scampered about and picked up a whole pocketful. I pretended they were some kind of strange coins. Exotic coins from China. I can remember wondering how high those bullets would rise before they arched and started back down. I remember wondering if the fish would be able to dodge them when those bullets hit the river.

Another grand attraction was also planned before the grand fireworks show. My dear old departed dad had in a moment of sublime inspiration hired a certain Chief Soaring Eagle to perform a thrilling stunt to really give the folks something to remember. Old Chief Soaring Eagle was a part-time wrestler and circus daredevil quite famous in that day. He claimed to be a bona fide Aztec Indian war chief, although there were a few dastardly rumors to the contrary. Dastardly rumors that Chief was actually a wop from Dayton, Ohio. At any rate, my dear old departed dad hired the great Chief to dive off the bridge into the dangerous river far below. His splashing entrance into the dangerous current was to signal the first flares of the grand fireworks show. Ah, squirt, Chief Soaring Eagle looked magnificent, his eagle-feather headdress gleaming in that late afternoon sunlight. And when with great solemnity he removed his beaded and brightly feathered ceremonial chieftain's cape there was no doubt in my squirt mind. That beautiful, brown, sleekly muscled body was no Dayton, Ohio, wop's body. He was truly an Aztec war chief. An Aztec god.

You have to picture this, squirt. Chief Soaring Eagle carefully removes his cape and headdress and with grave dignity prepares to daredevil dive into the dangerous river far below. Barefoot, he balances on the narrow railing, his head tilted back as though in worship, his long, black, gleaming hair falling straight back almost to his waist, sunlight golden on his calm, brave face. The highschool bands' drums roll. My dear old departed dad, resplendent in his World War One infantry captain's uniform, stands ready to fire the first rocket personally. The crack army reserve drill team is poised to fire a final volley. Slowly, Chief Soaring Eagle raises his powerful arms above his head. Suddenly, bursting through the crowd, yelping and hooting like a movie redskin devil savage, your dad, the captain of all the squirts, jumps up on the railing beside Chief Soaring Eagle. Your dad is bareback and his body and face are streaked with bright red and yellow paint and he is wearing a bandanna with several old bent chicken feathers stuck in it. Listen, squirt. Old Chief Soaring Eagle looked down at that painted, feathered, yelping dad of yours with an expression of such bug-eyed, open-mouth, goofy astonishment as I've never again seen on another human face. The crowd gasped. The drums stopped rolling. My dear old departed dad squealed. Your dad laughed and jumped.

Then suddenly I was jumping too. And damn if I know why. I don't even remember thinking about it. Just suddenly I was watching the river rise up to greet me. I don't remember being afraid or anything. Actually, I think I was rather calm about the whole thing. I just remember being rather astonished that here I was jumping into the river behind your dad. And, although I don't remember really thinking about anything in particular, I do remember how it all seemed so slow, like everything was happening in slow motion, and I remember how clear all my impressions were, how clearly I was seeing things, small things like branches floating along in the current. I remember seeing your dad below me in the water and I remember giggling when I saw the amazed look on his face when he spotted me. There I was giggling and I was probably going to drown. Probably going to take the big drink. Hell, I could hardly swim. I don't remember hitting the water at all. And I don't remember your dad pulling my ass out of the drink. But he did. He saved me. He pulled my ass out of the big drink. And you know, squirt, that wop from Dayton, Ohio, refused to dive after that.

Old Cap always protected me. Always. From the time we were squirts. Like a big brother. I was under his wing. And for no reason at all. I was always the puny squirt of squirts and old Cap was always the captain of squirts. I was nothing and he always took up for my worthless ass. And besides that time he pulled me out of the big drink there was another occasion when you might say he saved my worthless ass.

You mean he saved your life another time?

You might say that.

When was it? What happened?

I was so drunk I can hardly remember it.

Come on, Boomer. Tell me.

Forget it, squirt.

Come on, Boomer. How did he save you?

He didn't shoot me.

What? He didn't what?

He didn't shoot me.

He didn't shoot you? When? What happened?

Forget it, squirt.

Fuck, Boomer! Come on.

Goddamn it, squirt! I said forget it.

Sure, Boomer. Sure.

Pass the goddamn bottle.

Sure, Boomer, Jimbo says and passes the bottle.

You want to camp out here tonight, squirt? I'll get out the other cot.

No.

Come on. Why don't you stay here tonight?

No, Jimbo says. He picks the toy soldier up out of the mound of salt and puts it in his windbreaker's pocket. No. I got things to do.

You're welcome to stay. But suit yourself.

I got places to go, Jimbo says and gets up. He walks slowly over to the door and opens it. Rain sweeps in. I need a big drink. That's what I ¬eed.

Plenty to drink here.

That's not the kind of big drink I need, Jimbo says, arching his eyebrows and wrinkling his forehead.

Now, now, squirt, don't get melodramatic.

Don't sweat it, Boomer.

Well, what can I tell you? Boomer says and tilts back in his chair. He blows a series of perfect smoke rings into the air. Wish I could give you some pearls of wisdom. Some food for thought.

Don't sweat it, Boomer.

Well, don't do anything I wouldn't do. Don't take any wooden nickels. Don't piss against the wind. Life is no bed of roses. By the yard life is hard, by the inch it's a cinch. Never use sobriety as a crutch. Behind every dark cloud there's a silver lining. Hitch your wagon to a star. A bird in the hand is worth two in the bush. The truth is always leaked. The highest motive is to be like water. Never go to reality stag. The good traveler leaves no tracks.

Thanks for the tips, Uncle.

You're welcome, squirt, Boomer says and smiles. The smoky air about his shadowed skullface is luminous in the flickering teevee light.

Catch you, Boomer, Jimbo says and walks into the rain.

On bare feet Jimbo balances himself carefully on the railing in the center of the old bridge. The rain is cold now and comes in gusts across his face. His eyes blur with water and he can taste rain in the corners of his mouth. He can hear the rushing dark river far below and he thinks about how terribly cold its water must be. His clothes are soaked and he shivers in the cold, rising river air. Farther up the river, lights from the new bridge shudder on the swift, dark current. For a time Jimbo watches the lights of the cars crossing the new bridge. Jimbo closes his eyes and tilts back his head.

The big drink, Jimbo thinks and smiles. Jimbo tries to imagine hitting that dark, cold water. How cold would the water be on the bottom? he wonders. Would he be able to see at all underwater in the dark? How long would he be able to hold his breath? He could hold his breath underwater longer than anyone he ever knew. He had always hated to swim on the surface, but he liked to swim underwater, to swim close to the bottom for as long as he could hold his breath. The colder the water the firmer the fish, Captain always said. The cocksucker. Jimbo would not even try to swim when he hit that cold water. He would not even try to swim underwater, and he would not hold his breath. He would practice his deadman's float, that's what he would do. And it might be days before they found him floating on his face far downriver. And by that time his body would be horribly bloated and fish would have eaten out his eyes. We found him practicing his deadman's float, the cops would explain when they brought Captain and Judy to identify his corpse. But he could swim like a fish, Captain would tell them. I taught him to swim like a fish myself. You can swim like a fish, soldierboy, I told him. Just jump in and swim to me, son. I'm right here, soldierboy. Jump, son. Jump. Jump. Jump. Jump, damn it! Jimbo curls his bare toes over the railing's edge. The deep end. The deep end. Jimbo shivers. Jump! Jump! Jump, goddamn it! Jimbo slowly raises his arms above his head and stands on tiptoe. Jimbo wants more than anything to be with Captain in the deep end. Jump! Jump! Jump, goddamn it! You're not going to drown, goddamn it! Captain shouts and slaps the water with a cupped hand. It sounds like a shot. Jimbo flinches. Jimbo falls. He breaks his fall back onto the bridge with his battered, bloody hand. He screams and rolls over. He can feel the metal soldier in his windbreaker's pocket stab painfully into his side. Oh Jesus oh Jesus oh Jesus, Jimbo cries and curls childlike about his bloody hand. Oh Jesus oh Jesus oh please Jesus oh please Jesus oh please Jesus.

When he comes to, Jimbo rolls slowly over onto his back. Jesus, he thinks. He holds his bloody hand up close before his eyes, trying to see it in the dark. Jesus, he thinks and rests his head back on the pavement. He opens his mouth, letting the cold rain hit the back of his throat. Wonder how long it would take, Jimbo thinks, letting rain puddle in his open mouth. To drown in the rain.

Jimbo sits up and for a moment feels faint again. He shakes his head to clear it. He feels around in the darkness until he finds his motorcycle boots. Jimbo throws away his wet socks and after emptying the rain from the boots he slowly and with great difficulty pulls them on with his left hand. He feels dizzy again and lies back down until it passes. When he sits up he carefully peels the blood-soaked sock off his hand. He tries to examine his hand in the darkness. He blows on the hand and then, gently, he kisses the smashed knuckles. He kisses them and softly licks them. The blood is still sticky in places and tastes salty. Jimbo holds the hand up and slowly turns it around and around in the rain. He tilts his head back and catches rain again in his open mouth. When he licks his knuckles again the salt taste is gone. Jimbo reaches across himself with his left hand and tenderly touches his aching right side. He takes the toy soldier out of his windbreaker's pocket and holds it up in the dark before his face. It seems to be bent but he can't be certain. Thanks a lot, cocksucker, Jimbo says aloud and tries to laugh. Well, Jimbo thinks, I guess I blew this burg all right. Look the fuck out, boondocks, 'cause old Captain Rebel Without a Cause is on his way. Jimbo picks up the bloody sock and stuffs the toy soldier into it. Consider yourself one drowned cat, cocksucker, Jimbo says. He tosses the sock and toy soldier far out into the darkness over the river.

part two ➤

jobs, 1960

9 ➤
on the lam

zoom in

on Jimbo Stark, refusing to remember. Jimbo Stark, one
week after his highschool graduation, roaring through a rainy
southern night, warm can of beer between his legs, window
down, radio on, his steely eyes on the shiny, wet road, his
sidekick Pace passed out in the seat beside him: Jimbo Stark
making the perfect clean getaway at last and refusing to
remember: refusing to remember slouching across the auditorium stage at his honorless highschool graduation ceremony after his hopeless year of boondocks banishment: refusing to give a shit that Captain was not there: refusing to
remember falling down drunk again and again as he tried to
bop at graduation parties, to remember stealing money from
girls' purses after coming to on a bed of coats, to remember
bouncing shirtless about the highschool's parking lot barking
fight challenges to all comers, then losing quickly to a
freshman football star in the dazzling headlights of circled
cars . . .

closeup

of Jimbo Stark's face, the tight, ironic grin, the steely eyes
searching the roadside unafraid in the flashing headlights
for ghost hitchhikers, headless truck drivers seeking their
smashed, long-rusted rigs: ghostgirls in prom dress shrouds
still trying to return home safely to Mother after that fatal

crash twenty years ago: Jimbo Stark's steely eyes sweep the haunted roadside and he refuses to remember the press of Judy's bare legs against his own at the picnic only days earlier when they had held each other in swimsuits under a tree during that sudden summer rain and she had told him tear-fully that this time it was real, this time she was pregnant for real. Jimbo Stark takes a sip of warm beer and listens to the tires purr on the wet pavement and refuses to remember his mother's quick, burning eyes, her face shining in the bright revival tent lights, as she slowly unbuttoned her blouse . . .

Jimbo Stark grins and fires up a Camel. He arches his eyebrows and wrinkles his forehead and refuses to remember. Jimbo Stark, who is going to live his life like holy lightning, who is going to be a holy mad one, mad to live, mad to be saved: Jimbo Stark, old Captain Rebel Without a Cause On the Road, steely eyed, grinning tightly, his soul whoopeeing, roars relentlessly through the rainy southern night as he makes the perfect clean getaway in the stolen Silver Ghost.

The gas tank was nearly empty and it was long after dawn. Jimbo turned the Silver Ghost off the highway onto a narrow blacktop road which he followed for a mile before pulling over under some trees by a small stream. He gave Pace's shoulder a perfunctory punch. Pace grunted and tried to curl into a smaller ball on the bucketseat. Jimbo fired up a Camel and for a time sat there smoking and listening to an all-night hillbilly music station. He had always thought he hated hillbilly music, associating it with those school bus country hicks everyone Cool made fun of. Right now he felt differently. Right now those sad songs of faded love hit the spot.

After a time the windshield covered with steam and Jimbo rolled down his window. He could see his breath in the cool morning air. He got out of the Silver Ghost and stretched in the warm sunlight. He walked slowly down to the small stream and took a leisurely leak into its shallow current. In the glistening morning light small spiderwebs sparkled from the damp grass along the bank. A hillside meadow on the far side of the stream was thick with wild early summer wheat and small blue flowers and Jimbo could see grasshoppers flicking through the high grass. Birds called and thrashed in the thick leaves of the trees around him. Jimbo zipped up his fly and then shut his eyes and just stood there on the bank feeling the warm sunlight on his face. It all starts right here, he thought. Right here.

I can't believe this shit, Pace said from the car.

What's the matter, amigo? Jimbo said and walked back to the car.

I'm so fucked up, man, Pace said. He had his cardoor open and was sitting bent far over, his feet flat on the ground, his face in his hands. I'm sick as shit, man. This is the one that kills me. Oh Jesus. Where the fuck are we anyway?

I'm not sure, Jimbo said and offered Pace a drag on his Camel. Somewhere in Virginia I guess. Or maybe North Carolina.

Why did you pull over, man? Pace asked. He frenchinhaled deeply, then handed the Camel back to Jimbo.

It's daylight and we're about out of petrol, partner.

Well, why in the fuck did you stop here, man? Pace asked, looking around. Jesus, this ain't a gas station. We're in the middle of the goddamn woods, man. *Woods*, man. Wolves. Fucking bears.

You don't know much about getaways, do you? You don't wheel a stolen getaway car into a gas station in broad daylight, man. Not a stolen getaway car like the Silver Ghost anyway. Partner, this is where we part company with the old Silver Ghost. We ditch it right here.

Oh, that's cute. Then what? Do we walk to fucking Florida? Pace said. He adjusted the mirror on the door and after studying his face for a moment began to methodically pop pimples.

You don't really think your hero would make you walk all the way to Florida, do you? We fly, amigo. We fly on the swift wings of the open road, Jimbo said and wiggled his thumbs winglike in Pace's face.

Oh, what in the holy shit am I doing here? Pace said and jumped out of the car. You really did it to me this time, Stark. What the fuck am I doing here? Why did I ever let you talk me into this shit?

Now, now, little amigo, Jimbo said. He hopped up on the right front fender. Where's that old spirit of adventure? We're soldiers of fortune, amigo. Soldiers of fortune don't whine around. You can't waste your time bellyaching when you're on the road in search of adventure. And you remember what I told you soldiers of fortune get plenty of, don't you?

Tell me again, Pace said. Convince me.

Pussy, Jimbo said. Soldiers of fortune get more pussy than they know what to do with. And amigo, I mean exotic pussy. Beautiful, exotic princess pussy.

I can hardly wait, Pace said and put his face back in his hands and moaned. I can't believe it. A week ago I had a beautiful bomb and a honey who loved me. Then you hit town. I get drunk. I wreck my bomb. My old man raises hell. I get drunker. I lose my honey. I get drunker. My old man kicks my ass. You ruined my life, Stark.

Now, now, little amigo, Jimbo said. Baggage. That's all baggage. You got to travel light to be a soldier of fortune on the road. Baggage just slows you down. And you leave tracks. The good traveler leaves no tracks.

Oh Jesus Christ, Stark! You and your goddamn beatnik babble, Pace said. He walked down to the stream, then stood there on the bank weaving and shivering while he groped with stiff fingers about his fly. I'm so fucking cold I can't even find my goddamn pecker. I think it froze and fell the hell off.

Now, now, Jimbo said. He hopped off the fender and began to bounce about on the balls of his feet flicking punches. Just think about exotic princess pussy. You'll find it soon enough, amigo.

Quackshit, Pace said.

Jimbo stopped shadowboxing and just stood there inhaling deeply. Whooee! Whooee, world! he yelled and pounded his chest.

Whooee my quack ass, Pace said and pissed a thin, quavering arc out into the water. A week ago I had a beautiful bomb and a girl who loved me and my whole life was planned out. College next fall. Then after college Penny and I would get hitched and I'd go on to law school. Then after law school we'd have a kid and I'd be a hotshit lawyer raking in the dough. My old man has been a cop for seventeen years and all he ever wanted was for me to grow up to be a hotshit lawyer. He's been saving for my college for years. And here I've been out of highschool less than two weeks and already I'm a criminal. A goddamn crook. A *car thief.* Thanks to you, Stark. Thanks to you.

What a bunch of crap, Jimbo said, firing up another Camel. None of that chickenshit crap means a thing, man. Don't you understand? We are *on the road.* Let me tell you something, amigo. Right now—right this very minute while we're standing here—an old man with flowing white hair and wide, knowing eyes is waiting patiently out there somewhere on the road for us to find him. He is waiting patiently for us with the *Word.* The *Word,* amigo. The *Word.* When we find him he will give us the Word and make us silent.

Oh Jesus fucking Christ, Stark! Give me a break. You and your goddamn beatnik crap. Give me a break, man!

Amen, amigo.

Jim, let's go back. Seriously.

Fuck that, man. Seriously.

Let's just get in the car and go back home. It's not too late. Not if we go back right now.

It's always been too late.

Quackshit, man. Listen, Jimbo. It was a joyride, man. We just got drunk and took a crazy joyride. Things just got out of hand, that's all. We'll tell them that. They'll understand. Hell, even Frankie will understand that. Frankie has done a lot of crazy things himself before. And Frankie likes you, man. I bet old Frankie will just laugh it off.

I'm not sweating old Frankie, pal.

I want to go back, Jimbo. I want to get Penny back. I want

to fix up my bomb. I want to be a hotshit lawyer and rake in the dough when I grow up.

Suit yourself. Go back if you want to. I'm not holding you down or anything.

What about Judy, man?

She doesn't exist.

Hey, Jim, that's not being fair. Just because of one dumb mistake.

There is no Judy.

I should have kept my big mouth shut as usual.

I would have told you if it had been the other way around.

Shit, man. Come on. Let's go back.

Like I said, suit yourself. I ain't stopping you. But I'm not going back. Ever. I'm on the road for good, man. Splitsville, daddy. Forever. This was no punk joyride for me. This was a clean getaway.

Using both hands, Jimbo picked up a large, egg-shaped rock from beside the road.

Hey, Jim, Pace said. Come on.

I'll tell you one thing, though, partner, Jimbo said and hoisted the rock up to his chest. If you go back you'll have to walk.

Hey, Jim. Come on, man. Just cool it.

I'll cool it all right, Jimbo said. As though shooting a set shot, Jimbo pushed the rock into the air. The center of the Silver Ghost's windshield, tinted green with reflected leaves and shivering like water with sunlight, collapsed inward when the rock smashed into it.

Jesus fucking Christ! Pace yelled and jumped backward. You're fucking crazy! You're insane!

Amen, Jimbo said. He walked over to the Silver Ghost. He ran his hands slowly over the warm metal of the hood. Well, that's that, he thought. He leaned over and peered into the hole in the windshield. The black leather bucketseats were covered with shining, broken glass. Jimbo suddenly felt dizzy, almost sick, and he shut his eyes.

I just can't fucking believe it, Pace said.

Dig it, Jimbo said.

Now what in the fuck can we tell them? Pace asked. How can we explain that? Jesus.

Who cares? Jimbo said. Tell them you got hit by a goddamn meteorite. Tell them you were just cruising the Silver Ghost along on a joyride minding your own goddamn business when all of a sudden out of the blue you got drilled by a falling star. Tell them the fucking sky is falling. Tell them any goddamn thing you want.

Jesus.

Well, I'll catch you around, amigo, Jimbo said. He took his small suitcase out of the Silver Ghost. I'll drop you a postcard from never-never land.

Jesus, Pace said, just standing there staring at the Silver Ghost. He shook his head.

Jimbo walked slowly up the blacktop road toward the highway. He could hear distant traffic.

Oh, fuck it anyway, Pace said. Hold up, Kemosabe.

What? Jimbo said and turned around.

Wait a goddamn minute, will you? Let me get my goddamn transistor radio out of the goddamn car. It's my old man's graduation gift. I don't want to leave it.

Dig it, Jimbo said, grinning.

Jesus Christ, Pace said as he trotted up to Jimbo.

Have a little breakfast, Jimbo said. He handed Pace a pint of bourbon he took from his suitcase.

I still can't believe this shit, Pace said and took a long pull.

Hey, partner, Jimbo said, draping his arm over Pace's shoulders as they walked toward the highway. Things are going to be cool. Take your hero's word for it, boy. First we'll get a little truck driver café grub in our soldier of fortune guts. Then we'll fly south on the swift wings of the road. Hey, amigo, things will be cool. It's going to be a piece of cake. Listen, Miami is hopping this time of year. It's tourist season, amigo. They'll be begging for busboys and bellhops. You know, we might even get on as lifeguards. Like at one of those big fancy hotels. We'll have room and board in one of those fancy hotels and plenty of dough in our pockets. That'll give us plenty of time to look around for something really interesting. Like on a boat or something. A sunken treasure expedition. Some smuggling. *Adventure. Adventure.* Just keep picturing a beautiful, exotic princess sitting on your face.

I could use some breakfast, Pace said. He pulled the collar of his highschool jacket up in back and pushed up its sleeves to his elbows. He clicked on his red transistor radio.

Listen, Jimbo said, just remember what old Alfred E. Newman always says.

What's that, man?

What, me worry? Jimbo quacked in his Donald Duck cartoon voice.

Quackshit, Pace said. Quackshit.

Jimbo shaded his eyes with his hands and gazed down the narrow, two-lane blacktop road. In the distance the hot blacktop looked strangely wet, as if covered with pools of shining, dark water. Not a car in sight. In either direction. The road was a secondary route back road which Jimbo had figured would be safer for their getaway, safer than the main highway from sleepy-eyed, slowly patrolling, southern deputy sheriffs with time on their hands to stop and ask questions— *Hey, boy, ain't I seen a poster out on you? Hey, ain't you Jimbo Stark? Christ! Pull your rod, Clyde, it's the Jimbo Stark gang!*—but Jesus, they had been stuck at this shadeless crossroads for nearly two hours. Sun blazing in a cloudless sky: flat, hot fields spreading to horizons: the air, hot, still, smelling of steaming cow dung: a single wretched-looking crow perched on a nearby speed limit sign evil-eyeing them like potential crowlunch.

Pace was doing a little dance in the roadside's dust while holding his red transistor radio tightly to his ear. Alley Oop Oop, the radio played and at each *Oop* Pace snapped his fingers and grunted and Jimbo flinched. The bottoms of Pace's pegged jeans and his black penny loafers were powdered pale with the dust he stirred. Jesus, Jimbo thought and coughed in the rising dust. Some gang. Some getaway.

Do you have to kick up all that goddamn dust? Jimbo said. He was squatting in the feeble shade of a dust-covered bush beside the road.

Gee, Kemosabe, I'm so sorry, Pace said and continued dancing. I'm just having so much fun at this adventure I've got me an uncontrollable case of the happy feet.

We'll never get a ride, man, with you flitting around like a goddamn fag.

Tra la la, Pace said, dancing on tiptoe. Oh, tra la la.

Why me, God? Jimbo said and spat into the road.

Hey, hero, Pace said and looked intently at his watch. It's almost two o'clock, man. We ain't had a lift in a long time. Stuck in the middle of nowhere. Hungry. Hot. Hung over. Hey, man, this adventuring is a real kick.

Glad you dig it.

Hey, Kemosabe, let me ask you a question. Have we had an adventure yet, man? I mean, you'd be sure to tell me if we were having an adventure, right? I'd hate like hell to miss out on adventure.

I'll tell you all right, turdface. Some sturdy sidekick you are.

Yeah? Well, some hero you are.

Turdface.

Asshole.

Turdface, Jimbo said. He hit the nearby speed limit sign with a small stone. The wretched-looking crow flapped to a fencepost across the road from where he resumed his glare. I guess the turdface has a point all right, Jimbo thought. Some adventure. Some getaway. Maybe he should not have ditched the Silver Ghost after all. Maybe he should have driven it to the end. Maybe he should have pulled the Silver Ghost out into that stream and floated off on it. Made a raft out of the old Silver Ghost and he and Pace could have perhaps floated it safely all the way down the Mississippi to New Orleans. Now, that would have been some getaway. No, Jimbo thought. He was right about ditching it. The old Silver Ghost, Jimbo thought, suddenly picturing its smashed windshield. He wished with all of his heart he could take that back. Frankie didn't deserve that. Frankie didn't deserve any of this shit. Frankie had always done right by Jimbo. He had even gotten Jimbo and Judy back together last summer. Frankie had told Judy what Hutch Bodine was saying when Jimbo had drilled him with the perfect punch at the Beacon that night. And after Pace had given her the ring and poems Judy had called Jimbo at his grandmother's in the boondocks. I feel *so awful*, she had wept. *So guilty*. They had begun writing daily and calling weekly then and Jimbo was certain their love was more true than ever. He was certain this time their love would grow and grow until the end of time, until the twelfth of never. Well, the old laugh had been on him once again. But never again, Jimbo thought and spit into the road. The old laugh would never be on him again. Jimbo would never again believe in truelove.

A car appeared in the shimmering watery distance of the road and Jimbo jumped up. He brushed off the back of his pants. He carefully took his glasses out of his shirt pocket and put them on.

Glasses, amigo, Jimbo said. Glasses are the trick. Makes you look smart. Sincere. Safe. Makes you look like a college boy.

Captain Fag Foureyes is more like it, Pace said.

Christ, Pace, why do you have to wear that highschool hoodlum jacket all the time? Even in this heat. At least put the collar down. Try to look like a nice college boy. Not a goddamn punk highschool hood.

Bang bang bang, asshole, Pace said, hiking his leg high and farting loudly.

Just as the car approached, Jimbo smiled broadly and waved his thumb and hoped he could fasten his sincere eyes onto the driver's. The car, a 1956 red and black Ford Victoria with jeweled white mud flaps and several squirrel tails tied to its aerial, was packed with teenage girls who yelled and waved furiously as they roared past. Jimbo flipped them the finger.

>   >   >

The air inside the drugstore was cool and had a fresh icecream smell to it. Jimbo and Pace walked to the fountain area in back and sat on stools. Pace immediately began to spin himself around and around on his stool while trying to imitate the buzz of a helicopter. Jimbo ordered applepie with icecream and black coffee. Pace ordered his usual three hotdogs with everything and a large double cherry Coke.

Don't you ever eat anything else? Jimbo said.

Not if I can help it, Pace said. I got to think about my figure.

Christ, Jimbo said and laughed. Listen, partner, how much money do you have left anyway? We better do some accounting.

Not much, man, Pace said and took out his wallet. About six bucks and some change is all.

God, Pace, where the fuck is all your graduation loot?

In the bank, man. My old man made me put it there for college next year.

For college? Jesus.

Well, I ain't got no rich Uncle Boomer, man. I ain't got it made in the shade.

Made in the shade. Sure thing. I'm not going to any fucking college myself, man. The road of life is going to be old Captain Rebel Without a Cause's college.

That's just peachy if you want to be a bum. Get a degree in bumism. I'm going to be a lawyer myself, daddy. Make the bucks. Bail bums out of jail.

Well, anyway, college boy, I have about twenty bucks left. Here, take seven. That keeps us even.

Hey, speaking of loot, what the fuck happened to all your wad, man?

A two-week drunk for one thing. Anyway, hoard this cash, man. It's got to last us until we get to Miami and land jobs.

I ain't worried about it, man. I don't expect to ever see Miami. I expect to be starved to death long before then.

Well, I'll give you a decent burial. Then I guess I'll have to be a handsome lifeguard at one of those fancy hotel pools getting pussy all by myself. And when I get on a sunken treasure expedition I'll think of you.

I'll never see Miami, Pace said. No way.

Not if you keep eating nothing but shit, Jimbo said and took a bite of applepie.

Jimbo and Pace both got popsicles for dessert and Pace ambled over to a revolving rack of comic books. Jimbo found a paperback bookrack, which he spun slowly, scanning titles. Well, well, Jimbo thought and smiled when he spotted a copy of *On the Road*. He had given his latest copy away a month ago, the sixth copy he had either bought or stolen and then given away to someone since he had first read the book. He had given two copies to Judy, both of which she had lost before ever opening. Jimbo casually glanced around the drugstore. The waitress was busy washing dishes and only a fat girl looking at movie magazines was anywhere nearby. Holding the popsicle to his mouth with his left hand, Jimbo picked the paperback from the rack with his right and with a quick move smoothly slid it up under his loose shirttail and stuffed it in his pants waist. Jimbo arched his eyebrows and took a long sweet suck from his cherry popsicle. When he glanced around again he saw that the fat girl was looking at him. She was wearing tight black pedal pushers and her hair was up in huge yellow rollers and when Jimbo looked at her she grinned. Jimbo looked back at the paperback rack. Caught in the act? he wondered. Well, it was too late now. If she said anything he would just pay up and try to talk his ass out of it.

A group of teenagers, three girls and two boys, came into the drugstore and walked back to the fountain stools. The two boys were tall and thin and had long greasy ducks. The sleeves of their white T-shirts were rolled up high on their arms and in the tight folds both carried packs of cigarettes. Punk local-yokels, Jimbo thought with a sneer. They were cracking stupid jokes and trying to flirt with one of the girls who was blond and very pretty. She was wearing red short shorts and when she sat down on a stool the flesh of her tan thighs spread softly over the black vinyl top. One of the other girls was carrying a large blue plastic radio by its handle like it was some sort of musical purse and she set it on the countertop and turned it up. The pretty blond began spinning around on the stool, snapping her fingers in time to the music and kicking out her smooth legs. She glanced toward Jimbo.

Jimbo held the popsicle down at his side and slowly edged over to where Pace was intently reading a Little Lulu comic.

You want this popsicle? Jimbo said.

What? What? The man don't want his popsicle?

Jesus. Just take the fucker, Jimbo said and looked around. The fat girl was watching him and grinning. What's with her anyway? he thought. Jimbo walked over to the postcard rack and began spinning it slowly. He took his glasses off and put them in his shirt pocket. He ran a hand slowly through his hair and then rubbed the back of his neck and rolled his head around in a little circle. Ah, yes, the handsome, mysterious stranger from the road looks world weary all right. Jimbo arched his eyebrows and wrinkled his forehead and examined the postcards intently through his squinted eyes. He took out his pack of Camels and tapped it lightly against the edge of one hand, smoothly sliding a cigarette out, which he then took from the pack with his lips. With his right hand he got out a book of paper matches and flipped it open with his thumb. Using only his right hand, he folded over a match and flicked it against the striker with his thumb. He lit his cigarette and frenchinhaled deeply. Glancing up, Jimbo saw that the pretty blond was sitting with her back to him and talking intently with one of her girlfriends.

Fuck her, Jimbo thought. She was chattering about a date she had for tonight with this real cute boy who had a tough red convertible. Red convertible, shit. Fuck her. Jimbo was certain this information was for his benefit. Her voice was just too loud to be natural. He wondered if she really did have a date with a guy who had a tough red convertible or if she was just trying to make him jealous. He wondered if she screwed, if she banged like a screen door and went down like a submarine. He wondered if the guy in the tough red convertible would have her down in the seat tonight. Wonder what old Judy would be doing tonight? Probably still waiting for him to pick her up. He'd left her cooling her heels once and for all. That was for sure. He wondered if her suitcase was still hidden in the bushes beside her house where he was supposed to pick it up and stash it in the Silver Ghost before he came to the door to get her for their heavy date. A heavy date Frankie had loaned him the Silver Ghost for. A heavy date that little did Frankie know was supposed to be a getaway for Jimbo and Judy to find their perfect summerplace where Judy could have their baby and they could frenchkiss forever in peace. Well, he had made a getaway all right and this time the joke was on old Judy. The joke was on everyone but Jimbo. Let Hutch Bodine fuck her all he wanted. Jimbo didn't give a royal shit anymore. Let her run off with Hutch Bodine somewhere and have the goddamn little bastard. One thing was for sure. The joke was not going to be on old Captain Rebel Without a Cause On the Road this time.

Come on, Pace, let's cut out, Jimbo said and picked out a postcard of a local Dixie Court Motel. He could write "Wish you were here" on its back and mail it to old Judy. Now that was abstract. Jimbo liked being abstract. It went along with being cute. Jimbo grinned and ambled to the counter up front near the door and paid for the postcard.

Hold up, man, I'm going to get some shades for the Florida rays, Pace said and pointed to a revolving rack behind the counter displaying sunglasses.

You better hold on to your cash, man, Jimbo said. He glanced at the rack himself. It looked like a weird little tree with flat, dark eyes instead of leaves.

Hard rays in Floridaland, man, Pace said. A cat needs shades.

Suit yourself, amigo, Jimbo said and picked up the suitcase and walked out the door. The hot air nearly took his breath away. His skin felt immediately sticky again and he had to blink back salty tears in the bright sunlight. The sidewalk was dazzling with small bright points of light and heat waves quivered up into the air from the blue metal of a Pontiac parked at the curb. Jimbo fired up a Camel and studied the drugstore's display window. Taped to the bottom right corner was a hand-painted poster announcing a revival meeting at the Grace Baptist Church Sunday night which would be broadcast live over a local radio station. *Broadcast live.* It made Jimbo think strangely of bait stuck on a hook and cast live into water. Live bait is the best, Captain always said. Live bait wiggles. Broadcast live. Broadcast live into the airwaves. Like his mother had almost been.

The gang had been cruising around in Pace's midnight blue '49 Ford drinking and hunting for something to do for kicks. They were celebrating. Jimbo Stark was back from the boondocks and buying all the booze they could drink with his highschool graduation loot. Hey, there's a tent revival at the edge of town, Boots had said. Well, let's just cruise out there and get a few laughs at the Christians, Jimbo had said. They had gotten a few laughs all right. Christians testifying live over the radio about what they had been cured of by the love and grace of Jesus amen. I was cured of a deformed foot amen. I was cured of the piles thank you Jesus. The gang had stood at the back of the hot, brightly lit tent near a door passing a pint in a paper bag and getting lots of laughs. I was cured of throat cancer, the tall, gaunt man had croaked into the microphone. Sounds like he's got a frog in his throat, Boots had said and the gang snickered. I was cured of wearing slacks, a young woman in a demure dress shyly said. Lots of laughs all right. Get a load of that, Boots had said and punched Jimbo's arm when a middle-aged midget woman beating a tambourine lightly against her leg walked down the sawdust aisle toward the stage. Probably cured of bad breath, Boots said and the gang snickered. Hey, Jimbo, look over there, man, Pace had said and pointed to a far aisle. Her face was glistening in the tent's heat. Her eyes were wide and bright and a strange smile was frozen on her face. She was walking down the far aisle toward the stage.

Jesus, Jimbo thought and shut his eyes and pressed his

forehead against the display window's warm glass. He had to refuse to remember. That was the trick. When you are on the road you just refuse to remember. That's what being on the road was all about. Memory was like tracks. The good traveler left no tracks.

I seen what you did in there.

Jimbo blinked open his eyes and looked around. The fat girl was standing behind him holding a flabby armful of movie magazines. When he looked at her she gave a little nervous laugh and glanced away.

What? Jimbo said and blinked his eyes.

I seen what you did in there, the fat girl said and winked.

What's that supposed to mean? What's with you anyway?

I seen you steal that book in there, she said and laughed nervously and winked again.

You don't sweat much for a fat girl, do you? Jimbo said and arched his eyebrows.

Well, I like you too, the fat girl said and turned and hurried away up the street.

Hey, wait up, Jimbo called and trotted after her.

Hey, listen, I'm sorry. I didn't mean anything.

Well, like I always say, sticks and stones can break my bones but words can never hurt me.

Listen, I'm sorry. Here, Jimbo said and took the book from under his shirt. You want it? It's a good book.

You're all heart.

Really. It's a good book. It's one of my favorites.

Stick it up your ass, the fat girl said and walked away.

Jimbo and Pace had been let out after a long ride at the edge of a small city and after a local copcar had slowed down as it had passed them, the one cop in it giving them a long once-over, they had walked for a couple of miles to get out onto the open road before hitchhiking again. They were on a straight stretch and could see car headlights at a distance so they walked in the middle of the road, clomping along in cadence on the blacktop. Jimbo could hear frogs from the brush on both sides of the road and fireflies were blinking in the deeper shadows under the trees. To their left were stands of pines, which sent a clean resin smell into the air. To their right the land was mostly clear and in the distance at intervals across the open fields they could see lights from farmhouses.

Man, I'm really dragging my ass, Pace said.

Courage, amigo.

Man, I've never been so beat, Pace said, adjusting the sunglasses on the bridge of his nose.

You don't need those shades, amigo, Jimbo said. It's dark out.

I like to be Cool at all times, Pace said and adjusted the sunglasses again. I owe it to my fans.

Fans my ass, Jimbo said. The sunglasses had bright reflecting surfaces, as though Pace was wearing two little mirrors over his eyes. All afternoon Jimbo had stared at the two small images of himself he saw reflected in those glasses. He wished he had bought a pair himself.

You owe it to your ass not to fall on it in the dark, amigo, Jimbo said.

Cool cats don't ever fall down, man, Pace said and turned up his radio.

The car did not even slow down as it approached them. Jimbo and Pace hurried to the side of the road and stuck out their thumbs. Jimbo had to shut his eyes in the blinding headlights.

You dumb cocksucker! Jimbo yelled as the car sped past them. He rubbed his eyes with his fists.

Hey, man, Pace said, tapping Jimbo's shoulder.

The car had pulled to a halt up the highway and was slowly backing toward them.

Maybe he heard you, Pace said.

So what? Jimbo said. I'm in an ass-kicking mood, amigo.

When the car reached them Jimbo bent to the closed shotgun seat window and arched his eyebrows. The driver, a dark-haired middle-aged man, stared intently at Jimbo through heavy plastic-rimmed glasses.

Thanks for the ride, mister, Jimbo said and gripped the doorhandle.

The driver made no move to unlock the door or roll down the window. His intent stare made Jimbo glance away. What's with this guy? Jimbo thought.

Toss your suitcase in back, the driver said after finally opening the door. He still kept glancing at Jimbo.

Jimbo and Pace climbed in the frontseat with Pace in the middle. The car was a current model Chevy Bel Air and its interior had a good, new smell.

Do we know each other, sir? Jimbo asked the driver.

I don't think so, the driver said. He pulled the car back out onto the highway. I didn't mean to gape like that. You look like someone.

I've been told that before, Jimbo said and laughed. People tell me I look like this moviestar.

What moviestar is that? the driver asked.

James Dean. People say I look like a deadringer for James Dean. Except I have dark hair.

Is that a fact now? Well, sorry, James, but that's not who I had in mind. You know, everyone seems to think they look like this or that moviestar. In fact, people tell me I look like the late, great Humphrey Bogart. Can you see it? The world-weary face. The sad, knowing eyes. The voice. Listen. *Play it again, Sam.*

I guess so, Jimbo said.

You guess so, the driver said, still in Bogart's voice. Play it again, Sam. You're gonna have to take the fall, sweetheart. And you only guess so.

Sure, Jimbo said. I can see it. Who was it I reminded you of?

You don't know the party. What's your destination, sports?

Floridaland, Pace said. Gonna soak up rays. Suck oranges.

That's a long haul.

How far are you going, sir? Jimbo asked.

Oh, I guess I'll know when I get there. Where in Florida are you boys heading?

Miami, sir, Jimbo said. We have jobs lined up with my

uncle's construction company. We're saving up for college next fall.

Well, well, the driver said. Boys with ambition. I'm duly impressed. What's going to be your chosen profession?

I've been thinking about the ministry, sir, Jimbo said.

Bullshit, sonny, the driver said and laughed.

What makes you say that, mister?

Forget it. Let's try another one. What monikers do you guys go by? If you don't mind telling me that is.

We don't mind at all, Jimbo said. Not at all. I'm Sal. Sal Paradise. And my friend here is Dean Moriarty.

You don't say, Jake said, laughing. You don't say. Old Sal and Dean. Old Sal and Dean on the highroads of America. Searching high and low for old Dean's long-lost dad I bet. You guys must be on the lam. I thought so as soon as I saw you.

What gives you that idea, sir? Jimbo said.

What did you tough customers do? Rob a bank? Knock over an armored car? Snatch an old lady's purse? Hey, am I in danger? You tough customers wouldn't knock me off, would you? A fine fellow who picked you up and all?

No, Jimbo said. We'll give you a break. We won't knock you off.

That sure puts my mind at ease. How about a little drink on it, boys? Reach in that glove compartment, Sal boy. There's a little bottle of hooch in a paper bag. Help yourselves, boys.

This I can use. Thanks, Jimbo said. He got out the bottle and took a long hit. You want a drink, sir?

No thanks, Sal boy. I have my own special poison right here, the driver said and took a small medicine bottle from his shirt pocket. He opened it with one hand and took a deep drink.

Let me have a hit, Pace said and Jimbo passed him the bottle.

Old Sal and Dean on the road, the driver said and laughed. Jack will get a real kick out of this all right. When I tell him I ran into a couple of real tough customers named Sal and Dean on the road. He'll get a real kick.

I don't get you, sir, Jimbo said.

Old Jack is a pal of mine.

Jack? Jack who? Oh, you don't mean . . . Oh, come on now.

What are you all talking about anyway? Pace said.

Do you really know him? Really?

Jack and I go a long way back, the driver said. He'll get a real charge out of this.

Who? Pace asked. Who in the hell is Jack?

I'll be goddamned, Jimbo said and laughed.

Some aliases you came up with, Sal boy. Some aliases.

Will someone tell me what the hell you guys are talking about? Pace said.

Jack Kerouac, Jimbo said. He knows Jack Kerouac.

Who's that? Pace said. So what?

Jesus, turdface, Jimbo said. He wrote that book I gave you last year. *On the Road.* My goddamn favorite book. Sal Paradise and Dean Moriarty are the heroes of *On the Road.* Well, sort of the heroes I guess.

Sort of is right, the driver said, laughing. Why don't you run some more aliases by me.

I'm Jimbo and he's Pace, Jimbo said. And I guess you could say we are sort of on the lam. Hey, who are you anyway? How do you know Kerouac?

I'm Jake. Jake Barnes. You ever hear of me?

No. I don't think I have anyway, Jimbo said. Should I have? I mean, are you famous or something?

Not lately.

Well, I'm glad to know you, Mr. Barnes, Jimbo said.

Hey, cut the mister crap. Please. The mister and sir crap makes me feel old. I'm only forty, for Christ's sake.

Well, how do you know Kerouac? Jimbo said. What do you do?

Oh, I guess you could call me an engineer of sorts. Something of a troubleshooter. When there's trouble on a job I hop in and clear it up. Good thing about my job is I have to bust ass for a few weeks or maybe months sometimes but then I get to lay off with pay for long spells. Get a lot of free time to myself this way. Anyway, I met old Jack about ten years ago when I was hanging out in the Village pretending to myself and to the world I was a poet. The world knew better. Jack and I have done our share of shitkicking together since then I'll say.

I'll be damned, Jimbo said. I write poetry myself.

I'm not surprised, Jake said.

Do you mind if I turn on the radio, Jake? Pace asked.

Feel free. Feel free. Listen, can both you boys drive?

Sure, Jimbo said.

Well, to tell you boys the truth, it so happens that I'm heading for Miami myself. And I'm in something of a hurry, see. So if you boys can give me a hand with the driving we'll just team up for the rest of the trip.

Jesus! Jimbo said. That's great!

Hot shit! Pace yelled and rapped furiously on the dashboard in time with a rock-and-roll song on the radio. We got it made in the shade.

Really, Jake, Jimbo said. This is just great.

Well, it works both ways. You sports are doing me a favor too. I could use the company and you boys both look like you can hold up your end of a deal. You seem like boys I can count on.

You better believe it, Jimbo said.

We'll do our share all right, Pace said.

Hey, Jake, let me ask you something, Jimbo said.

Shoot.

How come you're in such a hurry to get to Miami? Jimbo said, laughing. Are you on the lam too or something?

Jimbo, everybody is on the lam from something, Jake said. It's part of the human condition. Actually, I just finished up a big job and I'm taking a well-deserved, extended vacation. Now the reason I'm in such a hurry is that I'm horny as hell. And there's a sweet, beautiful, willing woman waiting for me in Miami. You'll find out, boys, when you get to be an old dog like me that sweet, beautiful, willing women are hard to come by. And this lady is something special. Cuban lady, with dark flashing eyes and long black hair and mystery in her laugh. I met her during my smuggling days and she's held a piece of my old heart ever since.

Jesus, you were a smuggler? Jimbo said.

In a manner of speaking. I wasn't a pro. I didn't do it for profit. Arms to Castro when he was still in the hills and I still believed in him. And I really did believe in him once. That commie cocksucker.

Does your Cuban lady have any beautiful sisters? Jimbo said.

Don't worry about that, Jake said, laughing. Stick with me and I'll fix you up good.

Hey, turdface, Jimbo said and punched Pace in the shoulder. This is it. We're adventuring, amigo.

Dig it, Kemosabe, Pace said and turned up the radio. Dig it. Miami, look out. Miami, here we come.

Damn right dig it! Jimbo said, laughing. Jake, mind if I roll down the window for a while?

Feel free, Jimbo. Feel free.

The window had a sticky new-car feel to it as Jimbo rolled it down. Jimbo shut his eyes. The rushing night air was warm on his face. Well, this is it, Jimbo thought. On the road. *Really* on the road. Roaring through the sweet southern night with a mysterious madman poet toward Miami. *Miami.* God, how that name burned in his brain. Wild tropical nights in smugglers' beachfront bar hangouts. Glasses of dark rum poured by black-haired Cuban beauties with mystery in their laughs. Jimbo opened his eyes and watched the white line in the middle of the road reel them relentlessly south. He was leaving confusion and sadness and bullshit behind at last. He had found the groove of his life at last. Sure, there were things he felt bad about. But there wasn't anything he could do about them now. He couldn't do anything for his mother. No more than he could that horrible night when he spotted her walking down the aisle unbuttoning her blouse. He had charged out into the darkness and run until he collapsed, exhausted. And Judy. But she had made her own bed. Even if she had fucked

Hutch Bodine only once. I swear it only happened once, she had sobbed over the phone. It's you I love. Please. It's *our* baby. I swear to God it's *our* baby. Sorry, Judy. Once was once too often. Sure, he still loved her. But he would get over it. At least there was nothing about old cocksucking Captain to make him feel bad. He had spent a year in the fucking boondocks just like Captain had ordered. And he had kept his nose clean. No fights. Drank alone secretly. Kissed his crazy grandmother's ass. Got good grades. Had not asked for a thing. Had even returned the allowance Captain had sent. Then Captain had not even asked him home for Christmas. Captain had not even come to his highschool graduation. Well, so what? Who gives a big shit? Anyway, Jimbo had gotten the last word. He had kissed off old Captain and his chickenshit once and for all. Last night. God, was it only last night? It seemed like a year ago. Ten years ago. Blaring the radio and beating crazily on the horn, Jimbo had roared the Silver Ghost up Captain's street. He had pulled the Silver Ghost up over the curb right into Captain's frontyard. Leaving the radio blaring and the bright headlights on, Jimbo had stalked out in front of the car. He had stood there in the bright headlights shouting for Captain. Come on out and play, Captain old boy, Jimbo had shouted at the dark front of the house. Come on out and slide your ass down my cellar door, Captain old boy old pal. Neighbors' porch lights began to flash on. Pace yelled from the car for him to get the hell back in. Someone is gonna call the cops, Pace yelled. Hey, Captain, come climb in my rain barrel, Jimbo shouted. Hey, Captain, let's be jolly friends forevermore. No light came on in the dark house, no sign of Captain at all. The goddamn BozoBoat was parked in the driveway so old Captain had to be home. So what's the story on old Captain? Jimbo had wondered. Well, either he's hiding in the dark behind one of those windows too chickenshit to come out and play or he's passed out down in his chickenshit bomb shelter. Neighbors came out onto their porches. Come on, Pace yelled. The cops will be here, man! Jimbo had fired up a Camel, then slouched slowly over to the BozoBoat. He had taken a long, leisurely leak into the BozoBoat's open front window. Flashing the finger at all the nosy neighbors, Jimbo had slouched back to the Silver Ghost. He had backed it out into the street and, blasting the horn, had roared it off into the night.

10 ➤
deadringer

Jake Barnes had been about everywhere and done about everything all right. As they drove south that night and the following day, taking turns behind the wheel, Jake told one story after another about his wild youth. When they passed a chain gang chopping brush beside the road in the early morning, Jake told about the six months he had once spent on just such a chain gang before finally escaping with a big spade through the Georgia piney woods. He had been in on an assault charge after a roadside tavern fight in which he had beaten a bullying off-duty deputy sheriff silly. Those six months on the chain gang had been a living hell, Jake told them. He and the big spade had been lucky in their escape and before the hounds tracked them they had made it to the railroad tracks where they had hopped a freight north to freedom. All that had happened years ago but if he was ever stopped for anything in Georgia and they ran a check on him he would probably end up right back beside that hot highway, chopping brush until he dropped. So drive carefully in Georgia, boys, Jake had said and laughed. When Jimbo was stopped for going through a caution light in a small Georgia town by a local redneck cop, Jake said, Well, boys, this might be the end of the ride and he got out of the car to do the talking. Somehow he soon had the redneck cop laughing and they got to go on without even having their licenses checked. Early that afternoon they picked up a hitchhiking soldier whom Jake talked with at great length about his own days in the service. He had seen a lot of action in the South Pacific and had been wounded at Okinawa. He had reenlisted when the Korean conflict broke out and had been wounded again at Pork Chop Hill. Jake insisted on turning inland west for nearly fifty miles to take the soldier to his hometown. "Not many guys would do this, mister," the soldier said when Jake let him out in front of his parents' home. Jake had been stopping for cold six-packs all day and when they crossed the Florida line in the late afternoon Jimbo and Pace were high and happy. They yelled and cheered and from the windows tossed confetti they had made by tearing up a newspaper.

Damn, but I wish my boy Nick was with us right now, Jake said.

You have a son? Jimbo asked.

Yeah, Nick. Old Nick just turned twenty. Let me tell you he's a pisser. That goddamn kid is always into some kind of goddamn beef.

Where is he? Jimbo asked.

Atlantic City. My wife passed away a few years back. Nick stays with my sister most of the time. Comes up to stay with me at my place in New York every now and then but we always end up tangling over something and he takes off. I've got a cottage over on the Jersey shore and he stays there during the summer sometimes. Real independent kid. He gets around all right that kiddo. Gets in a beef in Atlantic City, then hightails it up to the cottage to hide out. Or comes up to New York until he gets his ass in a jam there. Then he takes off again. Some kid.

He sounds like a tough customer, Jimbo said.

Tough customer is right. But he'll be all right. I was worse when I was his age. He'll settle down. Meanwhile, though, all he thinks about are fast cars and chippies. Just like his good-for-nothing old man used to.

Just like me I guess, Jimbo said and everyone laughed.

Pace turned up the radio and Jimbo rolled down his window. The evening air was hot and moist and smelled heavily sweet like rotting fruit. Jimbo had a sudden picture of rotting oranges glistening with flies. Through the insect-smeared windshield he watched the carlights illuminate the high walls of trees looming at the narrow road's edges. From his side window Jimbo stared intently into the close, dark swamp. The Everglades, he said to himself. Jungle. Tropics. Tropical. Even the word was mysterious, magical. Deadly snakes camouflaged among the twisted roots of mangroves. Dead, still, black water. Showers of exotic insects. Glowing swamp gas. Shimmering apparitions. Lost Spanish spirits. Ancient, unknown Seminole villages. Indian holy men chanting in firelight. Low drums. Voodoo. Jimbo shut his eyes and breathed in the hot, moist night air deeply. He was getting closer and closer to the true beginning of his life. Somewhere near a tropical rebirth waited for him. He would be someone new, nameless, mysterious. His life was unfolding now like an opening black orchid.

Moths swooped in from the darkness about the brightly lit SAVE sign above the gas pumps. The rambling, one-story, wood-frame building was blazing with neon beer signs and two old men were sitting in rusted lawn chairs on a narrow concrete front porch. One of the old men got up and walked slowly over to the car as Jake lined it up at a high-test gas pump. Jake told him to fill it up and check the oil and don't forget to clean the dead bugs off the windshield. They all got out of the car and walked around stretching.

Boys, I have some calls I better make before it gets too late. Why don't you sports go in and grab some snacks? Jake said. He walked over to a phone booth at one end of the porch.

The old man sitting on the porch silently stared at Jimbo and Pace as they crunched across the gravel to the moth-encrusted screen door. There was a DRINK NEHI sign on the door and along both sides were signs advertising FRESH RIVER FISH: CATFISH, PERCH, DRUM, EEL, BUFFALO. What in the hell is a buffalo fish? Jimbo wondered, getting a crazy picture of a shaggy, big-headed fish with a huge hump.

Pace let the screen door bang behind him when they entered and several men standing around a pool table in the back of the long, low room looked up. The front part of the room had several narrow aisles of shelves stacked with canned and packaged goods and along one wall were pop coolers and racks of silvery potato-chip packages. Along the other wall a counter ran almost the length of the building. Pace headed directly for the pop coolers. Jimbo browsed among the aisles until he spotted a swivel bookrack of paperbacks. He fired up a Camel and idly glanced through the titles. A jukebox blared hillbilly music from the back and Jimbo hummed along with a tune as he turned the bookrack. Most of the paperbacks were westerns or thrillers with words like *naked* or *lust* or *virgin* in their titles and had covers with half-naked voluptuous women lying tangled in sheets on damp-looking beds. Miami, Jimbo thought. This time tomorrow night they would be in Miami. Black-haired harlots. Cuban mulatto lovers.

You gonna buy that book, boy?

Jimbo looked up from the bookrack. A young, heavyset blond man in a military uniform was leaning against the counter only a few feet from him. Two other men from the back were standing nearby watching. The young soldier grinned at Jimbo and took a long pull on his bottle of beer.

What book? Jimbo asked.

That book you stole, the soldier said and pointed his beer bottle at Jimbo's copy of *On the Road* in his hip pocket.

I had that book when I came in, Jimbo said. He looked back to the bookrack.

I saw you slip it in your pocket, boy, the blond soldier said.

I told you I already had this book, Jimbo said and arched his eyebrows.

Yeah, he had that book before he came in here, Pace said. He was sitting on a pop cooler sipping an orange soda. Hell, man, he swiped that book yesterday.

You mind your business, the soldier said to Pace. Now, I say I saw this boy stick that book in his pocket. He stole it off this rack. Hell, this is my old friend Sam Harlin's store. I can't let you steal something from old Sam.

I didn't steal it here, man, Jimbo said.

You see, boy, I just got out of M.P. training. I'm with the Military Police, don't you see. I got a duty. I'm gonna arrest your ass, see. I'm gonna put your ass in custody.

You know what? Jimbo said and wrinkled his forehead.

What, pretty boy?

You read too many comic books, Jimbo said.

Oh Jesus! Pace muttered. He hopped off the pop cooler and rushed over beside Jimbo. Hey, man, he really did have that book when he came in. Honest, mister.

Too many comic books, huh? the soldier said. He put his beer bottle down on the counter. Well, like I said, I got my duty. Let's you and me take us a little stroll on out front, pretty boy. I got all kinds of brand-new judo tricks I want to show my buddies. Hell, I been home on leave two goddamn weeks and I ain't had the chance to kick one single ass with all my new judo tricks. Until now that is.

Hey, come on, mister, Pace said. We just came in here to get some snacks.

Shut up, Jimbo said to Pace.

Come on, now, the soldier said and crooked his forefinger at Jimbo to follow. Let's get to it.

You boys get everything you need? Jake said. He was standing in the door.

This guy claims Jimbo stole a book, Pace said.

Must be some mistake, Jake said.

I say I saw him, the soldier said and squinted his eyes at Jake.

Must be some mistake, friend, Jake said, smiling. That's my son you're accusing. He wouldn't steal anything. I've raised him to be a real good boy. Churchgoing. An Eagle Scout. Did you boys get anything?

I got an orange pop, Pace said.

How about you, son? Jake asked Jimbo.

I don't want anything, Jimbo said.

This should cover things, Jake said and spread a dollar bill on the counter. He walked over and put an arm around Jimbo's shoulder and moved him toward the door. Jimbo turned his head and glared at the blond soldier.

Come on, now, Jake said and herded Jimbo through the door. Pace scooted after them.

That prick, Jimbo said as they walked across the gravel lot to the car. I could take his ass, man. He'd be sucking soup till his teeth grew back in.

I believe you, Jimbo, Jake said. But what's the percentage? Why bother? It's just trouble, sport. One thing you don't need when you're on the lam is trouble.

The screen door banged in back of them.

Hey, buddy, I ain't quite done talking to your boy, the soldier said. He was standing at the edge of the porch. Several of his buddies leaned against the building. They were all grinning. The soldier took a swig from his beer bottle, then tossed it out beyond the front lights. He hopped off the porch.

I got a duty to my cronies here, don't you see? the soldier said. I promised to show them some of my brand-new judo tricks.

Hey, friend, Jake said, laughing, let me buy you a drink. Listen, I've got a little bottle in a paper bag right here under my frontseat. Great hooch. Twelve years old. What do you say, friend? Have a shooter with me, OK?

I ain't gonna bang your little boy up too much, buddy, the soldier said and walked slowly toward them. I'll just toss him around a little while. Just till I work up a little sweat, OK? Just for a little exercise.

I want him, Jimbo said and moved toward the soldier.

Jake shoved Jimbo back against the car.

Get the hell in the car, sport, Jake said. I mean it. Either get in the goddamn car or get out of here. If you don't get in the goddamn car you can walk to Miami for all I care.

Fuck, Jimbo said. He slid into the frontseat and sat there pounding a palm with a fist.

Hey, buddy, let your boy come play.

Listen, friend, we don't want trouble. Come on over and have a shooter of this great hooch with me, Jake said and reached under the frontseat.

Hell, maybe I'll just toss your ass around awhile instead of your boy, buddy, the soldier said. He walked slowly up to the car. I kinda hate to throw old guys around though. I hate to hear them old bones breaking.

Using the open cardoor to shield its sight from the men standing on the porch, Jake took a shiny, nickel-plated pistol out of the paper sack. Holding it low, he leveled it at the soldier and cocked it.

The soldier's eyes popped wide and he just stood there looking back and forth from Jake's face to the pistol.

Well, you went and bought it, boy, Jake said quietly, smiling.

Oops, the soldier said.

Oops is right, friend, Jake said and chuckled. Well, friend, just how serious do you want to be about this situation we have on our hands? Do you really want to get down to some serious cutting and shooting?

Hey, listen, mister, I ain't nearly as serious about this situation as I thought I was, the soldier said.

Well, good, friend. It's such a nice, pleasant, balmy night out for any serious cutting and shooting. So we'll just say good night now and be on our way. Is that perfectly all right with you?

Listen, mister, that's fine with me.

Good night, then. Say good night to your friends for us.

You bet. Good night, mister, the soldier said. He began backing slowly away from the car.

Jake uncocked the pistol, put it back in the paper sack, then stuck it under the frontseat. He got in the car, started it up, and pulled it slowly out onto the highway.

Jesus Christ, Jake, Jimbo said. Were you serious?

Oh, I can get as serious as I need to be.

I mean, would you have shot that guy?

I didn't figure it would come to anything like that. A punk

kid like that doesn't have it in him to get too serious. You see, I believe spitting teeth is for suckers. Hell, I don't believe in any kind of trouble unless there's a percentage in it. You can usually talk or bluff your way out of trouble. Thing is, never call a bluff unless you're able to back it up if you have to.

Then you would have shot that guy if he'd come on?

Oh, probably not, Jake said and laughed. I would have probably just slapped his punk ass around a bit. I guess I was just sort of showing off to you guys by pulling the rod. Give you something to tell your friends back home.

You did that all right, Jimbo said. Hey, what kind of pistol is that? Can I shoot it sometime, Jake?

A .45 automatic. Sure, you can shoot it sometime. I'll give you sports some pointers.

Really? Jimbo said.

Sure, why not?

Now we really are armed and dangerous I guess, Jimbo said, laughing.

You better believe it, Jake said.

Late that night when they reached the outskirts of St. Augustine Pace was asleep in the backseat and Jimbo was trying to stay awake. Jake yawned and said that he just was not the hard charger he once was and that they would have to stop for the night. That sweet, black-eyed woman will just have to wait a little longer, Jake said and laughed. It's hard to be an old dog, boys. Jake pulled into a motel called the Ponce de Leon Motor Court whose elaborate pink neon signs advertised a garden pool and free teevee.

Well, what do you think of old Jake? Jimbo asked Pace when Jake went into the motel's office to check on a room.

I thought he was totally full of bullshit until back at that beerjoint, Pace said. I don't know, man. He's a strange cat. I don't know. He's OK I guess.

Yeah, I think he's all right. At least he's not queer or anything. He's got that son and all. And he was a marine.

So he says.

Well, like you said, the way he handled that situation back at the beerjoint was pretty cool. I have a feeling he can back up a lot of his bullshit.

Yeah, me too I guess. I agree he sure ain't any queer. Like, those tattoos on his arms? I don't think queers go for tattoos.

Right, Jimbo said and fired up a Camel. Anyway, what harm could he do us? I mean, if he would pull anything we'd just cold-cock him.

He looks pretty tough to me, man.

I could handle him if I had to. But, like I said, I think he's all right. Hell, he's been paying for everything. And he tells great stories whether they're bullshit or not. I think he's a kick to be with. I think we really lucked out when he picked us up. I really do, amigo.

Time will tell.

Hey, turdface, why be such a pessimist?

You're probably right, man.

Jake came out of the office with a thin, middle-aged woman whose hair looked orange in the pink neon light. They were talking and laughing as they followed a flagstone walk from the office to the semicircle of Spanish-style, pink stucco cottages in back. Jake waved for them to bring the car. He stood in front of a cottage near the center of the semicircle and directed Jimbo into a slanted parking slot.

This is Sally, boys, Jake said, introducing the lady when they got out of the car. She owns and operates the Ponce de Leon Motor Court.

How do you do, ma'am, Jimbo said.

Howdy, Pace said.

I hope you all will be real comfy now, Sally said with a twitter. She smelled of whiskey and heavy Jungle Gardenia perfume. Just holler if you all need more towels or anything. And if you boys would like to take a refreshing dip I'll turn the lights back on around the pool.

I could sure dig a dip, ma'am, Pace said.

Well, I'll just go turn the lights on then. Just try to be a teensy bit quiet as most of my other guests have retired for the night.

The room was paneled in imitation knotty pine and its pale green ceiling glittered in the lamplight. Jake tossed his suitcase on the bed nearest the bathroom and opened it. Jimbo clicked on the teevee. Pace sat on the other bed and bounced up and down.

I hope you sports don't mind sharing a bunk, Jake said.

It's all right, Jimbo said.

Oh, we'll just *love* it, Pace said and fluttered his eyelashes. We'll just have the best old time.

I've got to get the hell out of this smelly goddamn shirt fast, Jake said. He took off his flower-print sportshirt. There were several long purple scars across his chest and stomach. Both of his large biceps had elaborate tattoos on them and there was a small tattoo of a heart over his left nipple.

Jesus Christ, Pace said. You really did get some war wounds.

Pretty, aren't they? Jake said, laughing. The ladies don't seem to mind, though. Seems to intrigue most of them in fact. Between the scars and the tattoos my whole body is a conversation piece. I usually don't tell the ladies I got the wounds in the service, though. That's boring. War wounds are a dime a dozen. I usually make up some real exotic bullshit baloney about how I got them.

I can believe that, Pace said and Jimbo punched his shoulder.

Right, Jake said, laughing. I can dish up the bullshit all right. But the thing about being a big bullshitter is that you develop a built-in, shockproof bullshit detector of your own. Nothing wrong with bullshit, boys, as long as you never bullshit yourself. And speaking of bullshit, Jimbo boy, I just adopted your ass.

You just what?

Adopted you, sonny boy. You're my boy now.

I don't get you, Jake, Jimbo said and arched his eyebrows.

When I signed the motel register, Jake said and laughed

again, I put you down as my son. My son and his best pal
Pace. So it wouldn't look queer, sport. An old dog like me
teamed up with a couple of kids could look a little odd, right?
And since we're all on the lam we don't want to draw attention to ourselves, right? So as far as old sweet Sally is concerned you're my boy. All right, kiddo?

Sure, Jimbo said. Sure thing, daddy-o.

Hey, I'm jealous, Pace said. How come I couldn't be the son
and Jimbo the pal?

Here's one reason, sport, Jake said. He took a small gold-
framed picture out of his suitcase. He looked at it for a
moment, then handed it to Pace. What do you think of that?

Holy cow, Pace said. He handed the picture to Jimbo. It
could be your twin brother, man.

Jimbo studied the picture. It was of a boy about his own age
sitting on the front fender of an old Chevy. The boy did
resemble him.

Who is he, Jake? Jimbo asked.

That's old Nick, that's who, Jake said, laughing. That's why
I skidded to a stop last night and then kept staring at you after
I picked you up. Can you believe it? You two almost could be
twin brothers. When I spotted you in my headlights as I shot
past last night it startled the hell out of me. For a minute I
thought you were old Nick himself out there hitchhiking.

I'll be damn, Jimbo said. He handed Jake the picture.

Yeah. I'll have to get a snapshot of you before we split up to
show Nick, Jake said and set the picture on the small table
between the beds. Old Nick will get a kick out of it.

Well, gang, I'm gonna hit that pool, Pace said and took his
trunks from the suitcase.

I'll be right behind you, amigo, Jimbo said.

Hell, I might even take a dip myself, Jake said.

Last one in is a rotten asshole, Pace said, pulling off his
jeans.

Hey, boys, Jake said. Listen, hold up a minute. I better tell
you there's been a little change in my immediate plans.

What's that, Jake? Jimbo asked.

It's those calls I made back at that roadside joint. I talked to my Cuban honey, see. And to a couple of other friends I have down Miami way. It's not a good idea for me to hit town for a couple of days. There are a couple of characters around town right now I'd best avoid if I can. Including my honey's husband. So I'm going to hang out here in old St. Augustine for a few days before I head down the coast. Now you sports are more than welcome to stay with me and head on down in a few days. I enjoy your company. Hell, it's almost like having old Nick and one of his pals along. Except we get along better than me and old Nick. But, if you boys want to shoot on down to Miami that's all right. And since I told you I'd take you all the way I'll spring for the bus tickets. Either way, sports, it's up to you.

Hell, we're not in that big a hurry, are we? Jimbo asked Pace.

I'm with you, Kemosabe. Whatever you want to do.

Hell, Jake, then we'll stick with you if it's really all right, Jimbo said. The only problem is we're short of dough. We might have to borrow some from you till we land jobs in Miami.

You guys don't have to worry about dough. I figure you even have some salary coming for helping me drive. And don't worry about jobs in Miami. There are a lot of people in that town who owe me favors. Anyway, we'll just sort of lay low and play tourists in old St. Augustine for a few days. I'll give you sports a regular guided tour.

I've never been much of a tourist myself, man, Pace said.

Listen, the only way to go through life is like a tourist. You should be a tourist every goddamn minute of your life. Every second.

I dig it, Jimbo said.

You know, Jimbo old boy, Jake said, I hope I get the chance to introduce you to old Kerouac someday. He'd love you, kiddo.

11 ➤

borned to win

The pool was in a garden of palms and flowering plants in the center of the semicircle of pink stucco cottages. It was kidney shaped with a marble fish-shaped fountain at its smaller end, a fish shaped like a leaping porpoise with a thin stream of water arching from its pursed lips into the pool. Blue spot-lights were arranged in the palms with their beams playing on the pool and the fish fountain. Here and there in the thick flowering bushes under the palms stood brightly painted plaster-of-paris peacocks and flamingos. Pace's red transistor radio played softly from a poolside table while Pace sat at the pool's edge idly kicking his dangling feet in the water in time to the music. Jimbo floated on his back in the center of the small end of the pool. He was looking up through the thick palm fronds at the black, star-filled sky and thinking about the loss of love.

If only Judy had not tried to con him. That was the real rub. If only *she* had told him about Bodine instead of Pace. And if Judy had not told Penny who told Pace, Jimbo would not know about it even now. God, how he had loved her. What went wrong? They had written and called each other all year. Then, just when he was so confident in her love, Judy had mailed back the only ring in the whole wide world and had asked Hutch Bodine to be her lucky escort to the Valentine Ball. Why? Why would she do it? He had loved her so much, so truly.

Enough to hitchhike through a dangerous blizzard with snowflakes as big as goddamn bats to take her a sappy box of valentine candy even after what she had done. And even though he had been half frozen and surely near death he had leaned that box of candy against the back french doors and had tried to bolt, to disappear, for he wanted only to show her the depth of his love and he wanted nothing in return. He had fallen and slid facefirst into a snowdrift; but somehow, just as he heard the doors fly open, he had pulled himself up and staggered out into the snowdrifts in the yard. And he would have kept on staggering away too, staggering away into the dangerous dark never to be seen again, if Frankie had not tackled him from behind. Then, while Judy stood coatless at the edge of the yard weeping and begging for them to stop, Jimbo and Frankie had rolled about in the deep snow wrestling furiously until Frankie finally got him in a headlock. Come on, Jimbo, Frankie had said, calm down, boy. Calm down. Everything is going to be all right. God, how sweet Judy's love had then once again been. More sweet and intense than ever. Every night during the week he remained at her home snowbound and recovering, they had slipped down to the basement gameroom after her family was asleep to go all the way relentlessly. He had forgiven her everything, for sending the ring back, for asking Hutch Bodine to the Valentine Ball. Judy had never been so passionate. I don't have any protections, Jimbo had warned her. I don't care, Judy had said. I don't care.

How's the fishing? Jake said. He was standing by Pace at the edge of the pool in swim trunks.

Perfect, Jimbo said. He rolled over and swam to them. I just landed that monster myself, he said and pointed to the fish fountain at the other end of the pool.

Christ, what is that anyway? Jake said. Some kind of fish tombstone?

It's a buffalo fish, Jimbo said. There used to be a lot of them around. Over sixty million once. But they're real rare now. Now you can only find them real deep down in pools with no bottom.

Well what do you know! Jake said. I don't think I ever heard of a buffalo fish before. I guess you learn something new every day. Are buffalo fish good to eat, sport?

They're pretty hard, Jimbo said.

That doesn't mean they aren't good to eat.

Yeah, I think niggers like them.

Well, all you ever need to eat anything in the old world is the right recipe.

Dig it, Jimbo said, laughing.

Hey, Jake, Pace said. Do tattoos hurt?

Usually only after the fact, Jake said. Like when you sober up the next morning and see what you've done.

Did you get all those when you were drunk? Pace asked.

Just about. I got most of them back in my old merchant marine days, Jake said. This one on my right forearm I got in Hong Kong. It's supposed to be a black panther. Looks more like a sewer rat. And the dame in the grass skirt here on my right bicep is supposed to swing her ass when I flex my muscle. Watch. Looks more like she's got a corncob up her ass.

Did you get that one back in your old pirate days? Jimbo said and pointed to the tattoo on Jake's left bicep. It was a skull and crossbones with a striped snake curling in and about the crossbones, then emerging from the hollow of the skull's left eye. Above the skull was the word BORN with a pair of stars before the B and another pair after the N. Below the crossbones were the words TO WIN.

Right, Jake said, laughing. Back in my old pirate days. Back in my old black buccaneer days of blood and buried treasure.

Crazy, Jimbo said.

Actually, Jake said, there is a pretty good story behind it. I got it in Frisco. In a tattoo parlor up in North Beach. Huge Hawaiian cat ran it. Had copies of all the different designs you could select from up on the walls. Had dozens of skull and crossbone variations to choose from. Only they all had BORN TO LOSE around them. I wasn't born to lose, see. I was born to win. I finally picked out this particular design with the snake. I told the fat Hawaiian to ink in WIN instead of LOSE. He didn't like the idea. He wanted me to stick to the original design. BORN TO WIN around a skull and crossbones upset his personal aesthetics. Too much cheap irony for him. After I acted like a tough customer and paid him an extra five bucks he agreed. I was falling down drunk, see. I'd been on a three-day binge. I passed out even before he finished me. That goddamn fat Hawaiian bastard got the last laugh. When I sobered up the next day I found he had inked in the WIN instead of the LOSE all right. He had made another slight design change in the design himself though. A slight change of spelling. The tattoo now said BORNED TO WIN. Can you believe it? BORNED TO WIN. That's why there are two stars before the B and two after the N. I'm sorry now I had the ED covered up. I wish I'd left it like that. I think that fat Hawaiian cat had my number good.

Borned to win, Jumbo said, laughing. That's great. I think I'll get a tattoo when I get to Miami.

Sure, Pace said. What kind? A frilly heart with JUDY in it on your ass?

I'll tattoo your teeth if you're not real careful, amigo, Jimbo said.

Oh my, I'm so scared, Pace said and slid into the pool. He fluttered his hands about in the water. I'm gonna shit my pants I'm so scared.

You better be, boy.

I'm the creature from the black lagoon, Pace said and contorted his face. And I ain't afraid of anyone. Anyone I catch swimming in my black lagoon I eat raw.

Yeah, well, I'm the atomic monster from beneath the sea and this pool ain't big enough for the both of us.

Then I guess it's a fight to the death.

May the better monster win, Jimbo said. He stalked toward Pace.

Grunting like monsters, they grabbed each other and began wrestling in the water. Jimbo quickly got Pace in a headlock.

Some chickenshit creature you are, Jimbo said. Do you give?

Shit no, Pace said.

Jimbo ducked Pace's head under the water.

You give? Jimbo said. You give?

Pace tapped Jimbo's shoulder, signaling that he gave up. Jimbo laughed and kept Pace's head underwater.

I can't hear you, Jimbo said.

Pace began to struggle violently and Jimbo let him loose. Pace surfaced spitting water.

You asshole. Pace coughed.

I'm the King Kong of the pool, Jimbo said and pounded his chest. King Kong of the pool!

Not quite, Jake said, laughing. He slid into the water.

Bullshit, Jimbo said. I'm not going to wrestle you, Jake.

Go on, King Kong of the pool, Pace called. Or are you just King Kong Chickenshit?

I just don't like to hear old bones break, Jimbo said.

Come on, King Kong, Jake said, smiling. I'll let you get a hold on me. Any hold you want.

Any hold at all?

Any hold you want. No holds barred.

I hate to do this to you, Jake old pal, Jimbo said and waded around behind Jake. Using his forearms he wrapped Jake's neck in a choke hold.

You got your hold, sport? Jake said.

I got it.

You sure now?

You'll see.

You ready?

Ready teddy.

Say when.

When.

What?

When!

Jesus Christ! Jimbo thought, his head suddenly underwater. He had not even had a chance to get a good, deep breath. *What the fuck happened?*

You give, sport? Jake called.

Jimbo tried to pry Jake's arm from around his head. He couldn't budge it. He tried to get an arm around one of Jake's legs but Jake tightened his grip and pushed Jimbo's head down. *Fuck this!* Jimbo screamed in his head and began to thrash wildly, trying to break free.

You give? Jake called. You say uncle?

Jimbo's lungs were bursting.

Come on, sport, give it up.

The pressure behind Jimbo's eyes was intense.

Give it up, Jimbo boy.

Jimbo shut his throbbing eyes.

Give up, son.

Jimbo relaxed and breathed in the water. It was not as painful as he had always imagined it would be.

Jesus Christ, Jimbo! Jake said, jerking Jimbo's head from the water. He pounded Jimbo's back. You crazy kid.

Jake helped Jimbo to the side of the pool. He massaged Jimbo's shoulders as he continued to cough up water.

Maybe I ought to give you a little mouth-to-mouth resuscitation, Jake said and laughed quietly. Are you going to be all right, sport?

Jimbo shook his head yes. His throat felt raw and his eyes were blind with tears.

You're a tough customer all right, sport, Jake said. He patted Jimbo's shoulder. You're all right. This pool is big enough for both of us any day in the world, kiddo. You're like me, kiddo. I never say uncle for anyone either.

Jimbo laughed hoarsely and pulled himself up out of the pool. He sat on the edge until all the dizziness had passed, then got up and walked shakily over to the table where he had left his pack of Camels. He fired one up and sat down in a lounge chair. Jake came over and sat down beside him.

You sure you're OK? Jake asked.

Sure, Jimbo said. You know some neat tricks, Jake.

I guess so, Jake said, laughing. I'm just an old dog with old tricks. That's me all right. But I'll tell you, kiddo, you aren't born knowing tricks. I don't know a thing I couldn't teach you too.

Would you?

My pleasure.

Is anyone coming back in? Pace called from the pool. Are you guys out for good? Hey, King Kong, come on back in. Give me a rematch.

I'll rematch your mouth, amigo.

I thought I heard splashing around out here, Sally said. She was standing at the end of the pool clinking ice around in a highball glass. In the blue light her hair looked green.

Were we making too much noise? Jake asked.

Oh my, no. Heavens no. I just wanted to make sure you all was guests of the Ponce de Leon. We got some nigger kids around here who like to try sneaking dips at night.

We're guests all right, Jake said. Paying guests.

You sure enough are, Sally said and twittered.

Jimbo started coughing again and Jake patted his back.

My gracious, what's wrong with your boy?

He swallowed a little hard water, Jake said. He's planning to enter the ministry, see. He got a calling for the Baptist ministry when he was just a boy. They believe in total submersion. Every chance he gets he practices baptizing. He just got carried away.

Amen, Jimbo said and laughed.

I'm a Methodist person myself, Sally said.

That sure looks like a nice, cool drink for such a hot night, Jake said.

It's a gin and tonic. And it does hit the spot.

I bet it does, Jake said.

I just might be able to scare up another one.

Well, you just let me go get decent and if you can scare up another one of those I'm just liable to drink it, Jake said and stood up. I'll be back in two shakes, he said, walking off toward the cottage.

Sally strolled over and sat down beside Jimbo. She was wearing a frilly lavender dress and at least a dozen dangling bracelets on each arm. Your daddy sure seems like a nice fellow, she said to Jimbo.

He's a peach, Jimbo said and frenchinhaled deeply.

Your daddy says you all just might spend his whole two weeks' vacation right here with us in St. Augustine.

Two weeks? Jimbo said.

I think that would be just grand. I just know you all will simply love St. Augustine. By the by, did you all happen to stop and visit the Oriental Gardens in Jacksonville on your way down?

No, ma'am.

Oh, they are just so lovely. Oh, so lovely. But you know, I think in my small way I have a lovely little garden right here. Nothing really grand, of course. But I do have some just lovely blooming azaleas and bougainvillea and some beautiful hydrangea and I have a gorgeous flame vine going strong. I get comments all the time. I did most of the garden myself. My husband passed on about five years ago, you know. He had cancer, you know. I have some postcards made up with pictures of the little fountain and garden that are just lovely. I have a little gift shop off the office in front and you'll have to come in and look at the postcards. Maybe you'll even want to send some to friends. If you don't mind me asking, honey, how long ago did your mom pass?

A long time ago.

My, my. If you don't mind me asking, honey, what did she pass of?

Cancer.

My, my. Oh, you know a place you all will just have to visit while you're taking in the sights around here is Silver Springs. It's just south a ways from St. Augustine and my goodness, it is such a treat. The water is just crystal clear. You can see way down to the very bottom. They have what they call Jungle Cruises that you can take in these glass-bottom boats and they are so interesting. The captain of the glass-bottom boat points out things of interest as you float along and it is all just as fascinating as can be. He tosses food out in the water and the fish come up to feed and he tells you all about them. Oh, and there's one real sad story that the captain tells. At the very deepest spot at the Springs there's this big open hole. It's where the spring water bubbles out of I believe. Anyway, years and years ago this handsome young man who had been horribly wounded in a war, wounded in such a way that he could never ever marry his sweetheart, well, this handsome young man went out on one of the Jungle Cruises one day just like any other tourist, and when they got directly over the top of that hole he jumped off the glass-bottom boat and while all the other tourists watched in horror he dove all the way down and disappeared into that hole never to be seen again. And you know, just a week later his beautiful sweetheart went and did the same thing. She dove off a glass-bottom boat to join him forever in that hole. Now, isn't that the saddest story you ever heard? Honey, if you don't mind me asking, why hasn't such a nice fellow as your daddy ever remarried?

It's a sad story, Jimbo said. When the Korean conflict broke out Daddy reenlisted. He's real patriotic, you know. Well, he was wounded at Pork Chop Hill in such a way . . . well, you know. Like in the story you just told me.

Oh, you don't mean it!

It's a sad story all right, Jimbo said.

Well, I'm all set for that tall, cool drink, Jake said as he walked up to the table.

Oh, you poor dear, Sally said and touched Jake's arm.

What? Jake said.

I think I'll take another dip, Jimbo said and got up. He walked over and sat on the edge of the pool. He watched Jake and Sally as they walked through the garden toward the office.

What the fuck are you grinning so hard about? Pace said. He was floating on his back in the pool.

Nothing, Jimbo said. Hey, amigo, I'm sorry I held you under.

Yeah, well, Jake held your ass under. That was a cute move he made.

He knows a few tricks I guess. Anyway, I'm sorry I held you under.

You better be. Next time it'll be me who baptizes your ass.

You and what army?

Me and this, Pace said and pointed his forefinger at Jimbo. He cocked back his thumb. I got you covered, you dirty rat.

Give me a break, pal, for old times' sake, Jimbo said and raised his arms in the air.

Not a chance, you dirty rat. Eat hot lead, you dirty rat. *Blam.*

Oh, Jimbo groaned and grabbed his chest. No! No!

Blam. Blam. Blam blam blam blam.

Oh Mother of God, is this the end of Rico? Jimbo gasped and clutched his spilling guts. He tumbled facefirst into the water and floated there like a dead man. He opened his eyes underwater. He arched and dove down to the small circular drain hole at the bottom of the pool. He pressed his face as close as he could to it and tried to peer in. He kicked his feet against the pool bottom and surfaced with a big splash.

I'm gonna get out, Pace said and swam to the poolside. I'm getting wrinkled as a goddamn prune. This fucking water is turning me into an old turd before my time.

Jimbo paddled over to the poolside.

Yeah, me too I guess. Did you ever think about the fact that fish fuck in water?

Nope.

Hey, have you ever seen a movie called *Sunset Boulevard?*

Nope, Pace said and pulled himself out of the water.

Crazy movie, man. Stars William Holden. Starts out with Holden floating facedown in a pool. His eyes are bugged open and he's dead as a doornail. It's sort of like the camera is underwater shooting up at him, see. And up above him you can see cops and reporters shooting off their flashbulbs. The crazy thing is, he's telling the story of how he ended up floating dead in this pool. I mean, in his own words. In William Holden's voice. He's dead as a mackerel and he's telling his story in his own voice. It's real strange.

Yeah, crazy, Pace said and stood up. I'm gonna go in and watch teevee, man.

Yeah, I'll be there in a minute, Jimbo said. He arched and dove, then swam slowly underwater to the pool's small end.

When he surfaced he felt the spray from the fish fountain splashing on his head. He rubbed his neck. His throat was still sore. He tilted his head back and let the fountain spray splash over his face. He opened his mouth and let it fill with the spray. Wonder how long it would take to drown in fish breath? he thought and grinned. Jimbo turned and kicked off against the poolside and deadman-floated slowly back toward the pool's deep end. He felt suspended in water. He felt warm and relaxed. *The baby in the bottle.* Jimbo suddenly pictured the baby in the bottle. It was the one bottle in Uncle Boomer's Grand Scientific Specimen Collection which Jimbo would never touch. The bottle with the human fetus. Its head all swollen and sour cream colored, looking more fish than human. Years, years, earlier, on that first night Jimbo had ever camped out with Boomer in the old, haunted caretaker's house, he had had horrible dreams about that unborn baby in the bottle. He had dreamed all night that somehow that baby had broken free from its bottle as though being finally born. He dreamed he could hear small barely formed feet slapping like flippers across the floor, as the baby stumbled blind and dripping around the dark room, its greenish swollen fish head bumping painfully against table legs, its soft, stunted hands groping before it, feeling, touching, searching for Jimbo.

Jimbo shivered violently. He swam quickly to the poolside and pulled himself out of the water.

Jimbo was stretched out on Jake's bed smoking and watching the palms move in a warm, morning breeze through the open door. He was trying to remember last night's strange dreams. He had not had the strange dreams for a long time: not since he had taken the silver cones down and ripped them apart that morning a year ago before he boarded the bus to the boondocks. Last night he had had trouble sleeping in the same bed with Pace. Pace tossed and turned and talked about Penny in his sleep. After getting one of Pace's arms flopped across his face for the fifth time, Jimbo got up and just sat in the dark smoking and thinking sadly about Judy. Jake had not come back yet. After a time Jimbo decided that Jake was not coming back at all so he climbed into Jake's bed for the rest of the night. He had fallen asleep immediately and had dreamed strangely once again, had dreamed gangster dreams of getaways and shootouts and of gangster deaths.

I'm gonna grab a shower, man, Pace said. He was bent over the chest of drawers studying his face closely in the mirror.

Feel free, Jimbo said and blew a series of smoke rings.

Looks like old Jake got some nooky, Pace said and popped a pimple. A bead of pus hit the mirror.

Jesus Christ, turdface, that's disgusting.

Crazy, man, Pace said and continued searching his face with his fingers.

At least wipe that shit off the mirror, man.

I need some breakfast. Where's that cockhound at? Old Sally must have fucked him blind. I'm gonna take a dump, man, Pace said and went into the bathroom.

You could've shut the goddamn door, turdface, Jimbo said. He got up to shut the bathroom door. He flopped back down on Jake's bed and fired up another Camel.

Jake walked up to the open door. He stopped in the doorway and just stood there looking at Jimbo. He did not say anything and he was not smiling.

Hey, Jake, Jimbo said. Get any?

You're a real cute one, joker boy, Jake said and just kept staring at Jimbo. He held one hand behind his back.

I'm what?

This is for you, joker boy. You got this coming, Jake said and suddenly tossed something at Jimbo.

Jimbo jumped and Jake started laughing.

The coconut bounced on the bed. Jimbo grinned and picked it up, looking it over. A face with shell eyes and teeth was carved into its brown, shaggy hull.

Just what I've always wanted, Jimbo said.

His name was Yorick. Alas, poor Yorick. He was a fellow of infinite jest. He was a joker like you, see. That's the way jokers sometimes end up.

Hey, come on, Jake. Did you get any?

You don't have any class if you brag about your lady. I'll tell you this though, that cute story you spun for old Sal about my horrible war wound worked out for me all right. Old Sal is probably the most flattered gal in Florida this morning.

Gee whiz, Jake, glad I could help out your sex life.

I'll do the same for you some day, sport, Jake said, grinning.

What's that thing? Pace said as he came out of the bathroom buckling his belt.

An ancient skull, Jimbo said. He tossed the carved coconut to him. It's Ponce de Leon's petrified head. Jake found it floating by the fountain.

Crazy, man, Pace said. Where'd you get it, Jake?

Old Sal has quite a little gift shop out there, Jake said. I also ended up with about a dozen postcards of the Ponce de Leon motel.

Crazy, man, Pace said. As though shooting a hook shot he tossed the carved coconut back to Jimbo.

Well, listen, boys, Jake said. I have what might be some bad news.

What? Jimbo said.

I'm going to have to change my immediate plans again. I won't be cruising to Miami in a few days after all. See, old Sal and I have decided to tie the knot today.

Oh, sure, Jimbo said.

Right, Jake said and laughed. Actually, I'm not going to be able to get down to Miami right away. I have to cruise back north. I just talked to my sister on the phone, see, and it looks like that goddamn Nick has his ass in another jam. Seems some punk was sniffing around one of his chippies and old Nick beat the holy hell out of him. Put the punk in the hospital. I have to get up to Atlantic City and try to iron things out.

Well, hell, Jimbo said.

Yeah, it's a pain in the ass all right. But he's my goddamn kid so I have to do it. What I'm going to do is get Nick and bring him back down here to Florida where I can keep my eye on him until things cool down. Here's what I want to talk to you sports about. Like I told you I'm good for bus tickets and some pocket money if you want to head on for Miami. And I can give you some people to look up there. On the other hand, I'd like to offer you sports a deal. I'm going to be cruising back down again later. The thing is, I'd sort of like to offer you sports jobs helping me drive. I have to get up there in a hurry. You boys have shown me I can count on you. You both pull your weight. So this is a straight job offer, see. I'll pay you each a couple hundred bucks. Hell, make that two fifty. An even five hundred bucks to split between you. Now that isn't half bad for a couple of lousy weeks' work. Easy work. And we'll probably have a few laughs along the way. Maybe we can spend a couple of days at my cottage on the shore. Hell, if we get a chance maybe we'll just cruise up to New York. And Jimbo, if old Kerouac is in town, which he probably is, you can bet I'll get you two together. Anyway, when we get down to Miami I'll see that you guys are set up good. Don't worry about that. So, boys, that's the deal. As I told you before, no hard feelings if you want to head on for Miami.

I don't know, Jake, Jimbo said. It's so fast. What do you think, Pace?

Beats me, man.

You boys talk it over. I'm going to the bank with old sweet Sal. She's going to cash a personal check for me. I'm running a little short on cash. I have an account at a Miami bank which I had planned on tapping but obviously I can't do that now. Anyway, we'll be back in a half-hour or so. You boys talk it over and let me know. Do what you think is the best for you guys.

Sure, Jake, Jimbo said.

Old Sal wants to cook us all up a big southern breakfast so try not to starve to death before we get back. Yeah, and by the way, don't let it slip to old Sal that I'm heading back north today. Damn women anyway. You get them all lathered up and they fall in love. I don't want any scenes so as far as old Sal is concerned we're just going out sight-seeing after breakfast, see.

Sure, Jimbo said. Dig it.

OK, boys, see you in a bit, Jake said and left.

So now what, Kemosabe? Pace said.

What do you think, amigo?

I don't know, man. Shit. I'd sure like to see Miami. Shit, even St. Augustine. Here we are in Florida at last and all we've seen is the goddamn Ponce de Leon motel. Yippee shit, man!

Well, hell, we'd be back down this way in a couple of weeks, amigo. I don't know, partner. Two hundred and fifty buckeroos ain't chicken feed. Just for driving around and seeing the countryside and probably raising our share of hell. Hey, man, I've never been to Atlantic City either. Or, Jesus, *New York City*. The Big Apple, amigo. New York fucking City!

I don't know, man. I don't care I guess. To tell the truth I'm homesick as hell, man. I miss Penny.

Hey, don't start that punk shit again.

Yeah. Yeah. I don't care what we do. You decide, man. I'm with you, Kemosabe. What I'm going to do is go take a long hot shower and think about Penny and whack the fuck off.

Jimbo fired up a Camel and stood in the doorway for a time looking at the garden. He turned back into the room and clicked on the teevee. He sat down on the end of Jake's bed and started changing the channels around. *Damn* but he wished he had Boomer around right now to talk to. He wished he could have seen Boomer before he made his getaway this time. Boomer had not been around though. Boomer had been at the Green Glenn Rest Home for his annual spring dry-out. Old Boomer, Jimbo thought and smiled. Jimbo sat there on the end of Jake's bed clicking the teevee channels around, from cartoon to game show to morning movie to soap opera to cartoon. *Doppelgänger.* That's what Boomer said teevee was. Ghost images, squirt, Boomer would say. Teevee *is* a *medium.* Watching teevee is like being at a séance. *Doppelgänger,* squirt, the ghostly double of our world. That's teevee. Old crazy Boomer, who looked like the old teevee detective Boston Blackie. He would sit there night after night in front of his silent teevee (Why do I need the sound on? I know teevee by heart!), calling himself an intertidal teevee detective, claiming he was collecting ghost images like starfish between the high and low tides of teevee's currents, claiming he was searching those oceanic images of teevee's tides for clues. Where are you when I need you, crazy Boomer? Jimbo said aloud. Jimbo sat on the end of Jake's bed and changed the teevee channels faster and faster.

12 ➤
fish in the sea

Looking into the awesome excavation site here where a life-size pottery army was recently found is like looking back more than 2,000 years at an ancient battlefield.

The site, near the tomb of a Chinese emperor who reigned from 221 to 207 B.C. and who was attended in death by pottery legions, is strewn with hundreds of realistic figures of fallen warriors and horses.

No two warriors look alike. Most are in armor and long tunics, wearing varied types of headdress. They are almost exactly six feet tall.

So far 314 warriors and 24 horses have been unearthed and the whole army is believed to consist of a complete phalanx of 6,000 warriors. The horses and men were buried in military formation 15 to 20 feet underground.

Jimbo carefully tore the article from the newspaper. He folded it and put it in his wallet. Old Captain would get a kick out of the article, Jimbo thought and grinned. And Father's Day was coming up soon. He would have to get a nice Father's Day card, one with a poem in it, and he would slip this interesting article in it and shoot it off to Captain.

Jimbo stood up from the picnic table and stretched. Sometime late last night Jake had parked by a roadside park and
Pace had piled into the backseat with Jimbo to sleep and it had
been miserable. Pace's feet smelled rotten. With the windows
up they had roasted and with them down millions of mos-
quitoes swarmed in. Just before dawn Jimbo had given it up
and gotten out of the car. He had sat at a picnic table and
smoked and thought about the Big Apple. He had once seen
Kerouac on the Steve Allen show reading poems while someone in the background played cool jazz. Jimbo pictured himself in a Village coffeehouse. He had a beard and he was
wearing a beret and a black turtleneck sweater. He was sitting
on a stool in the center of a small stage. A single naked
lightbulb at the end of a long cord swayed gently overhead,
glowing deep shadows over his intense face. From somewhere
in the dark room a soft bongo beat accompanied a tenorman
blowing low blues while Jimbo read his poems. When Jimbo
had read his last poem he thanked the audience for listening
so patiently. He just sat there then on the stool with his head
bowed. The room remained hushed. Someone stepped from
the darkness onto the small stage. Yes, yes, yes, Kerouac said
softly and just stood there at the edge of the stage grinning and
lightly snapping his fingers.

Jimbo bounced about on the balls of his feet flicking
punches. After a time he just stood there looking around. A
half-dozen tables were scattered about under the pines and
beside the entrance to a path which led back through the trees
to rest rooms was a large stone-basin water fountain. Jimbo
walked over to the water fountain and rinsed out his mouth
with the tepid water. He splashed several handfuls of water on
his face and he ran his wet fingers back through his hair. He
wiped his hands off on his pants, then fired up a Camel.
Almost to Atlantic City at last, Jimbo thought and smiled. Jake
had decided when they left Florida to take an inland route
instead of the coastal road. Being an old moonshine runner he
knew the inland roads like the back of his hand, Jake had
declared. He knew all the shortcuts and all the backcountry

roads seldom patrolled so they would really be able to fly. They had gotten lost a dozen times. And, although Jake had said he wanted to haul ass north nonstop, they ended up staying in motels nightly. Jimbo had tried to remember all he saw along the road so he could record it each night in his journal. But he soon gave this up, being either too tired to write in his journal at night or discovering that most of his impressions had hopelessly blurred anyway. Jimbo spent most of the time when he was not driving just lying in the backseat watching the green reflection of trees wash over the rear window, or, at night, watching approaching carlights streak across the curved glass. On the radio Nashville hillbilly stations played Hank Williams endlessly or Negro stations out of Memphis played Muddy Waters and advertised White Rose Petroleum Jelly. Jake told endless stories about the back roads and low-down honky-tonks and lost barmaid loves of his youth. Jimbo would lie in the backseat smoking and listening to Jake's stories and he would think about the fact that here he *was: Jimbo Stark* snaking north along forsaken ridges on secret, backcountry roads through the eastern wilderness of America with a madman poet, a holy con-man character who could be right out of Kerouac.

Jimbo rinsed his mouth once more with the tepid fountain water, then walked back to the picnic table. He began glancing again through the day-old newspaper he had found under the table. Traffic began picking up on the road beyond the picnic ground's parking area. Finally, Pace climbed out of the car yawning and stretching. He strolled over to the picnic table and sat down across from Jimbo. His face was greasy and there were clusters of yellowtipped pimples on his cheeks. He put his mirror sunglasses on the table and began studying his reflection in them.

Got a weed, man? Pace said and began squeezing a bump.

I only have three left.

Oh, come on, man.

Here, Jimbo said and flipped him a Camel. You know something, amigo, your feet smell like shark breath.

Yeah, well, you're no rose yourself.

Why didn't we stop at a motel last night? I was sound asleep until you piled your ass in on me.

Beats me. He pulled in a couple of places but always came back out. Said there were no vacancies. They didn't look full up to me though. And he kept stopping at gas stations to make phone calls. Hey, man, I'm going to call Penny today.

Suit yourself, amigo. It ain't my dime.

Hey, Jimbo, I have to call her.

Yeah, I know. Listen, amigo, ask her about Judy.

Yeah, man. Sure.

I still love her. I don't want to but I do.

I know, man. You never fooled me.

I've really fucked things up.

Hey, Kemosabe, it'll be cool. It's not too late. Listen to the kid, man. Things will work out.

Pace, tell Penny to tell Judy that if she wants me to I'll come back and get her. Tell her that, amigo.

I'll tell her all right, man.

Jake climbed stiffly out of the car. He walked slowly over to the picnic table rubbing the back of his neck. He sat down and fired up a cigarette. His hands were shaking slightly.

Sure is a pretty spot, Jake said and gazed about the park. Smell that air. Boys, we made it.

Made what? Pace said.

A safe continental cruise. No mean cops. No major Indian attacks. No one eaten by wolves. Forty days and nights in the wilderness and here we are safe and sound.

Let's get rolling, Pace said. I'm starved.

First things first, Jake said. He took his small brown medicine bottle from his shirt pocket and drank from it. He held it up in the light and shook it. Damn, I'm out of my magic potion, he said and tossed the bottle away.

What is that stuff anyway? Jimbo asked.

Like I said, my magic potion, Jake said. I drink enough of that stuff and I can do just about anything I want. Jump high buildings with a single bound. Fly faster than a speeding bullet.

Hey, what is it? Jimbo said. Come on.

Dope, Jake said. I'm a dope fiend, see.

Come on, Jimbo said.

No fooling, sport. It is dope. Has codeine in it.

Why do you take it?

Pain.

Pain from what?

I got started on this stuff in a VA hospital. Still need it. I'm not a sport who believes in pain. Look at this, Jake said and took out his wallet. From one of its pockets he took a thick bundle of cards and spread them out on the table. They were all ID cards, driver's licenses, Social Security cards, even union membership cards, and they all had different names on them.

I don't get it, Jake, Jimbo said.

When I buy my dope at a drugstore I have to sign for it and sometimes show identification. So I collect ID cards. Sort of my hobby I guess. Collecting aliases.

How did you get them all? Jimbo said.

Listen, sport, getting a phony ID is an easy thing to do in this country. For a few bucks you can be just about anyone you want to be.

Isn't that illegal? Jimbo said. I mean, to sign those phony names at a drugstore.

It's just another game, sport. Just another version of hide-and-seek, Jake said and put the ID's back in his wallet. He glanced in his wallet's bill pocket. Boys, we made Atlantic City by the skin of our asses. I'm about broke.

No kidding? Jimbo said.

No kidding, Jake said. What's more, it's Saturday so I can't cash a check. What's more, I made some calls on the way in last night. Found out my sister bolted for Boston. Went up to stay with a cousin of ours for a few weeks. So I can't hit her for any dough.

What are we going to do then? Jimbo said.

I can lay my hands on some quick dough tonight. We'll get a nice motel and rest up, then shoot up to the cottage tomorrow morning. Found out that's where that goddamn Nick is laying low. Meanwhile, sports, we have less than ten bucks. The car needs gas and oil. I need a bottle of dope. You sports will need beer. That about takes care of the ten.

Hey, man, Pace said, what about breakfast? I'm starving.

No problem. Trouble with you is that you've never had to live off the land.

You mean we're gonna go out and pick some fucking berries or some shit? Pace said.

Only if you want them on your Wheaties. You'll see. I was a great hobo once, boys. Rode the rails and thumbed the byways of this great land many times coast to coast, from sea to shining sea, and never went hungry.

I've seen pictures of hoboes, man, Pace said. Bunch of bums sitting around campfires in dump yards eating shit stew out of rusty cans. The hell with shit stew. Is there any baloney left, Kemosabe?

Yeah, Jimbo said. Look in the sack on the back floor.

Don't spoil your appetite now, Pacer boy, Jake said. Save some room for ham and eggs and hashbrowns and some biscuits dripping with pure golden honey.

Yeah, sure, Pace said. He stalked to the car.

Looks like old Pacer woke up on the wrong side of the carseat, Jake said, chuckling. Well, I best get busy with my morning meditations and devotions.

Come again?

My dawn dump, Jake said and winked. He got up and walked back the path to the rest rooms.

Ham and eggs my rosy ass, Pace said when he returned. He tossed the opened package of baloney on the table. He counted out three of the six slices for himself, then slid the package across to Jimbo.

What about Jake's cut? Jimbo said and took one of Pace's slices and added one of his own and set them aside. Two each, amigo.

Captain Hobo Bullshit is gonna eat shit stew, man. Didn't you hear?

Who put the corncob up your ass this morning, amigo?

Ah, fuck it anyway, man.

Come on, boy. Cool it a little.

Ah, man. If I hear one more goddamn story about his long-lost youth or about his badass Nickie boy I'll puke.

Cool it, Jimbo said. He reached across the table to lightly punch Pace's shoulder.

Look what we have here, sports, Jake called. He was walking up the path carrying a small yellow puppy.

Hey, crazy! Pace said.

Where'd you get that? Jimbo said.

Poor little mutt was hanging around the shitter. Look at these ribs. Poor little mutt is damn near starved. Some asshole just dumped him here. I could blast someone for doing this sort of thing. I mean it, Jake said and put the puppy on the table. It stood there shivering.

He's got different-colored eyes, Jimbo said. One's brown and the other blue. I've never seen that before.

Look at those bald spots in its fur, Pace said.

Malnutrition, Jake said and petted the puppy. A few days of decent food and he'll look fine. Won't you, pupper?

No, that's mange, man, Pace said. I've seen it before. Hey, people can get that shit too. And your hair falls out just like that.

He just needs care, Jake said. Whose baloney?

That's your share of breakfast, Jimbo said.

Yeah, ham and eggs, Pace said. The hashbrowns ain't done yet.

Here you go, pupper, Jake said and fed the puppy a slice of baloney. Have an egg. Here, boy, have a nice slice of ham.

What are you going to do with him? Pace said.

Name him, for starters, Jake said.

You mean you're gonna keep him? Pace said.

Right. Every mob needs a mascot.

Some mascot, Pace said.

Some mob, Jake said.

How about Lassie or Rin Tin Tin? Jimbo said.

How about Mange Mutt? Pace said.

How about Pard? Jake said.

How about Pace? Jimbo said.

Very funny, smartass, Pace said.

I like Pard, Jake said.

How about Ponce? Jimbo said. Short for Ponce de Leon.

I'm going to call him Pard, Jake said.

I'm not going to call him shit, Pace said.

He's Pard to me, Jake said.

Ponce, Jimbo said.

Here, Pard. Here, Pard boy, Jake said and petted the puppy when it wobbled to him. See, Pard knows his name all right.

Yeah, sure, Jimbo said, laughing. That's just because you're the one with the baloney.

And don't you ever forget it, Jake said.

You have to have faith when you live off the land, Jake said and pulled off the main street of the small town they were passing through. He began to cruise tree-shaded side streets. After a short time he pulled up in front of a large brick church.

Yes, sports, sometimes you just have to put your faith in the Lord amen. You boys wait here, Jake said and got out. He followed a sidewalk along the church to a house adjoining it.

Wonder what he's got up his sleeve? Pace said.

Who knows? Jimbo said. Maybe he's gonna light a candle.

After a time Jake and a tall, distinguished-looking man came out onto the parsonage's front porch. They were talking and laughing. Jake pointed toward the car and walked down the steps and the man followed him.

This is my son Jim, Jake said to the man when they reached the car. And his friend Pace. Boys, this is Reverend Phillips.

Hello, boys, Reverend Phillips said and leaned down to stick his hand in the window for a shake.

Hello, sir, Jimbo said and shook his hand.

Howdy, Pace said.

Boys, Reverend Phillips has been kind enough to help us out. Looks like we won't have to go hungry today after all. Reverend, I really can't thank you enough.

Mr. Adams, it's no problem at all. You just take your boys down to Morrison's Café on 3rd Street like I explained. I'll call ahead so they'll be expecting you. Just have them stamp that food voucher I gave you with the total bill when you have finished your meals. Don't worry about the voucher, I'll just pick it up later today.

Again, Reverend, what can I say? Jake said. You've been too kind. When I discovered this morning that I'd lost my wallet I was afraid the boys would get pretty hungry before my sister's money wire arrives this afternoon. You've helped us salvage our little vacation.

That's what we are here for, Mr. Adams. I hope you enjoy your meals.

Rest assured, Reverend, you will be repaid for this, Jake said and shook his hand.

That's good of you, Mr. Adams. That is the spirit.

They all waved back at the Reverend as Jake pulled the car out.

Praise the Lord, Jake said.

Amen, Jimbo said.

Ah, yes, Jake said. Some ham and eggs and hashbrowns and biscuits dripping with honey will certainly hit the old spot about right now. Damn, old Pacer boy, it's a crying shame you've already chowed down.

Very funny, Pace said.

Yeah, Jake said, I guess I'm just a barrel of laughs. More fun than a monkey's uncle.

Well, what are we gonna do for money the rest of the day? Pace said. What about lunch? And dinner?

We'll hock something, Jake said. Then pick it up on our way back to Florida.

Like what? Jimbo said.

A watch would do the trick, Jake said. But I never wear one. The only ring I ever wore I buried with my wife.

I have a graduation ring, Jimbo said. My Uncle Boomer sprang for it. Thirty bucks.

Not much demand for highschool rings, Jake said. I was thinking of taking out the car radio. I could probably get a few bucks for it. Enough for some sandwich chow and some beer. Then we'll hit a beach for the day.

Hey, Jimbo said. What about our little red radio?

Screw that! Pace said. Where do you get this *our* radio shit, man? This is *my* radio, daddy-o! This is my old man's graduation gift.

Don't be so chickenshit, Jimbo said. We'll get it back. How much could we get for it, Jake?

Enough.

Come on, Pace, give, Jimbo said.

Shit.

Don't be so chickenshit, man.

Oh, screw it anyway. Take the goddamn radio. Take anything.

It's only for a few days, old Pacer, Jake said. OK, listen, sports, we'll chow down real good on our preacher buddy, then after I make a couple of calls we'll hock the radio and head for the surf.

Dig it, Jimbo said.

I got a phone call to make myself, Pace said. He flopped back in the seat.

Above the shining blue sea masses of white clouds moved. Far off on the horizon a vessel seemed absolutely still under a thin blue ribbon of smoke. Pace played in the waves. Jimbo and Jake sat back up on the beach drying in the sun while sipping cold, beaded cans of beer. The beach Jake had brought them to was secluded and there were few other swimmers.

Old Pard the pupper, Jake said and rolled Pard onto his back in the sand. Pard jumped up wagging his tail furiously. Tilting his head and barking, he tried to circle Jake but ran head-on into the beer cooler.

Old Pard here is blind as a bat, Jake said.

I thought something was wrong with him, Jimbo said. Poor little pupper.

That's probably why he was dumped.

Is there anything we can do for him?

I don't know, sport. I hope so, Jake said. He scratched Pard's head. I'm going to take him to a vet as soon as we get up the coast. Maybe they have drops or something.

What if they don't?

Then I guess I'll just be old Pard's seeing-eye person.

Dig it, Jimbo said.

So you're thinking about going back for your girl? Jake said.

Yeah. I've got a lot to make up for. A lot.

My opinion is that you're doing the right thing. What are you going to do when you get her? Where will you two go and everything?

I'll have to figure all that out.

I don't mean to stick my nose in your business or anything, but I've got a suggestion. Actually it's sort of an offer. Since I'm taking old Nick south to lay low for a while nobody will be using my cottage, see. So if you kids need a place to go it's yours gratis.

Christ, Jake! That's great. You have no idea what this could mean for us.

What the hell. You're a good kid. And I'm sure your gal is too. I'm just repaying the favors people have done me in the past. Listen, I'll tell you what. Nick has a real snazzy convertible, a '56 Ford Victoria. Solid white. You can use it to go get Judy if you want.

I can't believe it, Jake. This is just too much, man. Hey, but what will Nick say? It's his bomb.

Not for a while it ain't. I'm clipping that bird's wings. He's going down to Miami with me in my car so I can keep an eye on him. And when we get down there I'm going to park his ass until he figures a few things out. So use it. You'll be doing me a favor, sport.

I'll pay you back someday for all this help, Jake. I swear it.

Don't worry about paying me back, sport. Just pass it on.

Give someone else a hand someday when you get the chance.

I will. But I still want to pay you back somehow.

Bullshit. Listen, let me be best man at your wedding. Let me be your first son's godfather or something.

Hell, Jake. I'll name my first son after you, that's what.

You're a good kid, Jake said.

Hey, gang! Pace yelled as he ran up the beach. You all out for good or what?

I'm just gonna swill beer for a while, amigo, Jimbo said.

Yeah, all of it, Pace said and opened the cooler. Jesus, man. It was my ten dollars that bought this beer. I figure at least five of these left are mine.

You and your chickenshit ten dollars, Jimbo said. Don't sweat it, sport. You'll get your chickenshit cut.

Yeah, well, I better. I sure miss my radio.

It's kind of nice to have some peace and quiet for a change, Jake said and laughed. We can listen to the ocean instead of that bebop you play all the time.

Fuck the ocean, man, Pace said and opened a beer. He ran his fingers over his skin. Jesus, man, that goddamn salt water makes me feel more sticky than ever. This kid needs a shower baaad.

After I round up some dough tonight I'll get us a nice motel room, Jake said. Place with a big pool and free teevee like the old Ponce de Leon.

And with another Sally? Jimbo said.

Isn't it pretty to think so? Jake said.

Hey, man, Pace said, where are you going to round up this dough anyway? I thought you couldn't cash a check or anything.

I'm going to lark it up.

What? Pace said. What's that mean?

I'm going on an outlaw lark. Used to do it all the time in my wild and woolly youth. Did it as much for the fun as for the dough.

What's an outlaw lark? Jimbo said.

A job.

A job? Jimbo said.

Right, sport. I am going to pull a little job.

What do you mean, Jake? Jimbo said.

Listen, don't worry, Jake said. You sports won't be involved.

But what are you going to do? Jimbo said.

It's simple. It's a little operation I used to pull regularly when I was a kid and needed some safe, fast pocket change. I'll just drive around until I find a nice, quiet, dark spot, see. Then I'll have you sports drop me off downtown. Then you sports drive back to the spot and just sit there and enjoy yourselves until I get back. Simple, see?

I don't get it, Jimbo said. How do you get back to the car?

I take a cab.

A cab?

Sure. Only I don't pay the cabbie for the ride. He pays me.

You mean a holdup, Jimbo said. You mean armed robbery.

A job is a job is a job, Jake said and smiled.

But that's really serious trouble, Jimbo said.

Only if you get caught, Jake said. And I never get caught. It's against my code to get caught. I live by my code.

But why do you want to do it in the first place? Jimbo said. With all you'd lose. Your job and everything. Why risk all that? Can't we get the dough some other way?

Sure we could. But it wouldn't be as much fun. It wouldn't be an outlaw lark. I've been bored lately, sports. Bored with easy living. Bored. Hell, what it boils down to I guess is that I've been feeling old. Anyway, you sports won't be involved.

We'll be in the getaway car, Jimbo said. That's involved.

Hey, I want to be a lawyer someday, Pace said. I can't be in a robbery.

If a goddamn lawyer is really what you want to be, then you couldn't ask for any better experience than a robbery, Jake said, laughing. Anyway, if anything should go wrong, which it won't, but if it should, I'll just say I set you innocent young things up. That you didn't know beans about what I was up to.

A job, Jimbo said quietly.

Listen, if you really don't have the stomach for it just forget it. You boys can just wait for me somewhere if you want to and I can drive the car to the spot myself and then hop a bus back downtown to get a cab.

We'll drive you, Jake, Jimbo said.

I won't, Pace said. I want to be a lawyer.

Then you can park your chickenshit ass in a hole somewhere and wait for us to do the job, sport, Jimbo said.

Shit, Pace said.

Well, boys, Jake said and stood up, you do whatever you think is best. This old dog needs a little exercise. I'm going to trot down the beach a ways. Maybe I can get some pretty lady into a conversation about my body.

Jimbo and Pace sat smoking silently for a time after Jake trotted off. Jimbo watched two pretty girls in swimsuits toss a beach ball back and forth. Whenever one would miss a toss she would run giggling and cutely girlish to retrieve the ball. Sometimes they glanced in Jimbo's direction. *A job*, Jimbo thought to himself and arched his eyebrows and french-inhaled deeply.

Are you really going to drive for him, Kemosabe? Pace said finally.

Correct.

But why, man?

Kicks.

That's real dumb, Jimbo. I mean, real dumb.

Jake knows what he's doing.

The hell he does. Listen, man, that cat is trouble with a capital *T*, dig? He's total bullshit. Total quackshit. No goddamn grown-up engineer is gonna go out and stick up a lousy taxicab. He's been lying about everything. He's a total phony bullshitting quack and you know it.

He's going to loan me Nick's car to go get Judy, man. It's a '56 Ford Victoria. A solid white convertible. And he's going to let us use his cottage on the shore.

You can forget that, man.

I believe him, sport.

That's not exactly what I meant. I lied to you this morning when I said Penny wasn't home when I called. She was home, man. I talked to her.

I don't get you, sport. Why did you lie to me about that?

I got real bad news. I didn't want to tell you. It's Judy.

Jesus, Pace. What? Is she hurt?

Not exactly, Kemosabe. She's getting married. Judy is going to marry Hutch Bodine, man.

Pace tried to dodge but Jimbo's knee caught him in the chest and he fell back on the sand with Jimbo on top. Jimbo put his knees on Pace's shoulders and grabbed a handful of Pace's hair.

OK, punk, Jimbo said and drew his free fist back, you're going to be sucking soup till your fucking teeth grow back.

Hey, man! Pace yelled. Get off me! It's not my fault! I didn't do anything. What the hell did I do? I thought we were best buddies, man.

Are you lying to me, Pace?

Why would I lie, man? It's true. I swear it, Kemosabe. That's what Penny told me.

Why didn't you tell me this before?

I just didn't. I didn't know how I guess. You're my best friend. I didn't want to screw you up, Kemosabe.

Fuck, Jimbo said and got up off Pace. He squatted on his haunches and stared at the sea.

I'm really sorry, Jimbo, Pace said. He sat up and rubbed his shoulders. I know how you feel, Kemosabe. I'm sorry. I didn't want to tell you.

Fuck, Jimbo said and smashed his fist into the sand. Fuck her. There's plenty of fish in the sea.

Yeah, man. Fuck her.

It's a joke, Jimbo said, laughing.

No, it's true. I swear it.

That's not what I mean, sport. It's a big joke on Bodine. I get the last laugh after all, see. That stupid, fucking Bodine is going to stroll down the aisle with sweet Judy and she's got my cake in her oven. It's my kid, see. My son. I get the last laugh.

Bodine is going to get stuck with raising my son. Don't you see how goddamn hilarious that is, sport?

    Sure, Jimbo.

    You're going to drive the car tonight, Pace.

    Sure, Jimbo. But what about you, man?

    I got a job to do.

13 ➤
gangster death

Rico stepped cautiously out into the alley back of the court-house and took a look around. The alley was blind to his right; to his left it came out onto a main thoroughfare and there was a bright arc light at that end. Rico took out his gun and moved slowly toward the arc light.

You can't never tell, he said; then, in an access of rage: They'll never put no cuffs on this baby.

When he was within fifty feet of the main thoroughfare a man appeared at the end of the alleyway, a big man in a derby hat. He saw Rico and immediately blew a blast on his whistle. Rico raised his gun and pulled the trigger; it missed fire.

Rico was frantic. He wanted to live. For the first time in his life he addressed a vague power which he felt to be stronger than himself.

Give me a break! Give me a break! he implored.

The man in the derby hat raised his arm and Rico rushed him, pumping lead. Rico saw a long spurt of flame and then something hit him a sledgehammer blow in the chest. He took two steps, dropped his gun, and fell flat on his face. He heard a rush of feet up the alley.

Mother of God, he said, is this the end of Rico?

With a frantic burst of strength Rico pushed himself to his knees. He crawled back across the alley to the door. He butted it open with his head. Somehow he pulled himself to his feet. He stumbled down the dark hallway. When he reached the wall phone at the end of the hallway he was gasping for breath. He could taste blood in his mouth. Got to hang on, he thought. Just a little longer. Little longer. Got to tell her. Got to let her know the truth.

Somehow through his blurred vision he managed to dial her number. The phone rang and rang. Hold on, he thought. Hold on, baby.

Hello-ie, she finally answered in that incredibly cute way of hers.

I love you, he whispered. I love you, Judy.

His eyes milked over and he slid slowly down the wall. Blood streaked the wall's faded yellow paint. He crumpled onto the floor. At the end of the cord the phone swung slowly.

Hello-ie. Hello-ie. Is anyone there? Hello-ie.

Atlantic City, 1960. A warm June night. Jimbo Stark sat on a bench in a small park near the center of the city imagining gangster deaths. Oh Mother of God, is this the end of Jimbo Stark? he thought and grinned tightly. On the corner across the street from the bench was Capone's Bar, where Jake had gone to call the cab. Al Capone's real-life brother owned that bar, Jake had claimed, and that was why he had wanted to call the cab from there. Cheap irony, Jake had said, I really go for cheap irony. How did Capone finally get his? Jimbo thought, trying to remember that gangster death.

Jake came out of Capone's Bar and crossed the street to the park.

Well, the cab should be here in a few minutes, Jake said. He sat down beside Jimbo on the bench and fired up a cigarette. How are you doing, sport?

Fine as wine.

Are you sure you want to do this? Jake said. You can wait here if you want and I'll pick you up later. I'd understand.

No thanks.

You're really sure?

I'm sure.

You really are a tough customer, sport. You really are.

Thanks, Jimbo said. Hey, Jake, how did Al Capone finally get his? I can't remember.

Well, it wasn't with a bang, that's for sure, Jake said, laughing. It was with a whimper. He died that old unlucky lover's death. He croaked from syphilis.

Terrific, Jimbo said. He tilted his head back on the bench and gazed up through the trees at the stars. You know, I wanted to be an astronomer when I was a kid. I once even built a telescope. It was a four-inch reflector. I polished those mirrors for weeks.

What changed your mind?

It's all going to cave in someday. Who wants to watch it caving in through a goddamn telescope? Who needs a closeup of the end of the world?

That's a gloomy prospect, sport. Did you read it in a book somewhere?

I saw it in a movie. This lecturer at a planetarium was explaining how the world will end. He said a new star will appear and just keep getting closer and closer to us. And the weather will change. The ice caps will melt and after a while the oceans will even boil. And finally that new star will just blow everything to hell. It was like in 3-D or something. Stars colliding in 3-D and dying. Then there was nothing. The lecturer said that everything will just be still and cold again and that no one out there will even know. He said that man existed all alone and won't even be missed.

Well, perk up, sport, Jake said. He patted Jimbo's leg. Here's our cab.

For a moment Jimbo felt panic. He felt frozen to the bench.

You coming, partner? Jake said. He opened the cab's rear door.

Jimbo put on the mirror sunglasses he had borrowed from Pace and stood up. With his first step toward the waiting cab the panic vanished. He felt light-headed, dizzy almost. He felt strangely unstuck, as though part of him was outside himself, as though he was witnessing himself, audience and performer at once.

Jimbo slid into the backseat beside Jake and Jake gave the cabbie the address.

You got any dough on the fight next week, buddy? the cabbie asked, looking back at them in his rearview mirror. He was a heavyset man in his thirties. He moved a toothpick about in his mouth as he talked.

What fight is that? Jake said.

Why, the heavyweight championship of the world, buddy, the cabbie said. Patterson and Johansson.

Oh, right, Jake said. No, I don't have any bets down. To tell the truth I haven't followed the fights much lately. I used to. But I just sort of lost interest. Who are you picking?

Personally, I want to see Johansson kick that nigger's ass again. Now usually I root for the American. But not when it's a nigger. I always root for a white man over a nigger even if the nigger is from America. I got ten bucks down on Johansson. The papers call that right hand of his the hammer of Thor. That right hand of his is something. Hell, he knocked that damn nigger down seven or eight times in that last fight.

Some right hand all right, Jake said.

A *job*, Jimbo thought to himself. Jimbo Stark riding through Atlantic City in a cab on his way to work. Through the mirrored sunglasses he gazed at the traffic with his heavily lidded moviegangster eyes. Well, officer, he was tall, the cabbie would describe him. A good six-footer I'd say. And he was thin. No, lean. He was tall and lean. What you would call rangy I guess. And he had thick hair. He had hair like that moviestar who was killed when he crashed his silver Porsche on that California highway a few years back. And the kid had nerve. You could tell he had nerve all right. That kid was cool as a cucumber, officer. He was a little young maybe but you could sure tell he knew his way around.

I got to admit though I kind of learned to like old Joe Louis even if he was a nigger, the cabbie said. You know, I didn't always feel this way about niggers. What happened is that I used to drive a hack up in New York. In one single year I got stuck up four separate times by niggers. And twice the black bastards hit me over the head. That's one reason I moved down here in '53. Anyway, like I said, I did sort of like old Joe. Yeah, the old Brown Bomber. I sort of respected him. But to tell the truth I still didn't get too choked up when the Rock kicked his black butt. That Rocky was something else. Forty-nine fights, forty-nine wins, and forty-three KO's. Now he was my kind of fighter. No fancy shit. Just wade in and pound ass. Hell, I used to box a little myself in the service. Was pretty good too. Thought about turning pro when I got out.

I used to box a little myself, Jake said.

No kidding.

Right. I wasn't bad myself. I even thought about turning pro myself when I got out.

No kidding. I'll be damn. You fight in the service too, buddy?

No, Jake said. I took up the ancient art of pugilism in prison.

You don't say.

Right.

The traffic thinned as Ohio Avenue entered the residential area north of town. They turned left off the avenue and followed a narrow side street over a small bridge.

Prison, you say? the cabbie said.

Right.

What was you in for, buddy, if you don't mind me asking?

I don't mind at all, Jake said. Armed robbery.

You don't say.

And murder, Jake said. He took his pistol out of his belt from under his loose sportshirt.

You don't say.

They turned onto a street of wooded vacant lots.

Here's the street you wanted, mister, the cabbie said. But I don't see any houses.

Friend, how about pulling right up here under these nice, dark trees and clicking off your lights, Jake said and pressed the pistol against the back of the cabbie's head.

Oh God, I thought so, the cabbie said. He slowed to a stop under the trees.

Now, friend, Jake said, just behave yourself and I won't have to blast your brains out.

Please, mister. I got kids. I got lots of kids. I'm a Catholic, mister. A good Catholic family man with lots of kids.

I'm a Mason, sport, Jake said. And I hate kids.

Please, mister.

Just stay calm, Jake said, and you'll be all right. We're friendly crooks if you don't cross us. In fact, we usually rob the rich just to give to the poor. We're the famous James gang, see.

Whatever you say, mister.

Just keep your paws on that steering wheel and look straight ahead. Go to work, Frank boy.

Right, Jessie, Jimbo said and climbed into the frontseat. He felt through the cabbie's pockets, taking his wallet and a roll of bills.

Check his shirt pocket, Frank, Jake said.

Nothing, Jessie. I think I got it all.

So you don't like Negroes, sport? Jake said.

I don't know, mister. Please. I got lots of kids.

Pull out his radio's phone, Frank. And get his keys.

Right, Jessie, Jimbo said. He yanked the phone's cord loose. He took the keys from the ignition.

You know, sport, I've always considered myself as a sort of nigger, Jake said.

Hey, mister. Please. Please don't shoot me.

Oh, I probably won't.

Are you going to hit me over the head?

Well, now, I don't know. What do you think, Frank?

Whatever you think, Jessie. You're the boss of this gang.

You know, I heard the pope was queer, Jake said. What about that, sport?

Whatever you say, mister.

I say he is queer.

He's queer. He's queer.

OK, sport. Now you just stretch out here in the seat and don't move a muscle for an hour. We'll have someone watching.

Sure, mister. Sure, sure.

Frank, boy, give our good Catholic family man back a buck.

What?

Give him a dollar.

Jimbo took a dollar from the roll of bills and stuffed it into the cabbie's shirt pocket.

I want you to do me a little favor with that buck, sport.

Sure, mister. Anything.

Place a bet for me on Patterson.

Jake and Jimbo hurried down the dark road and turned the corner. The car was not there.

Oh Jesus Christ! Jimbo said.

That stupid punk, Jake said. I should have known better.

What the fuck are we going to do?

Wait a minute, Jake said. He pointed to a car parked under some trees in the next block. There. That's it.

Jimbo started to run.

Hold on! Jake called. Cool down, sport. There are some houses over there. Walk, boy. Walk.

That stupid punk, Jimbo said.

When they reached the car they found the doors locked. Pace was lying down in the backseat. The radio was playing. Jake knocked on the driver's side window. Pace jumped up. He quickly unlocked the front doors.

God, you guys scared me shitless, Pace said. I must have dozed off.

Have you been playing this goddamn radio all this time? Jake said. He slid behind the wheel.

I wanted to hear some music, man.

What the hell is wrong with you, boy? Don't you know this runs the battery down?

Jake turned the key in the ignition. The car started.

That's lucky, Jake said. He slowly pulled the car out.

I just wanted to hear some music. I don't have a radio anymore, you know.

Just shut up about that chickenshit radio, Jimbo said. Where in the hell were you anyway?

What d'you mean where was I? I was right there where you found me.

You stupid punk, Jimbo said. You were in the wrong place. You were a block away from where you were supposed to be. Jesus. You stupid shit.

It looked like the right place to me, man. I don't know my way around here. I didn't want to drive anyway. You made me, man.

You stupid shit.

Come on, sports, Jake said. Settle down.

Did you do it, man? Pace said. Did you really do it?

You better believe it, Jimbo said. It was a goddamn lark.

Jesus. Then you really did it. Now we really are crooks.

Outlaws, Jimbo said. Outlaws.

When Jake reached Ohio Avenue he turned back in the direction of town.

Now we'll just lose ourselves in the Saturday night traffic, Jake said. Hey, count the loot, Frankie boy.

Dig it, Jessie, Jimbo said.

Was there any trouble or anything? Pace said.

Didn't you hear the shot? Jake said.

God, no! What happened, man? You didn't shoot anybody, did you? Oh Jesus!

He thought he was a tough guy, Jake said. He made a move. I had to plug him.

Oh God, no!

But if you didn't hear the shot then probably no one else did, Jake said. That's a real break for us. He might not be found for hours.

Oh God, did he, Jimbo? Did he really, man?

No, I did, sport, Jimbo said. I had the rod. I count about ninety bucks, Jessie.

Ninety bucks! Pace said. Jake, you said he'd have four or five hundred bucks on him. You said since it was Saturday night he'd be loaded.

He must have checked it in, Jake said.

Jesus, Pace said. Ninety lousy bucks. My whole life ruined for ninety lousy bucks.

Shut up, Jimbo said.

Did you really hurt someone, Jimbo? Did you? Did Jake?

Not yet, sport, Jimbo said.

Listen, we'll get by on ninety bucks, Pacer boy, Jake said. It just has to last until Monday. Monday I'll cash a check and pay you sports your five hundred.

I'm heading home on Monday, Pace said. As soon as I get my radio out of hock. Then I'm going home no matter what.

Well, you and Jimbo will have the Victoria to drive back in, Jake said.

That's all changed now, Jimbo said. I'm not driving back now. I don't have any reason to drive back now.

Why don't you drive your big hot Victoria back and drag with Hutch Bodine? Pace said.

Listen, sport, that white Victoria would blow Bodine's punk Green Machine off the road, Jimbo said.

Yeah, maybe so, sport, Pace said. But that ain't what old Bodine is driving around these days, sport. Old Bodine got himself a new bomb, sport. Penny told me all about it on the phone this morning.

What new bomb?

The Silver Ghost, sport.

What?

The old Silver Ghost, sport. Frankie fixed it up and gave it to Bodine for a wedding gift, sport.

The fuck he did.

He sure as hell did, sport. Penny told me all about it.

You didn't tell me this.

I forgot I guess.

Well, listen, boys, Jake said, whatever you decide to do is all right by me. Jimbo, you can use the car if you want to. Or you can come on up to the cottage with me. Whatever. Listen, you're good boys in my book. I've enjoyed the lark. Made me feel wild and woolly again. Made me feel like a kid. Anyway, we'll get us a nice motel room out on the pike somewhere and just spend a couple of days lying around. I'll find us a place where we can have old pupper with us and we'll just settle in and rest up. Hey, where is old Pard the pupper? Wake old Pard up. He shouldn't be sleeping through the big getaway. What kind of mobster mascot is that?

I don't know where he is, Pace said.

What's that? Jake said.

I don't know where the damn dog is.

Now what in the hell does that mean? Jake said. Isn't old Pard back there?

No.

No! What in the hell do you mean *no?* Where in the hell is he?

I don't know. He must of gotten out or something.

He got out? How the hell could he get out?

I took a couple of pisses. I left the door open or something I guess. He got out I guess.

Jimbo's punch caught Pace high on the forehead. Pace bounced back onto the seat, then rolled quickly onto the floor.

You punk! You goddamn punk! Jimbo yelled. He leaned over the seat and pounded on Pace's back.

No, Jimbo! Pace cried. No! Please, no! Please, Kemosabe!

Jake pulled off the avenue onto a side street and parked in the dark under some trees. He fired up a cigarette and watched as Jimbo punched Pace's back.

He's had enough, Jake said.

Punk. Punk, Jimbo grunted. He continued hammering.

Come on, sport, Jake said.

Jimbo turned around in the seat and smashed his fist against the dashboard.

A little blind puppy isn't going to run off, Jimbo yelled. That's a bunch of crap. That punk threw little Pard out. He ran Pard off. I could kill him. I mean it.

I swear he got out, Pace said. He crawled onto the backseat and lay there crying quietly. I swear to God he just got out somehow.

I could kill him, Jimbo said. He smashed the dashboard again.

Settle down, son, Jake said and patted Jimbo's shoulder.

Let me kill him, Jake, Jimbo said. Let me use your gun.

That's not even funny, Stark, Pace said and sat up.

Let me use your gun, Jimbo said.

Is that what you really want to do?

Don't talk crazy! Pace cried. That's not even funny.

Do you really want to shoot him? Jake said.

Yes.

Come on, Kemosabe. Quit kidding around.

Jake handed Jimbo the nickel-plated pistol.

Jesus Christ, Jimbo! Pace cried. That's not even funny.

Cock it before you fire it, Jake said.

Jimbo cocked the pistol and turned around in the seat. Jimbo aimed the pistol at Pace's face. Pace yelled and rolled back onto the floor. He tried to cover his head with his hands.

He's not worth the lead, Jimbo said. He uncocked the pistol.

That's all right, Jake said.

Shit, Pace said. He got up from the floor. That wasn't funny.

Count out thirty bucks, Jimbo, Jake said.

Why?

Just do it, sport.

Jimbo counted out thirty dollars and handed the bills to Jake.

Here's your cut from the job, Pace, Jake said. He tossed the bills on the backseat.

Why give him a cut? Jimbo said.

I don't want it, Pace said. I don't want anything to do with this.

Take it, Pace, Jake said. It's your thirty pieces of silver.

I didn't want any part of this, Pace said. You made me do it, Jimbo. We were best buddies and you made me do it. Everything is ruined now.

You're cruising for another bruising, sport, Jimbo said.

Nothing is ruined, Pace, Jake said. Just keep your mouth shut, see. Keep your mouth shut and everything will be fine. Now put that money in your pocket.

Pace took the money and stuffed it in his shirt pocket.

OK, that's square, Jake said. He reached over the seat and opened a back door. Climb out now, Pace.

What?

Get out of the car.

What'll I do? I don't even know where I am.

Let me tell you something, sport, Jake said. If you were a grown man you would be bleeding right now for what you pulled. I'd have shot you in the gut. I'd have shot you just once. That way it would have taken you a long time to die. That way I could have sat and watched you suffer for hours. Get out of the car.

Yes, sir, Pace said. He climbed out of the car.

Hey, Pace, Jimbo called. You tell the folks at home that I'll be back myself one of these days. I'll be back to settle some scores.

I'll tell them all right, hero.

Jake pulled the car out. Jimbo looked back at Pace standing in the street.

Stop, Jake.

What, sport?

Stop. Please.

Jake pulled over to the curb.

I've got to go back, Jimbo said.

You want me to wait? Jake said.

Yeah. I've got to say something to him, that's all.

Take your time, sport.

Jimbo got out of the car and walked back toward Pace. For a moment Pace seemed to tense as though ready to run. Then he just stood there in the street looking down at his feet.

You change your mind about something? Pace said when Jimbo walked up to him. Did you decide to shoot me after all?

I couldn't shoot you, Jimbo said. You know that.

I guess you want to punch me some more then.

I don't want to punch you, amigo.

I swear I didn't mean to let that damn dog out, man.

I went crazy or something, Pace. It wasn't real. It wasn't me doing it. It wasn't me hitting you, amigo.

Who was it then, Ingemar Johansson?

I'm sorry.

Hey, Kemosabe, come on with me. It's not too late, man. Let's go home, Jimbo. Leave that quack.

I can't now.

Sure you can. Let's go home, Jimbo.

Listen, take care of your worthless ass, you old turdface.

So you're going off with that quack.

Hey, amigo, do me one last favor.

Your last wish, huh? Sure. Why not?

Tell Judy I'll be back for my son. Someday I'll be back.

I'll tell her.

And you know that fancy ring I got her? Get it from her. Keep it. It's yours, amigo. Give it to Penny or something. Just get it from Judy.

Can I hock it?

Hock the fucker. I don't care. Just get it from Judy.

Hey, man, will you do me a favor too?

Just name it.

Send me my goddamn radio.

It's in the mail, man. Listen, I'm sorry I went crazy, Pace. I don't understand it.

Don't get hurt, Kemosabe. Don't get your ass shot off or something.

I'll try, amigo. But who knows? Maybe getting plugged is how I'm meant to go out, Jimbo said, arching his eyebrows and wrinkling his forehead. He gave Pace a light punch in the shoulder, then turned and slouched toward the waiting getaway car.

14 ➤
the big kissoff

Then everything began to reel before my eyes, a fiery gust came from the sea, while the sky cracked in two, from end to end, and a great sheet of flame poured down through the rift. Every nerve in my body was a steel spring, and my grip closed on the revolver. The trigger gave, and the smooth underbelly of the butt jogged my palm. And so, with that crisp, whip-crack sound, it all began. I shook off my sweat and the clinging veil of light. I knew I'd shattered the balance of the day, the spacious calm of this beach on which I had been happy. But I fired four shots more into the inert body, on which they left no visible trace. And each successive shot was another loud, fateful rap on the door of my undoing.

Jimbo read the passage again. He marked the page, then closed the book. He fired up a cigarette and leaned back on the bench. He watched as three young, pretty girls walked by on the boardwalk. When one of them glanced at him he looked away. He smoked and stared at the sea. The morning sky was overcast and the ocean looked leaden gray. Highlights shone on the tips of the gray waves as they rolled in to break on the nearly deserted beach. And each successive shot was another loud, fateful rap on the door of my undoing, Jimbo thought to himself. The door of my undoing.

Jimbo spotted Jake hurrying down the boardwalk toward him. Old Jake really does look like Bogart, Jimbo thought.

Well, sport, looks like the shit has hit the fan, Jake said as he walked up. He sat down beside Jimbo on the bench.

Did you get ahold of your old cop friend?

I sure as hell did. It's lucky I called him before I tried to cash a check this morning. They would have nailed my ass. Sport, it looks like we're going to be on the lam for real. Your little buddy spilled the beans.

You're kidding. Jesus Christ.

I'm not kidding. Some state troopers picked him up hitch-hiking. He's singing like a canary. I was afraid this would happen. I should have plugged the punk.

I'm the one who should have plugged him.

Well, who knows, you might get another chance at him someday. Anyway, they're looking for us. They've got an APB out for the Jim Stark–Jake Barnes gang.

What in the hell are we going to do now?

Well, first we have to lay our hands on some decent dough so we can blow town.

Another job?

Are you game, sport?

Why not? What does it matter now?

I'm not talking about another punk taxicab job though, sport. I'm talking about something bigger.

Christ, Jake, what? A bank or some shit?

A stagecoach, Jake said, laughing.

Sure. Why not? Crazy.

Actually, I have a nice little tavern on the Black Horse Pike all picked out. It'll be a piece of cake and we'll cop at least a grand. Then we'll shoot north and get Nick. I know where I can get my hands on some real dough in New York. We'll get it and head west. Maybe go to California and lay low.

What about the Victoria?

We'll have to leave it.

What about your job? What about your cottage and apartment and everything?

I don't have any goddamn job. I don't need it. Listen, I have plenty of dough stashed. And most everything I own is in another name.

Another name? Whose name?

My real name.

I don't get you, Jake.

My real name is Morris. Morris Adams. Jake Barnes is the name of a character in a novel. Like your Sal Paradise alias.

Christ, Jake. I mean Morris. Why didn't you tell me this before?

Because I didn't trust Pace the punk.

But what difference did it make when you first picked us up? I mean, we weren't planning to hold up a cab or anything then.

The things I told you about the tough customers waiting for me in Miami were true, sport. You see, my *old* smuggling days are not really so *old*. There are some mean Castro Cubans who would love to get their paws on me right now. See, I set up a big gun deal just last March for some anti-Castro people. Like I told you, I'm not in it for profit. I'm in it for principle. But I am still in it. Anyway, I figured the less you boys knew, the better. For your own sake too. It was just a precaution. I always take precautions, sport. I always figure the less anyone knows about my business, the better.

But if the cops think your name is Jake Barnes how could they trace your bank account? Or the Victoria? Why can't you cash a check?

It so happens the Victoria and my bank account here in Atlantic City are in my Jake Barnes name. I have accounts all over the country in different names. Just in case I have to really disappear and lay low. Anyway, it's bad luck for us that Jake Barnes is my Atlantic City alias. On the other hand, it's plenty lucky I never told Pace the punk my real moniker. If they can't trace me they can't trace you. Listen, you think up a name you like. Any name. Sal Paradise if you like. And I'll get you every scrap of paper you'll ever need to prove you're that person. And I mean *every* document from your birth certificate on. Highschool records even. Hell, you could go to Harvard on a

scholarship if you wanted with the records I can get you. No
one will ever trace you. You're going to be perfectly safe, sport.

That's what I'm going to do, by God. Jimbo Stark is going to
disappear. Jimbo Stark is going to vanish from the face of this
earth.

It's as easily said as done, sport. Who do you want to be?
Your old buddy Sal Paradise?

Sure. Why not?

It's as good as done, Sal, Jake said and laughed. I'll make
some phone calls and your new ID's will be waiting for you in
New York.

Dig it, Jimbo said.

Now, we'd best get a hideout lined up and lay low until
tonight. I know an out-of-the-way motel that would be easy to
get to from the job tonight. So let's load up with beer and
sandwich shit and shoot out there. How's that for a scheme?

Sounds like a great scheme, Jake. Morris, I mean. Morris. I'll
have to get used to it I guess.

You'll get used to it all right, Jimbo. I mean Sal.

 . . . gazing up at the dark sky spangled with its signs and
stars, for the first time, the first, I laid my heart open to the
benign indifference of the universe. To feel it so like myself,
indeed, so brotherly, made me realize that I'd been happy,
and that I was happy still. For all to be accomplished, for me
to feel less lonely, all that remained to hope was that on the
day of my execution there should be a huge crowd of spec-
tators and that they should greet me with howls of execration.

Jimbo closed the book and set it beside him on the bed. He
clasped his hands behind his head on the pillow and stared up
at the motel room's ceiling, which sparkled in the teevee
light's reflection. The day of my execution, Jimbo thought to
himself. The French still used a guillotine. Meursault would
have his head chopped off. They hang you in England. To be
hung by the neck until dead. In the eighteenth century they
used to string up even kids, Jimbo had read somewhere.
Sometimes the kids were so light the hangman had to swing

on them to do the trick. In Utah you could choose between the noose and a firing squad. Caryl Chessman had been gassed in California. Jimbo had read Chessman's death row book twice. Death row. To be in a cell on death row. What did they do to you in New Jersey? Jimbo wondered. The electric chair probably. They fry you. Thousands of volts of electricity shot through your nerves. Jimbo gazed at the teevee set. To be fried by electricity until dead. To die by electricity. Jimbo shut his eyes. He pictured himself being led from his cell on death row. He pictured himself being strapped into the electric chair. His head was shaved. Among the viewers behind a window were Judy and Captain. Judy was holding a baby. Captain was wearing his old uniform. Judy lifted the baby up close to the glass and waved its little pink hand with hers. She blew Jimbo a kiss. Just as they were ready to pull the mask over Jimbo's face Captain snapped to attention and saluted. Someone threw the switch. Jimbo pictured himself glowing. He pictured his skin incandescent. He pictured his life imploding like the light of a suddenly turned-off teevee.

Morris came out of the shower with a towel tied around his waist. He studied himself in the dresser's mirror as he fired up a cigarette. He flexed his muscles in the mirror and chuckled.

Not in bad shape for an old dog, Morris said. Still a real conversation piece all right.

Hey, Morris, what novel was Jake Barnes in? Jimbo said. Did this guy Camus write it?

No, a guy named Ernest Hemingway wrote it.

I've read him. In *Life* magazine. They ran a story of his about an old man who caught this big fish. Hemingway's the guy who goes all over the place hunting and fishing.

Right, sport. He's the guy. Jake Barnes was the hero of *The Sun Also Rises*. It's a novel about the Lost Generation.

The Lost Generation, Jimbo said.

Listen, I have all of Hemingway's novels in that magic box of books out in the car's trunk. He'll be next on your reading list. Like I told you, you stick with me, sport, and I'll give you a real education.

The Lost Generation, Jimbo said.

You know, Hemingway was the reason I went to Cuba in the first place. He lived near Havana before Castro fucked things up. I went down there the first time when I was just a kid. Hemingway was my hero, see. You might say I went down there to sit at his feet.

Did you ever meet him?

I did more than meet him. He sort of took me under his wing. Gave me a job on his boat. The old *Pilar*. Pilar was the name of a woman in another novel of his. I spent several summers working on the old *Pilar*. I learned a lot from Papa. That's what everyone called him, Papa. Like he was everyone's old man. And in a lot of ways he was I guess.

Whatever happened? Do you still see him and everything?

No.

Why not?

That's a difficult thing to explain, sport. I was young. I didn't have much experience in the ways of this world. Too many things were just black or white for me then. Papa was an artist, see. A great artist. And artists explore experience. All levels and forms of experience. And just because they explore a certain experience doesn't mean they can be defined by that experience. That's what I didn't understand then, see.

I don't follow you, Jimbo said.

Let's just say that Papa wanted to explore a form of experience with me that I didn't understand. I was too naive to really understand what it meant. To understand everything it did mean and everything it did not mean. Anyway, I reacted foolishly and I hurt him and that was that.

You mean he was queer or something?

That's the way I reacted too, see. It's just not that simple, sport. Maybe after you meet Kerouac you'll understand more.

You mean Kerouac's queer too? I don't believe it!

You have a lot to learn about life, sport, Morris said, laughing. But you're a tough customer. You've got lots of heart. You'll make it.

Jesus. I always heard they were tough customers.

You better believe they're tough customers, sport. Papa could have been a professional boxer he was so good. I saw him cool six sailors in a barroom brawl in Key West once. He was the toughest customer I ever saw. And old Kerouac is no slouch either.

I just don't understand. How could they be tough customers and goddamn queers at the same time?

You'll learn, sport. Hey, you want that temporary tattoo before the big job tonight?

Damn right. Let's do it.

Let me get my trusty ball-point pen. Like I told you, I'm one hell of a tattoo artist. We'll just ink this in, then when you get your real one the tattooist can just follow the design.

Make it just like yours. And draw that snake in too. Only don't cover up the ED with stars. Make it just BORNED.

You sure about that? Morris said. He sat down on the bed beside Jimbo.

Damn right. BORNED TO WIN.

OK, sport, flex your muscle. One skull and crossbones with a sinuous snake coming up.

Atlantic City, New Jersey. Around midnight on a hot, humid Monday in June 1960. Jimbo Stark, a runaway, a teenage soldier of fortune, his left front pocket stuffed with poems, is standing at one end of a small bar in a ginjoint right off the Black Horse Pike. His partner, Morris, has gone back to the head. Besides the bartender, a surly, fat wop with a black patch over his right eye, there are only three other people in the ginjoint, two dudes sitting at the bar nursing drinks and a plump, middle-aged bleached blond in tight pink pedal pushers over by the jukebox punching Frank Sinatra torch-tunes and sort of dancing around with herself, humming. Now and then the bartender casts his cold fisheye in Jimbo's direction. Jimbo casually runs his fingers back through his hair and adjusts the pulled-up collar of his red windbreaker and pretends to ignore the glare. When Jimbo and Morris had first come into the ginjoint the bartender had given Jimbo a hard time about his age, as though Jimbo Stark was some sort of punk kid, as though Jimbo Stark had not been around. Smartass bartender. One-eyed wop. And what's more, when Morris had politely asked the bartender to please turn on the teevee above the bar the smartass had said it was against policy.

Against policy, Morris had said. My friend, the greatest gangster movie of all time is on the late show. *High Sierra*. Didn't you ever see it?

No, I never saw it, buddy, the bartender had said, wiping some bar glasses and giving Jimbo the fisheye.

Great, great movie, Morris said. Starring the lovely, luscious Ida Lupino and the late, great Humphrey Bogart. Whom I just happen to resemble. Can you see it? Everyone tells me I resemble the late, great Humphrey Bogart. People stop me on the street sometimes. Listen, friend, it's a great gangster movie.

Like I said, it's against policy.

What policy is that, friend?

A lady is playing the jukebox, the bartender said, nodding toward the bleached blond. When we got patrons pushing silver into the jukebox, buddy, the teevee remains off. Besides, the goddamn thing is on the blink as usual. The goddamn picture rolls all the time.

Well, friend, Morris said, a rolling teevee beats no teevee at all. That's a great movie, I'm telling you. An uplifting experience for all. Now you wouldn't want to deny your patrons an uplifting experience, would you, friend?

Just forget it, please, buddy.

Let him keep his goddamn teevee off, Jimbo said to Morris. Jimbo was getting nervous. He wished they had not bought that last pint.

No, my boy, no, Morris said, putting his arm around Jimbo's shoulder. You're just the one I want to see it. Uplifting experience, my boy. Hey, pretty lady, Morris called to the humming bleached blond. Would you mind switching dream machines, sugar? There's a great Bogart movie on the late show.

What's that? the bleached blond said, startled out of her dreamspace. What's that? She blinked her wet, round eyes trying to focus on Morris.

A great Bogart movie. On the late show, Morris said, pointing his thumb over his shoulder toward the teevee.

Oh, is it *Petrified Forest?* the bleached blond asked, tapping her lips with her fingers, all aflutter. I just love, love, love that movie! Bette Davis was in it. Oh, she was so beautiful.

No, sugar, Morris said. It's *High Sierra.* A great movie in its own right. Starring Bogie and the lovely Ida Lupino.

Leslie Howard was the man in love with Bette Davis in *Petrified Forest,* the bleached blond said, winking and blinking as she walked unsteadily over to the bar to where Morris sat. That movie was so so romantic, she said, putting a hand on Morris's shoulder as she tried to focus her eyes on his face. Leslie Howard made Humphrey Bogart who was playing this hoodlum named Duke Mantee shoot him in the end so that Bette Davis could collect this five-hundred-dollar insurance policy he had signed over to her and go to Paris to paint like she had always dreamed. Leslie Howard died for love. Duke Mantee shot him right down though he didn't really seem to want to. I almost died for love once.

The movie on the late show is *High Sierra,* sugar, Morris said. But there are lots of folks dying for love in it. Let me buy you a drink, sugar. Hey, bartender, why not click the old set on and let me set the bar up? The whole damn bar!

Gee, buddy, do you think you can afford it? the bartender said, nodding toward the two dudes sitting there. Look, buddy, that rolling teevee gives me a goddamn headache. I had a hard shift tonight. I had to toss two drunks and one wise guy out. I got a goddamn headache as it is.

If it ain't *Petrified Forest* with Bette Davis and Leslie Howard I don't care if I see it or don't, the bleached blond said. She stumbled back over to the jukebox.

If you wanna watch the tube, buddy, you'll just have to stroll elsewhere.

Stroll elsewhere my pink ass, Morris had said, laughing quietly, after the bartender moved down the bar.

When Morris bursts out of the head with his big .45 automatic drawn and cocked and yelling "freeze" everyone freezes. The fat, surly wop bartender's fisheye pops cartoon wide and the bleached blond's torchtune sizzles suddenly into a whine. Even Jimbo is surprised. They were supposed to wait until the joint was cleared out before making their move. For a moment Jimbo feels the panic, the sick surge in his stomach, that metallic taste of fear in his mouth. Then, quickly, the unstuck feeling comes over him and he is completely outside himself. Jimbo arches his eyebrows and wrinkles his forehead and looks out coldly at the stiffs in the scene through his lidded moviegangster eyes.

I'd like to welcome all you nice folks to a cordial little holdup, Morris says, speaking tightly from the side of his mouth in his Bogart gangster voice. He slowly waves the .45 around the room, leveling it on each person in turn.

Oh, please don't shoot me, the bleached blond whines, hugging herself.

Don't worry, sister, Morris says. Nobody is going to plug you. This is your basic friendly job, see. Our gang only pulls your basic friendly jobs. Right, Jessie?

Right, Frank, Jimbo says. He slides off the barstool.

I've never been in a honest-to-God holdup before in my whole life, the bleached blond says. Just think, I'm in a real live holdup just like on teevee or something. Just wait till I tell Mabel.

Jimbo walks calmly around the bar to the cash register. *Yes, officer, that kid was one cool customer all right. I never saw a kid with so much nerve.*

Hey, buddy, just take what you want, the bartender says. Just you-uns don't do nothing crazy, OK?

Like Big Clyde said, we're really friendly outlaws, Jimbo says in his quiet, calm Whispering Smith voice. Why, we even help the poor.

Joking, officer. They were making jokes about the whole thing. You'd think they were at a picnic or something.

Bonnie's got a golden heart as big as the Grand Canyon all right, Morris says, firing up a Camel with one hand. Always giving our ill-gotten gains away. Hey, my one-eyed fat friend, how's about you clicking on the teevee for me now? Would you do that for me if I ask you real pretty please? Channel six, jerk. I sure would like to catch the tail end of that great gangster movie. Yes, indeedy. There's just nothing in this world I enjoy more than a hit of good old cheap irony.

Oh, sure. Sure thing, buddy, the bartender says, quickly reaching up to click on the teevee set.

A honest-to-God holdup, the bleached blond says and giggles.

That's right, sister, Morris says. Now, how's about you forgetting old Blue Eyes for a minute and hunkering your cute behind up to the bar with the rest of these stickupees. Hey, bartending man, set everyone up. Doubles, pal. We'll have us a little toast to the late, great Bogie.

Just like Duke Mantee, the bleached blond says, giggling and winking and blinking at Morris like crazy.

It just takes practice and patience, sugar.

Just like in *Petrified Forest*. That movie I was telling about. That had Bette Davis in it. You ever been in a holdup before? the bleached blond asks one of the dudes at the bar who, looking straight ahead, does not answer.

Leaving the silver, Jimbo calmly cleans out the cash register, folding the bills and sticking them in his jeans' right front pocket. His left front pocket is stuffed with his poems, his dozen favorites, the poems which in one of his favorite capture fantasies the tough but understanding cop will read. Empty your pockets, son, the tough but understanding cop tells Jimbo. A perplexed look flickers over the cop's face when Jimbo puts the poems on the desk. Sit down, son, the cop says, nodding his head toward a chair beside the desk; then he begins to slowly read each poem. He rereads each one of them twice. The perplexed look on his face deepens. At long last he looks up at Jimbo. You wrote these poems, son? Yes, I wrote them, Jimbo quietly tells him. I don't know much about poetry, son, but these poems are beautiful. Just beautiful. The tough but understanding cop picks the poems up again and glances through them shaking his head, a look of real pain, of true adult guilt, twisting his face. How could such a sensitive, intelligent, talented boy like you get your ass into this mess? How could you pull those jobs, son? You're a poet, not an outlaw. I don't know, Jimbo says. I guess I'm just confused. I feel misunderstood I guess.

After cleaning out the cash register Jimbo walks over and takes the bartender's wallet.

By the way, Jimbo tells the bartender as he removes the bills, that ID I flashed you saying I was twenty-one was punk. Phony as shit, smartass. You ought to be more careful. You might lose your license, smartass. Actually I'm only eleven. That's why I'm famous far and wide as The Kid. My close pals call me Baby Face.

I'd rather call you Bonnie, Morris says.

Suit yourself, Dutch, Jimbo says and comes back around the bar to frisk the patrons.

I only got me ten dollars, mister, please, the bleached blond whines. And it's got to last me.

We don't need a lady's last ten dollars, Jimbo quietly says to her and smiles and then slips a couple of his own bills under her glass. If you ask me, officer, that boy wasn't all bad. I don't think he would really have hurt any of us. I think there has to be some good reason he's turned outlaw. There was just something about him. A strange and wonderful gentleness.

Just be sure to frisk the big cat on the end there good, Bonnie, Morris says. He's flush.

You boys wouldn't be so tough without that rod, the big cat on the end says.

Think not, sucker? Morris says. He uncocks the .45 and sticks it in his belt. Make your move, hero. I'll stick your goddamn hero ass down your goddamn hero throat.

Hey, come on, Jimbo says. Cool it, Jessie.

Forget it, Big Cat says.

Oh, come on, hero, Morris says, folding his arms on his chest. Get your name in the paper, hero. Hey, hero, I've got a dandy idea. You don't happen to have an old insurance policy stuck away somewhere, do you? Hey, hero, you could sign it over to sweet Bette here. Then when we make our getaway I'll blast you and sweet Bette can get a free trip to Paris. Paris, France. How's about that, Bette?

What's that? the bleached blond asks, trying to stuff the bills Jimbo gave her into her change purse.

Paris, sugar, Morris says. Paris, France. How would you like the once-in-a-gal's-lifetime chance to bolt to Paris, France. To while away rainy afternoons in the Louvre digging the Cézannes. To drop by 27 rue de Fleurus for little cakes and fruit liqueurs with Miss Stein.

What's that? the bleached blond asks, polishing off her drink.

Where would you like to paint your pictures, honey? Morris asks, his arms still folded across his chest, the .45 stuck in his belt. Hero here is going to die for love. Hero is going to finance the trip of your fondest dreams, sugar.

Well, I got me a sister in Dayton, Ohio.

Well, hero, how's about it? How's about setting Bette up for a lifetime's dream trip to Dayton, Ohio? Die for love, hero, once in your life.

Hey, just forget it, Big Cat says.

Come on, Jessie boy, Jimbo says, let's get going. Yes, officer, if it hadn't been for the kid the older guy might of blasted me away. You might say I owe my life to that kid.

Well, whatever you say, hero. What's the world coming to? Nobody wants to die for love anymore. But like I said we're your basic friendly little band of merry robbers if you don't push us. Bonnie, you be sure to frisk hero good and true. He's flush, Morris says, taking the .45 out of his belt.

Right, Clyde, Jimbo says, moving down the bar toward the big cat.

Hey, hold up there a minute, Bonnie boy, Morris says,

waving the .45 toward the teevee set as if he wants to hold it
up too. Let's us call a brief time-out on this here job. Time-out,
folks. Hey, mister bartender man, set everyone up again on me
and Bogie. I want everyone to check this scene on teevee. This,
folks, is where old Bogie makes the big crashout.

So this is the way this gangster movie ends, Bogie, firing up
a last Camel (or maybe Lucky) (medium shot), thinks to
himself, though not really in despair, for he is weary of it all.
Being on the lam is no life. A price on your head. The constant
fear of being fingered. The constant fear of being shot down
like a dog in the street. Then the inevitable gangster getaway
pell-mell over dusty backcountry roads. The dizzy spinout and
crash. The mad scramble up the rocky mountainside only to
be cornered at last like a rat in a hole. Nowhere to turn. The
end of the road. Curtains. Another star kissed good-bye. And
all last night, while the law waited armed for him in the
forests below, Bogie, freezing in the zero High Sierra darkness,
had curled childlike about his last dreams. Fearful dreams but
his own. Dreaming himself born, his dying mother's screams,
the July sun burning into the tar-paper roof, the bumping of
flies against the screened door, a primitive, chanting preacher,
the shadows that circled for three days about the camp. Then
his childhood dream of his childself lost in a narrow street of
fog, hearing something growling as it moved swiftly toward
him. Finally he had dreamed for a last time his ancient
gangster dreams, of jobs and shootouts and getaways and of
gangster deaths. Gangster deaths. Bullet ridden, leaking. The
last closeup. The last words, bubbling from his dying lips like
a cartoon balloon of blood. Mother of God, is this the end of
Mad Dog Roy Earl?

How did I ever get my moviestar ass in this goddamn scene
anyway? Bogie thinks, his grin tight, ironic, in a closeup. They
wanted Raft to begin with. Agents, he thinks. Producers.
Assholes. In a slow pan down the steep, rocky mountainside
Bogie watches the early morning light begin to glisten on the
granite cliffs and to shine bluish from the firs far below where

the armed law waits. There's a bullet down there with my number on it, Bogie thinks. I hope I don't piss or shit myself when I eat that hot lead. I hope mine ain't a kicking, snapping, foamy gangster death. Now, if only I was a fancy dan like Fred Astaire, I could just fox-trot my ass out of this movie. Hell, I could have been a hoofer. I could have been a song and dance man.

Then Bogie hears the barking, faintly at first, then quickly near. Pard, Bogie's moviedog, is barking crazily on cue as he races up the steep slope seeking his moviemaster.

Well, Bogie says to himself as he flicks his last fag out into the cold air, this is the big kissoff. He walks out now to the edge of the cliff to look for Pard, exposing himself to the deadly waiting aim of the lawman sniper who during the night made his way above Bogie's Mad Dog Roy Earl hideout hoping to get just such a clean shot as this to end the movie on schedule.

Sometimes I go around pitying myself like a punk, Bogie thinks as he waits at the edge of the cliff. And all the time I am being carried on great ghost wings across the sky.

Bogie laughs, his breath exploding like smoke in the cold clean air. Bogie laughs in that freezeframe just before the big kissoff, just before that long deadman roll down the mountainside, rolling, rolling down the screenscape of some teevee on the blink in some sleazy Black Horse Pike ginjoint forever.

What does it mean when a man crashes out? the lovely, luscious Ida Lupino asks in a dazed voice as she gazes upon Bogie's blasted, broken Mad Dog Roy Earl moviecorpse.

Quietly a reporter standing near her says, It means he's free, sister.

Free, the lovely, luscious Ida Lupino repeats in a whisper and gazes up toward that great starfield in the sky.

15 ➤
crashout

Atlantic City, New Jersey. After midnight on a Monday in June 1960.

Come on, be a sport, hero, Morris said to the big cat sitting at the end of the bar. Die for love just once in your miserable life. Finance sweet Bette here for her dream trip to Dayton, Ohio. Help her paint her pictures, hero. Come on, be a sport.

Hey, forget it. Please, Big Cat said.

What's the world coming to? Morris said. No one wants to die for love anymore. Bonnie boy, you give hero a real good frisk. Hero is flush.

After Jimbo collected all the wallets he backed toward the ginjoint's door. He could tell by the wop bartender's glaring fisheye he was thinking about making a move. Morris saw it also and he leveled the .45 at the bartender's face and quietly said, I wouldn't do anything stupid if I were you, sister.

When he got outside Jimbo hurried down the dark, tree-lined street to the car and after starting the engine huddled on the front floor as Morris had told him to do. By the dim light of the dashboard he did a quick count of the take. Around three hundred bucks, he figured. Some grand. We'll cop at least a grand, Morris had said. Sure. What the fuck was holding Morris up anyway? Jimbo thought. Just as he rose up to look out the window Jimbo heard the blast. Oh Jesus Christ! What in the holy fuck? Jimbo huddled back down on the floor. He was wrong. He had not heard a shot. He never dreamed he would hear a shot. He had not heard a shot. Oh Jesus Christ.

Morris opened the door and slid in behind the wheel. He tossed a bottle of whiskey on the seat. He pulled the car slowly out.

What the fuck was that? Jimbo said.

What was what?

The shot.

Nothing of importance, sport.

Come on, Jake, what was it?

Morris.

What was it? Come on.

The wop got cute. I threw him a scare. Have you counted the haul?

About three hundred.

What do you mean three hundred? That big slob at the end of the bar was flashing a wad big enough to choke a cow. He was bragging about hitting it big at the track today. That's why I came out with the gun early. Didn't you frisk him like I told you?

I got his wallet. It just had ID in it. He didn't have any big wad. Not in his wallet anyway.

Didn't you frisk him?

I got his wallet I told you.

Goddamn it! I told you to frisk the son of a bitch. The son of a bitch must have slipped it in a pocket. Why didn't you do what I told you? You can bet that slob son of a bitch is setting up drinks and laughing at our asses right now.

I got his wallet.

Swell. I should have shot that slob son of a bitch too.

What do you mean by *too*, Morris?

I threw a scare in the wop by plugging him in the gut.

Oh Jesus Christ, you're kidding. You didn't.

The hell I didn't.

Oh no. Oh God, no.

You should have seen the fat blond split her pants ducking.

God, Jake, did you kill him?

The name is Morris. I don't know if he croaked or not. We'll read about it in the funnies tomorrow.

I can't believe it. I can't believe this happened.

You're beginning to sound like your punk pal. I'm beginning to wonder if you're ready for the big time, sport.

Some big time, Morris. Listen, I didn't have anything to do with you shooting that guy. I wasn't even there. It wasn't my fault.

Let me tell you something, Jimbo boy. According to the law of this land you're as guilty as I am. You were in on the job and that's all the law cares about. It won't make a bit of difference that you didn't pull the trigger. It won't even make a difference that you were already out in the car when I pumped lead into that jerk. The only thing that will make any difference is that you're seventeen and I'm forty-three. And what this means is that if we're nailed for bumping the bum you'll probably only get twenty years to life while they'll probably fry me.

How did this happen? I never thought something like this would happen.

What did you think this was, Jimbo, a game? This is real. We're not characters in some goddamn movie, kiddo. This is real life. You've got to grow up, kiddo. Face up to things. We'll be all right if we keep our heads and stick together. I know what I'm doing.

Morris turned south off the Black Horse Pike and drove slowly through a small town. A light rain started up and Morris clicked on the windshield wipers. The lights of approaching cars flashed over his face.

Listen, Jimbo, I wouldn't let anything happen to you. We'll blow old Atlantic City tomorrow, Morris said. I'll ditch the .45 first thing in the morning. I've got several pistols up at the cottage. And we'll ditch this Chevy too. Hell, the only reason I picked this lousy Bel Air up in the first place was because it looks so goddamn inconspicuous. I wanted to look like your basic tourist when I was driving around Miami. I've got a real snazzy Jag up at the cottage. Sport, they'll never trace us. We'll just follow our original plan. We'll shoot up to New York and pick up your new ID and my dough and we'll cruise to California in my Jag and lay low for a while. We'll even get you in college out there somewhere if you want. It will be a piece of cake. And we'll have a goddamn ball while we're at it. Take my word for it, sport.

What about Nick now? Are you still going to stop and get him?

No.

Why not? Why can't he come with us?

It would be impossible. It would take an act of God.

Impossible? Why?

Nick is dead.

What? Nick is what?

Dead. Nick has been dead for years.

Oh Jesus, Jake, Jimbo said. What next? What next, Jake?

Morris, Morris said.

Jimbo opened the bottle of whiskey and drank from it until he almost choked. He shut his tear-flooded eyes and hunkered as far down on the floor as he could. He listened to the rhythmic clicking of the windshield wipers and the sound of the tires on the wet pavement. A pungent, rainy-night air smell flowed in Morris's open window, filling the car's rushing interior.

I wasn't there when Nick needed me, Morris said. He walked slowly back and forth at the foot of the beds. Jimbo sat on his bed with his back pressed against the wall. The only light in the room came from the small teevee on the dresser whose sound was turned low. Now and then Morris took a hit from the bottle of whiskey he carried at his side.

My wife and I had gotten a divorce, see. I had been away for a while. Quite a while as a matter of fact. My wife had remarried. Nick and I stayed in touch. We wrote each other. I sent him money. Nick never complained about anything. He never even mentioned his mother's new husband. Not a word.

I had no idea what was going on. If I had known anything I would have done something. But Nick never said anything. He was that kind of kid. So here was the score. My dumb cunt ex-wife had married a bum. And the bum's hobby was getting drunk and pounding hell out of my ex-wife. Which she probably asked for. But what would happen was Nick would try to help his mother and the bum would turn on him. I found out later that the bum had even put Nick in the hospital once. If I had known about it in time I could have done something. Even if I couldn't have done it myself, I know people. But I didn't know in time. One night Nick shot him. It was my job but I wasn't around. So Nick did my job for me. Then Nick shot his mother. Then Nick shot himself.

Morris stopped walking up and down. He took a long pull from the bottle, then put it on the dresser. He picked up Nick's gold-framed picture from the dresser and tilted it in the teevee's light. He stood there, weaving slightly, and looked at the picture for a long time. Finally he placed it back carefully on the dresser. He looked at Jimbo. He slowly unbuttoned his sportshirt and took it off. He traced his fingers slowly over the scars on his chest and stomach.

These aren't any goddamn war wounds, Morris said. I carved these myself. I cut myself up when they told me about Nick. I was in prison when Nick needed me. They told me what Nick had done and I carved myself up. Only I didn't do a good enough job. Nick did a better job than I did. Nick did my job. Jimbo, can you imagine how I felt when I saw you hitchhiking by the road that night? I thought my eyes were playing tricks on me. I thought I had gone crazy. There you were. Big as life. Like you were a ghost. Nick's ghost. It was like Nick was reborn. It was like I had been given a second chance. That's why I have to keep you with me. Can you understand what I'm talking about, son?

Yes, sir, Jimbo said.

Morris picked up the bottle and took another long drink. He put the bottle back down, then picked up the .45 from the dresser. He held it in both hands and looked it over. He began walking up and back again while holding the .45 loosely at his side.

Then something else started to come over me, Morris said. Something that is going to be difficult to explain to you. You're young, Jimbo. This is going to be difficult for you to understand. You see, you started meaning a lot to me. A lot. And it wasn't just because you reminded me so much of Nick. In fact, it wasn't because of Nick at all. In fact, you started meaning more to me than Nick ever did. That's hard for me to say. Hell, it's hard for me to believe. But that's what happened. You started meaning more to me than anyone ever has. Anyone in my life. And I didn't know how to tell you. I was afraid you would react like I did with Papa years ago. You are so young. Like I was young. I didn't understand things when I was young. I was afraid of what you would do. There have been many nights when I've sat up watching you sleep. I've put this goddamn .45 against your head while you were sleeping. You just don't know, Jimbo. Goddamn it, you just don't know.

Morris raised the .45.

Jesus, Jake, Jimbo said.

It's Morris, Morris said. He turned and smashed the pistol's barrel through the teevee screen. It sounded like a shot. Jimbo jerked violently. In the sudden darkness afterimages of the teevee screen floated before Jimbo's face. Morris moved silently to the window and with the pistol's barrel parted the shades. In the faint slant of light Jimbo could see that Morris's hand was bleeding. Morris stood there with his back pressed against the door and peered through the parted shades.

They won't take us alive, Morris said.

Jimbo shut his eyes. Oh please, God. God is great, God is good. Now I lay me down to sleep. I pray the Lord my soul to keep.

Jimbo felt Morris sit down on the bed beside him. He felt Morris's fingers touch his arm and squeeze gently. Morris's fingers were warm. Jimbo opened his eyes and blinked in the darkness. Morris was a dark form sitting there. Jimbo could smell whiskey. Morris's fingers were damp.

Listen, old sport, Morris said quietly. You know I wouldn't hurt you, don't you?

Yes, sir.

Do you trust me?

Yes, sir.

Listen to me then. Listen closely. Try to understand. I like to fuck women, see. But I was in prison a long time. Nothing is ever just black or white. I love you, Jimbo. I love you more than I ever have anyone else. More than Nick. I love you more than I could ever just love a son. I won't hurt you. I promise I won't hurt you. You're not going to hurt me like I hurt Papa, are you?

Can I think about it, Jake? Please.

Morris. I'm Morris. No, Jimbo. I can't wait any longer. I can't wait any longer.

Can you wait until tomorrow, Morris? Just until tomorrow. Please.

No, old Jimbo, I can't, Morris said. He put the pistol on the table between the beds. He began undoing Jimbo's belt buckle.

Please, Jake. Morris. Please, Morris.

I'm not going to hurt you, old sport, Morris said. He unzipped Jimbo's jeans.

Don't take my pants off, Morris, Jimbo said and clutched his belt with both hands. Please, Morris.

Just relax, son, Morris said. He tugged gently. I won't hurt you. You know that. Think of your girl if it helps.

Jimbo shut his eyes. He tried to picture Judy's face. Judy's mouth. He couldn't do it. Oh my God, how did I ever get in this? Jimbo thought. First he was a thief. Then he was a killer. A murderer. And now he was a queer. A goddamn fag. A sock. Jimbo suddenly pictured a sock. An old athletic sock with blue and green stripes around its top that was stiff as a corpse. Suddenly the sock was soft. Suddenly Captain came stomping into the room. Captain came stomping into the room to square off once and for all with Jimbo and he caught Jimbo cold with his sock. Suddenly the sock was bloody. Jump, Captain called from far below. Jump! Jump, goddamn it! You're not going to drown, goddamn it! Captain slapped the water with a cupped hand. It sounded like a shot. Jimbo flinched. Jump! *Slap.* Jump! *Slap.* Jimbo jumped at last. In the deep end's swift current the blood-soaked sock gave way. Jimbo fell loose.

Morris sat on the edge of the bed smoking. He had clicked on the small lamp on the table between the beds. He had wrapped a handkerchief around his cut hand. Jimbo lay on the bed with his hands clasped behind his head. He stared at Morris's profile.

I told you I wouldn't hurt you, Morris said after a while. I didn't, did I?

No.

I wouldn't hurt you, sport. I'm sorry it happened like it did, though. I got too drunk. I don't want you to feel bad about it. Do you feel bad about it?

I guess not.

I hope not. I don't want you to feel bad. It would bust me up. Christ, look what I did when I lost Nick. If I lost you it would be tough, sport.

Morris turned and looked at Jimbo.

You have a strange look on your face, Jimbo, Morris said. Are you upset, son? Tell me the truth. Please.

A little I guess.

Listen, if it will make you feel better I'll tell you something. I didn't plug that wop bartender tonight.

Jesus Christ, Jimbo said. Why, Morris? Why did you tell me you did?

To keep you with me.

What was that shot then?

What else? Morris said and laughed. The teevee. I fixed that surly wop's rolling teevee. You should have seen the blond's britches split ducking when I plugged that teevee. You should have seen it, old sport.

Yeah. Sure.

Listen, I'm going to take a long hot shower. I'm still a little
drunk. I don't suppose you'd like to join me, would you, kiddo?

I'm tired, Morris.

Sure, kiddo. Been one hell of a long day. Why don't you just
crawl into bed then? Listen, sport, let me tell you something
else. This won't happen again if you don't want it to. I won't
come near you again unless you want me to, see. I promise you
this. I mean it. Do you believe me, Jimbo?

Sure. I believe you.

Good enough, old sport, Morris said and patted Jimbo's
thigh. He got up and took off his trousers and tossed them
onto his bed. At the bathroom door he turned to look at Jimbo.
You're still a tough customer all right, sport. Don't ever worry
about that.

You better believe I'm a tough customer, fag, Jimbo thought
to himself and arched his eyebrows. As soon as he heard the
shower water Jimbo sat up on the bed. He picked up the .45
from the bed table. He walked quietly over to the open bathroom door. Morris was humming in the shower. Jimbo
cocked the .45. Jimbo raised the .45, holding it with both
hands like Morris had taught him. He aimed it at the shower
curtain's center. *Blam!* Jimbo fired the .45 in his mind, the
trigger giving, the smooth underbelly of the butt jogging his
palm. He pictured Morris clutching the shower curtain desperately as he fell out onto the bathroom floor. *Blam blam
blam blam*, Jimbo fired four shots more into the inert body.
And each successive shot was another loud, fateful rap on the
door of his undoing.

No, Jimbo thought. Not my undoing.

Jimbo uncocked the .45 and stuck it in his belt. He moved
quickly now. He took Morris's wallet from the trousers on the
bed and stuck it in his own hip pocket. After peeling off a
single dollar bill and tossing it on the dresser, he stuffed the
roll of bills from the job in his front pocket. Not ready for the
big time, am I? Jimbo thought. He slid Nick's picture from its
golden frame and tore it into pieces which he scattered around

the dresser. He picked up the carkeys and the whiskey bottle from the dresser and backed toward the door. Morris was still humming in the shower. Jimbo took the .45 from his belt and looked at it. He didn't need to be armed and dangerous. He didn't want to be armed and dangerous ever again in his life. He tossed the .45 on the bed. He picked up his unopened suitcase at the foot of the bed and quietly opened the door. Besides, Jimbo thought, he really should leave old Morris something. Old Morris might need that .45.

Jimbo stared through the rain-streaked windshield at the phone booth on the closed gas station's corner. He took another long hit from the whiskey bottle. No use hurrying this now, he thought. Just a few more drinks to steady the old nerves. He just needed to calm down some more. It would be all right then. Dad, he would say, I want to come home. I'm sorry, Dad. I'm sorry for everything. I'll make it all up to you somehow. I love you, Dad, he would say. Come on home, son, Captain would say. We'll work everything out. I'll stick by you, son, no matter what you've done. Jimbo took another drink. Hell, Morris the fag had probably lied about Pace squealing, just like he'd lied about everything else. Maybe Jimbo was not in that much hot water at all. And maybe Judy had not married Bodine yet. Maybe she had changed her mind. Jimbo took another drink. It was warm inside the car so he cracked his window and took off his windbreaker. BORNED TO WIN, Jimbo said aloud, looking at the inked tattoo on his upper arm. Sure. He spit on his fingers and began to rub at the skull and crossbones. That goddamn fag, he thought and rubbed as hard as he could. Jimbo poured whiskey onto the tattoo and began scraping his skin with his fingernails. He scraped and rubbed the tattoo until his skin was bleeding.

The phone began ringing.

Jimbo opened the phone booth's folding door to turn off the overhead light. His hand was shaking. He closed his eyes and pressed the back of his head against the cool glass. He breathed deeply. The rainy night air smelled sweet and clean.

Everything was going to be all right. Somehow he would make everything up to everybody. I love you, Dad, he would say.

Hello.

This is a long-distance collect call from Jim Stark to anyone there, the operator said. Will you accept charges, please?

Yes. Yes, of course.

Go ahead, sir, the operator said.

Hello. Hello, Dad.

Hello. Jimbo. Jimbo. Jimbo, is this really you, squirt?

Boomer. Boomer, is this you? I was calling home I thought.

You are calling home, squirt. Where are you?

I'm up in New Jersey. What are you doing there anyway, Boomer? Is Mom all right, Boomer?

She's doing all right. She's better. She needs you home, squirt.

What are you doing there this time of night, Boomer? Is the old man drunk? I want to come home, Boomer. I want to talk to Captain. I love him, Boomer. Boomer, I've really fucked up. I've really fucked everything up. I got Judy knocked up. I'm in some real trouble, Boomer. Will Dad let me come home?

Squirt, don't worry about the trouble. I'll take care of things. Just come home. Where are you exactly? I'll send someone for you. Your mom needs you, Jimbo.

I want to come home, Boomer. I want to make things up to everybody. Will Dad let me come home, Boomer? Will you talk to him for me? Tell him I'm sorry, Boomer.

Listen, squirt, wherever you are, sit tight. I'll wire you money to get home.

I've got money, Boomer. And I've got a car.

The police are looking for you, Jimbo. Did you know that?

I knew it I guess. So Pace really did squeal. Where's Pace now, Boomer?

He's with the juvenile authorities in New Jersey. You boys have gotten yourselves in a little trouble. But don't worry about it, son. It can be taken care of. Let's just get you home for now. We'll worry about everything else later.

So Captain knows. He really knows. I guess I can't come home now.

Yes, you can come home, Jim. Your mother needs you.

Not unless Captain says I can. He has to tell me to come home himself.

He can't, Jim.

I don't care how goddamn drunk he is, Boomer. Get him to the goddamn phone. He has to tell me himself. I won't come home unless he asks me.

Jim, I'll tell you this straight. There's no other way. Your dad is gone, Jimbo. And your mother needs you like never before. Come home, squirt.

He's what?

He's dead, Jimbo.

Goddamn it, Boomer.

Your mother needs you, Jim.

All right, Boomer, tell me the truth. Straight out. Tell me how it happened.

A heart attack, Jimbo.

I might have known. So I guess everyone thinks it's my fault or something.

It was no one's fault, Jimbo.

So that's how he died. Stupid fucking heart attack.

His funeral is Wednesday. We need you home, son.

You sure didn't waste any time, did you, Uncle Boomer?

Will you talk to your mother, Jimbo?

Business always has been brisk, right, Uncle Boomer? Old sport?

I loved him, Jimbo.

Right. Did you lay him out yourself, Uncle Boomer? Did you pump him full of that embalming shit with your own hands?

Come on home, Jimbo. We need you.

You need me? You need me? What the fuck for? Oh, I'm coming home all right, Uncle Boomer. Yeah, sport, you better believe it. I've got some scores to settle, see. Didn't you hear? I'm armed and dangerous these days. I'm coming home all right, Uncle. I've got a lot of unfinished business back there. I might even finish up some business for the old Captain. I owe him that at least.

Settle down, squirt. Don't be melodramatic.

Right. Right, old Uncle Boomer. Old sport. Well, you be looking for me. And you tell them for me. They'll have to shoot me down like a dog. They won't take me alive.

Sleep it off, squirt, Boomer said and hung up.

zoom in

on Jimbo Stark pushing the pedal relentlessly down as he roars the Bel Air through the rainy New Jersey night, the open bottle of whiskey between his legs, the radio on, the window down, his steely eyes sweeping the shiny, wet road, unafraid in the flashing headlights as he searches the haunted roadside for ghost hitchhikers.

Jimbo fires up a Camel and frenchinhales deeply. Old soldiers aren't supposed to die. They were supposed to just fade away or some shit. Fade away. Wonder if he was down in his shelter when he dropped dead. Dropped dead. Goddamn him. Now who could Jimbo make everything up to? Now it was too late to make everything up. Except to Morris maybe. Maybe Jimbo should go back and make everything up to Morris. I'm sorry I swiped your soldiers, Morris. I'm sorry I knocked you up. I'm sorry I smashed your Silver Ghost windshield. I'm sorry I tore up Nick's picture. I'm sorry, Morris. I'm sorry. Let me make everything up to you. I'll do anything. Here, you can suck my cock all you want. You can suck my cock for a hobby. Oh God, Jimbo said aloud, what can I do now? What can I do? Where can I go? Maybe I should turn myself in and get it over with, Jimbo thought. Turn himself in and pay his debt to society. Go to prison and make license plates for twenty years. Sure. Turn into an old fag like Morris. Well, fuck that. No way. Not old Captain Rebel Without a Cause On the Road. They would have to catch him first. This crummy Chevy Bel Air was no Silver Ghost but it would do, by God. He would make his getaway west. West to California. To Hollywood. He would outlaw-roar over every shortcut backcountry road to Califor-

nia he could find. Sure. Why not? Goddamn right. Maybe he
would be discovered. Become a star overnight. And he would
get a pony with a silver-trimmed saddle. And on a hilltop he
would build a mansion with walls of gleaming glass and a
swimming pool, its heated water California sky blue. And his
mother would come to live with him. And he would satisfy her
wildest dreams. Make everything up to her at least. And no
one would ever see through his moviestar disguise. He would
lay low safely in Hollywood forever. Sure. Sure thing, sport,
Jimbo thought and flicked his half-smoked Camel out the
window.

the last closeup

of Jimbo Stark's face, the tight, ironic smile, the arched
eyebrows, the wrinkled forehead, as he pushes the pedal relentlessly down, as he tries with all of his heart to hit 110,
escape velocity: as he tries with all of his heart to become
perfectly himself: as he tries with all of his heart to blast off to
that great starfield in the sky.

epilogue ➤

the boy
in the planetarium

I am addressing the boy in the planetarium, the tough but understanding cop says into the loudspeaker. I am speaking to the boy inside. This is Frank Framek from the Juvenile Division. You are surrounded. You are surrounded by many armed police. Whoever you are, drop your weapon and come outside.

Do you think the end of the world will come at night, Jim? Plato asks. He is shivering.

Here, you're cold, James Dean says and offers his red windbreaker to Plato. Hey, can I see your gun? Just for a minute. I just want to see it. I'll give it right back. I promise.

James Dean slips the bullets out of the gun while Plato puts on the red windbreaker.

Here, James Dean says as he hands the empty gun back to Plato. Friends keep promises, don't they?

The movie is almost over.

But what a movie it has been. Daring to moo at stars: daring to pick up the switchblade just for being called chicken: daring to follow the soft, sloping signals of Natalie Wood's breasts as you roared that stolen car crazily toward the cliff's deadly edge in that wild, incandescent moment of headlights: daring to run away from America to an old, deserted mansion high in the haunted Hollywood hills with sweet Natalie, with confused but innocent Sal Mineo, an old deserted mansion where you dared to believe you could form a secret, new family and could begin the world over again.

Yes, it has been a great movie. But this is what you have come at last to know about this movie. For it to go on forever you would have to remain perfectly seventeen. Just imagining yourself perfectly seventeen forever would not be enough. You should have soared off that cliff, instead of Buzz, to vanish in flames on the rocks below. You should have been gunned down like a dog outside the planetarium instead of Plato.

On the front lawn of the L.A. Planetarium, you kneel weeping beside Plato's bullet-blasted body. I had the bullets, you weep. I had the bullets, you weep and open your outstretched hand full of bullets. There was no reason for the cop to fire when Plato panicked in the blinding searchlights. The sky begins to lighten above the planetarium. It is almost morning and the movie must end on schedule. You slowly zip up the red windbreaker on Plato's corpse. He was always cold, you say to no one in particular.

It is years later. You are drinking alone in your last-ditch ginjoint at the edge of the Mission, one of those ancient Irish ginjoints, with old Christmas decorations hanging about and green dancing leprechauns pasted to the bluetinted mirror behind the long, polished mahogany bar.

You are killing time. You look up at the Hamm's beer sign above the bar. It is one of those huge Hamm's beer signs with a rustic outdoors scene flowing across its surface. Moving from left to right, prismic points of light slowly shimmer a campsite and river and waterfall into view like an electrically charged pointillist painting. It is as though some strange teevee camera is taking a slow pan around some shivering, luminous landscape. Only some of it is lost. Some of it has disappeared. You sit in your last-ditch ginjoint at the edge of the Mission drinking alone and you watch the campsite with its tent and smoking fire flow slowly by; then you watch the blue water of the river as it becomes slowly the white, foamy waterfall; then somehow you are back at the campsite. At least 180 degrees of the pan have been lost somewhere in space and time.

Sometimes when you do not want to go home you sit drinking and looking at the Hamm's beer sign for hours. Killing time. You imagine fishing it. You fish it very carefully in your mind as it flows slowly by. You fish very carefully under the log sticking out in the current in front of the campsite, then sometimes you fish where there might be deep holes or sometimes, depending on the time of day, shallow stretches in the shimmering current, sometimes catching trout and sometimes losing them.

Sometimes you fish the visible 180 degrees of that Hamm's beer sign until closing time when you have no choice but to go home. You never, however, try to imagine fishing that 180 degrees of current lost in space and time. You know better. You know you would have to wade in too deep to hook trout in places impossible to land them. In that invisible 180 degrees, in that fast, deep, lost current, in the dark, where all forms have faded, have dissolved, have become shadowy fish shapes no eye can reel, the fishing would be tragic.

It is years later. You are sitting alone drinking in your last-ditch ginjoint at the edge of the Mission. You become weary of fishing the Hamm's beer sign but it is not yet closing time. You stare at your reflection in the bluetinted mirror behind the bar. You see a face you hardly recognize. You arch your eyebrows and wrinkle your forehead and look out through squinted eyes at your unknown face. You let your lower face collapse into smiles. Nothing works. You stare intently at your unknown face in the bluetinted mirror's visible 180 degrees and you wonder seriously if perhaps your life has finally broken down for good. You wonder seriously if it would not have been better, really, to have vanished that night years ago when you pushed the pedal relentlessly down until your getaway car actually hit 110, and you found out it was not, after all, escape velocity. Not your escape velocity, anyway. Maybe if you had just pressed the pedal a little harder.

Or, maybe, if you had been driving the Silver Ghost when you hit 110. Maybe you could have escaped at 110 in the Silver Ghost. Years ago. Years ago when you learned it is always too late to make anything up to anyone.